The Desperate Gamble

ALSO BY MARION BLACKWOOD

Marion Blackwood has written lots of books across multiple series, and new books are constantly added to her catalogue. To see the most recently updated list of books, please visit: www.marionblackwood.com

CONTENT WARNINGS

The *Court of Elves* series contains violence, morally questionable actions, and later books in the series also contain some more detailed sexual content. If you have specific triggers, you can find the full list of content warnings at: www.marionblackwood.com/content-warnings

THE DESPERATE GAMBLE

COURT OF ELVES: BOOK SIX

MARION BLACKWOOD

Copyright © 2022 by Marion Blackwood

All rights reserved. No part of this book may be reproduced in any form or by any electronic or mechanical means, including information storage and retrieval systems, without permission in writing from the publisher, except by reviewers, who may quote brief passages in a review. For more information, contact info@marionblackwood.com

ISBN 978-91-987259-8-8 (hardcover)
ISBN 978-91-987259-1-9 (paperback)
ISBN 978-91-987259-0-2 (ebook)

Editing by Julia Gibbs

This is a work of fiction. Names, characters, places, and incidents either are the product of the author's imagination or are used fictitiously. Any resemblance to actual persons, living or dead, events, or locales is entirely coincidental.

www.marionblackwood.com

*For everyone who laughs easily, loves freely,
and shrugs off problems with a mischievous wink*

CHAPTER 1

Mist swirled like a white veil between the trees. I leaned to the side and watched as the ground got closer. There was some kind of camp up ahead, and what looked like a sprawling city a bit farther away, but we were descending into an open clearing a short distance from the camp instead of approaching either of them. Fear and excitement fought in my chest.

A thud echoed through the silent forest as Captain Vendir's air serpent landed on the fresh green grass. I had gotten better at anticipating the movements over the weeks we had been traveling, but the impact still sent me rocking forward in the saddle.

Metal clinked faintly as Vendir unbuckled the straps over his legs and then gracefully swung himself down from the green serpent's back. Turning to face us, he spread his arms wide.

"Welcome to Valdanar."

Theo sucked in a breath.

For a moment, no one moved. All eight of us remained

frozen atop the great air serpent as we stared between the High Elf before us and the dense woods that surrounded the glen. My heart pounded in my chest.

Valdanar. The home of the High Elves and the birthplace of our ancestors.

"Cool," Valerie announced with a wide grin on her face.

That broke the spell. A ripple of laughter spread among our group and then we all bent down to unbuckle the straps that had kept us in the saddle.

My fingers trembled slightly as I undid the final one. Drawing in a shaky breath, I slid down from the serpent's back and landed on Valdanarian soil for the first time. After giving my body a good stretch, I moved a little farther away and turned in a slow circle to take in our surroundings.

The morning sun was just visible over the treetops, an orange ball of flame burning away the night's fog. Leaves rustled softly as a warm summer breeze stroked the canopy around us. The air smelled like damp soil and blooming flowers, and it tasted like mist and… something flavorful. And sparkly. Surprise fluttered through me. Magic. It tasted like magic.

A dark shape moved at the corner of my eye.

"You can taste it too, right?" I said without even turning to look.

Mordren Darkbringer came to a halt next to me. "Yes."

"What is it?" Hadeon asked from a few steps away while he squinted at the air as if he should be able to see something in it.

On his other side, Idra shrugged. "Magic, I presume."

"It's the Great Current," Ellyda supplied. Her sharp violet eyes slid to Captain Vendir. "Isn't it?"

"Yes." Vendir patted his air serpent on the neck before

turning back to us with a shrug. "Now you know how barren the air on your island is to us. There is no native magic there, only what you brought with you from here. That's why it's so starved, empty, and tasteless."

Eilan studied him while a thoughtful look passed over his gorgeous face. "And we would never have known the difference."

"Are we seriously talking about what the air *tastes like* when there's a whole continent to explore?" Valerie flapped her arms to indicate the forest around us. "Let's go already."

Chuckling, Theo hiked a thumb in her direction. "I agree with the spinning spatula over there. We just spent two and a half weeks flying across an ocean on the back of an air serpent to get to this place, and I for one am eager to see what 'this place' actually is."

The rest of us turned to the two thieves and then nodded. They did have a point. When we all shifted our gazes back to Vendir, and Mordren spun a lazy hand in the air, the High Elf captain blew out a sigh. Shaking his head, he motioned for us to follow as he started in the direction of the camp we had seen from above.

We followed. As did his winged serpent.

"Those extra four days are on you," Captain Vendir muttered.

Valerie narrowed her eyes at him. "What was that?"

Even though Vendir still wore the black bracelet that suppressed his magic, he had stopped walking on eggshells around us about a week into our journey. He still chose his words carefully when addressing Mordren or Idra, but he no longer displayed the same amount of caution around the rest of us.

"I said, those extra four days are on you," Vendir repeated a bit louder as he met Valerie's gaze. "It would only have taken two weeks if you lot hadn't had to stop all the time."

"It wasn't all the time," she protested.

"We took a lot more breaks than we should have."

"Well excuse me for not being used to flying or to holding it in for like more than ten hours." She threw out her arms. "What do you have? A bladder made of steel?"

"I am not discussing my bladder with you."

"Why–"

"Please," Vendir interrupted. Dragging a hand through his long blond hair, he heaved another deep sigh and shook his head as we weaved between the thick tree trunks. Brown eyes full of exasperation met us as he swept his gaze over our group. "There is an air serpent camp up ahead. I need to leave Orma there first so that they can take care of her after the long journey while we sneak into the city."

As if she could understand what he was saying, Orma swung her large green head towards Vendir at the mention of her name. He reached out and scratched her jaw before shifting his attention back to us.

"At the camp, we can also send word to the palace," Vendir continued.

"To request an audience," Ellyda filled in.

It was more of a statement than a question since we had already discussed this, but he answered anyway. "Yes. No one can just walk up to the Palace of the Never Setting Sun and demand a meeting with the emperor and empress."

A grin spread across Hadeon's lips. "We'll see about that."

"Need I remind you that this is *my* homeland? You know nothing about the customs here. But I do." Vendir lifted his hand and shook the black bracelet around his wrist. "After all, that's why you blackmailed me into this suicide mission. I put your overall chances of success at less than five percent. Without me, those odds drop to zero. So if I tell you to do something, or not to do something, you need to listen to me."

Mordren shot him a brief glance as we came to a halt at the edge of the camp. "Watch that tone."

"He's right, though," Eilan said, and lifted one shoulder in a casual shrug. "We need someone to navigate their customs for this to work."

"Exactly." Captain Vendir motioned towards the camp. "So, can I go in there to leave Orma and send that message?"

"If you try anything…" the Prince of Shadows began.

"I know." Vendir glanced down and adjusted his now rather dirty bronze armor in an effort to hide the flicker of annoyance in his eyes. "I'm quite familiar with your threats by now, Prince Mordren."

A sharp smile spread across Mordren's lips but he simply inclined his head. Vendir took that as permission to leave and strode forward with his air serpent beside him.

"I'll go with him," Idra announced.

"Me too," Hadeon said.

"I don't need your help." A slight scowl creased her pale brows as she shot him a glare before stalking after Vendir.

Hadeon did the same. "I don't care."

"Then why are you following me?"

"I'm not doing it for you."

"Then why…"

Their voices grew fainter as they disappeared towards the cluster of buildings up ahead. High Elves appeared from doorways a few moments later, calling out greetings and waving to Vendir.

Surprise shot through me when I realized that they were wearing normal clothes. It was the first time I had seen a High

Elf in something other than bronze armor, and the sight made them seem almost... ordinary. They were all tall and sculpted like gods, with long pointed ears that stuck up through their hair, and features that would make anyone jealous. But seeing them out here in the woods, in normal clothes, with a steaming mug of tea in one hand and a colorful blanket in the other, made them seem like real people. Not like a near mythical race hell-bent on conquering us. But as actual people.

"I thought they would make the Low Elves do these kinds of jobs," Ellyda said. Her eyes were fixed on the small group that had gathered to talk to Vendir and unsaddle Orma. "Based on the diaries and accounts from our ancestors, the High Elves made them do all the work while they just lounged around like nobility."

"Maybe they don't trust them with their air serpents," Theo offered.

"Maybe."

Silence fell for a few minutes as we studied them from beneath the bright green canopy. The sun had almost burned away all the mist, and small birds now chirped merrily in the trees. A gentle wind caressed my cheeks and brought with it another cloud of fragrant air. I watched as Idra read the note Vendir had written, before he handed it off to another High Elf.

"I do not trust him," Mordren said.

"Me neither." I glanced up at the Prince of Shadows before shifting my attention back to the captain. "He's far too loyal to Anron to actually sell him out. The first chance he gets, he will betray us."

"I suppose it is a good thing that we are all well-versed in the art of betrayal."

"Indeed."

"And blackmail," Valerie chimed in. "And manipulation, burglary, theft, assassination, deception, lyin–"

"Are you just listing every shady quality there is?" Theo interrupted.

"I'm just saying." She slapped his arm with the back of her hand before motioning at the rest of us. "This might be Vendir's homeland, but this kind of mission is our home ground. Between all the shady shit the eight of us can bring to the table, our dear dutiful and upstanding Vendir won't stand a chance."

Eilan looked at her for a long moment before raising his eyebrows and giving her an impressed nod. "She's right."

"Bah." She smacked him in the ribs. "Stop sounding so surprised. How many times do I have to tell you that I'm the brains of the operation?"

He rolled his eyes, but there was a smile tugging at his lips as well.

Next to me, Mordren was still staring at the camp in silence. Captain Vendir was on his way back, flanked by Idra and Hadeon. I watched the neutral expression on his face and wondered just how he was planning to betray us.

"Watch every move he makes," Mordren said as if he could read my mind. His silver eyes flicked to Eilan, Ellyda, and the two thieves as well. "All of you. We cannot allow him to betray us until we have convinced the emperor and empress to kill Anron for us. Otherwise, all of this will have been for nothing."

The gravity of the situation hung like a heavy shroud over the otherwise bright summer morning. Vendir, completely oblivious to the conversation we'd just had, came to a halt before us and then motioned in the direction of the sprawling city we had seen while flying.

"Let's go," he said. "We need to get to the capital."

"When can we expect a reply?" I asked. "To our request to meet?"

Vendir tilted his head back and looked up at the blue sky visible between the branches before replying. "If we're lucky, we should have a reply from the emperor by tonight." Raking his fingers through his hair, he met our gazes again. "We'll stay at an inn at the edge of the city until we hear back so that we can clean ourselves up and rest before we head to the palace."

"Yeah, taking a bath that isn't in the actual ocean would be pretty nice," Theo said.

"When we get to the city," Vendir continued as if he hadn't interrupted, "keep your head down and don't draw attention. And you might actually survive this."

Mordren gave him a smile that seemed to suggest that if we didn't survive, neither would he, but all he said was, "Lead the way."

With one last look at his great green air serpent, Captain Vendir turned around and started forward. I flashed my friends a grin. And then I followed.

Our boots left faint imprints in the soft moss as the nine of us strode through the forest and towards the huge city waiting ahead.

The capital of Valdanar.

The home of the High Elves.

And the two all-powerful beings that we were about to manipulate.

CHAPTER 2

"Stop drumming!"

Silence fell across the crowded living room as Valerie jerked upright and whirled to face Idra. With her eyebrows raised in challenge, the lethal warrior stared back at the thief. The midday sun streamed through the window and cast Valerie's face in a warm glow as she leaned back in her chair and raked her hands through her loose brown curls. Then she started drumming her fingers on the table again.

"I said, stop that," Idra repeated as she narrowed her eyes at Valerie once more. "You're going to give us all a headache."

"Staying cooped up in this room is giving me a headache," Valerie countered. Her brown eyes slid to Vendir. "You said we'd hear back by nightfall."

He shrugged. "I said *if we're lucky* we'll hear back by nightfall."

"But we didn't hear back by nightfall. Or by this morning. And now we're halfway through the day and we still haven't heard anything."

Impatience bounced around inside me as well, but I forced

it down and instead said, "I know. But there's not much we can do about it."

"But we can do *something*." Wood scraped against wood as she pushed up from the chair and started pacing the room. "We just spent two weeks flying–"

"Two and a half," Theo interrupted.

"Two and a half weeks flying here," Valerie amended, "and all we've seen is a forest and one street." She stabbed a hand towards the window. "*That* street."

Captain Vendir leveled an exasperated stare at her. "As I have already explained, you need to keep a low profile. High Commander Anron is a war hero. If any of his supporters find out who you are and why you're here, it will not end well for you."

"I can keep a low profile."

Eilan let out something between a snort and a chuckle.

Narrowing her eyes, Valerie shifted her gaze to him. "What was that?"

"Keep a low profile?" Amusement danced across his handsome features. "You?"

"I'm a thief."

"You're like a mix between a ball of energy and a box of fireworks." Sunlight from the window made his pale green eyes glitter as he held her gaze. "I have never met anyone who is as…" He flexed his fingers as if trying to pluck the word he was searching for from the air. "… impossible *not* to notice as you."

Valerie opened her mouth to retort but then stopped. With her brows slightly furrowed, she studied him as if she couldn't quite figure out if that had been an insult or a compliment. Then a devilish smile flashed across her lips.

Reaching into her clothes, she withdrew a knife.

Shock slammed home on Eilan's features. Sitting up straighter, he patted his own clothes before finally meeting Valerie's eyes again. "When did you...?"

"Three hours ago." She tossed him the knife she had stolen from him and then shrugged. "I was bored."

Catching the knife in his left hand, Eilan shook his head in disbelief and then returned the blade to its proper place.

"So what are we–" Valerie began again.

"Do you ever stop talking?" Captain Vendir interrupted with an exasperated groan.

"Nope." Shifting her gaze to Eilan, she wiggled her eyebrows. "Unless you want to gag me."

That time, a collective groan rippled through the room. All except Eilan. He just chuckled and shook his head once more.

Leather creaked as Hadeon shifted in his chair on the other side of the table. "I hate to say it, but I actually agree with the restless human over there. There's a strategic advantage to at least being a little familiar with the city and its people before we go talk to the guys at the top."

"That is a valid point," Mordren admitted.

Valerie grinned. "Ha! Told you."

I shifted my gaze to the blond High Elf in the corner. "Vendir?"

The crowded living room tucked away at the top of the tavern fell silent as Vendir considered whether it was worth the risk of letting us go outside. Or the risk of denying us. Indecision swirled in his brown eyes.

"Fine." He blew out a long breath. "But move only in pairs. Big groups attract too much attention." His gaze snagged on Valerie and Theo. "The people here have never seen humans before, so if you keep your ears covered, you should be able to pass for less attractive Low Elf children.

Valerie harrumphed. "Who are you calling ugly?"

"What she said," Theo chimed in, but he restyled his short blond hair so that it at least covered the top of his ears.

"We will meet back here in three hours," Vendir continued as if they hadn't interrupted. "And I can't stress this enough. Do not draw attention to yourselves."

"Alright," I said.

Anticipation burned in Valerie's eyes as she not-so-subtly slid over to pair up with Eilan. He blinked in surprise but then only inclined his head. On the other side of the table, Idra and Hadeon scowled at each other for a few seconds before the white-haired warrior demonstratively stalked over to Theo. Hadeon rolled his eyes but then elbowed his sister.

"What?" Ellyda snapped as she tore her gaze from the wooden wall she had been staring at for the past half hour.

"We're going outside."

Her eyes went in and out of focus a few times before they settled on Hadeon. "Now?"

"Yes."

Mordren and I exchanged a glance before we both turned to Captain Vendir. "You're coming with us."

It looked like he was about to sigh, but then he caught the wicked smiles on our faces. Clearing his throat, he simply inclined his head instead.

"Alrighty, let's go!" Valerie called and started towards the window.

"No." Eilan's hand shot out and grabbed her arm before she could get far. "We're taking the stairs."

"Amateurs," she muttered, but followed him towards the stairwell.

The rest of the inn was empty. I wasn't sure if it was because we were at the very edge of the city, or if the standard was considered subpar. But after two and a half weeks of sleeping on the ground on tiny islands and bathing in the ocean, the accommodations in this modest establishment felt like a luxury resort. I ran a hand over the wood panels as we descended the stairs and made our way towards the front door.

Bright sunlight met us when we finally stepped across the threshold. My heart rate sped up. I knew that we were here on a vital mission to save our home, but there was something irresistible about exploring a new city. And not just a new city. A part of our history.

"Remember," Captain Vendir began before everyone split up. "Three hours. Don't do anything that attracts attention."

"Got it!" Valerie called as she dragged Eilan down the street.

The others gave similar replies before drifting off as well.

Mordren jerked his chin at Vendir. I fell in beside him as the three of us started down the street.

The summer in Valdanar was similar to the one in the Court of Trees. Warm but not the sweltering heat that my own court offered at this time of year. I rolled up the sleeves of my thin black shirt and tied my hair back before brushing a hand over the dagger strapped to my thigh. My sword would have drawn too much attention, so I'd had to settle for only one blade. But it didn't matter. We weren't expecting trouble anyway. I glanced at Captain Vendir. Or so I hoped.

Mordren caught the look and gave me a small nod as if he was thinking the same thing. He had taken off his suit jacket and only wore a black shirt, but I knew he had blades concealed underneath it as well. Besides, with our magic, we should be able to survive if any trouble came our way.

As if he too could hear our thoughts, Vendir met each of

our gazes in turn before saying, "Whatever you do, don't use your fire and shadow magic. Low Elves on this continent don't have access to elemental magic. The pain thing and walking through walls? Fine. They're incredibly unusual abilities over here, but still explainable. But if you start throwing fire or shadows around, then we're going to have some real problems."

"Got it," I said.

Mordren nodded to show that he had heard him as well.

Chatter came from up ahead. My heart thumped in my chest as we left the deserted street behind and finally moved towards an area filled with people. At last, we were about to see how the High Elves really lived.

I had to force myself to keep breathing normally as we rounded the final corner and poured out onto the bright road ahead.

Three-story buildings made of wood and stone stared down at us as we joined the stream of people strolling along the neat cobblestone street. Flowers in yellow, blue, and pink had been planted in small boxes that hung from the windows up above, and the colorful petals swayed gently in the warm breeze. Vines with fresh green leaves clung to the side of a pale marble house up ahead and climbed all the way up to what looked like a rooftop terrace.

My pace slowed as I turned around and looked at the people around me. High Elves in skirts, and pants, and dresses of various styles and hues shared the street with Low Elves in similar clothes. The High Elves looked just like Captain Vendir, with their godlike physiques and long ears, and the Low Elves looked… just like us.

I stared at a pair of female Low Elves, one wearing a dark purple dress and the other a pair of brown pants, as they called up instructions to someone in a window above. They didn't look scared or beaten down, and they didn't bow and cower before the High Elves who passed them.

The elf in the dress tipped her head back and laughed at something the person in the window said. It made her violet eyes sparkle like amethysts in the sun. I glanced down at her wrists. No black bracelet.

"Not what you expected?" Captain Vendir said.

I realized that I had stopped in the middle of the street. Snapping my mouth shut, I gave my head a couple of quick shakes before turning to face him. There was a hint of amusement drifting over his mouth.

"No," I admitted.

Mordren's silver eyes swept across the street again before he turned to Vendir as well. "We were led to believe that your people kept our people as slaves."

"They did." Vendir looked back at us with a steady gaze. "But a lot has changed in the millennia since your ancestors left these lands. The High Elves of old used to lord over your people like gods. Sitting back and enjoying the fruits of the Low Elves' labor while doing none of their own."

"So what changed?" I asked.

Vendir shrugged. "My guess? Our ancestors eventually realized that a life without purpose is a life not lived. I think they discovered the wonder in doing something that brings them joy." His eyes took on a faraway look for a second. "The rush of happiness that comes from creating something."

He shook his head quickly as if catching himself, and then motioned for us to keep walking. After one last glance at the pair of elves I had been studying, I fell in beside Mordren and Vendir again as we moved down the street.

A gentle breeze washed over me and ruffled my hair. It

brought with it the smell of summer flowers and baking bread. I drew in a deep breath before shifting my attention to Vendir once more.

"No magic-siphoning bracelets?" I asked, and nodded towards a group of Low Elves who had gathered around a table that appeared to contain some kind of game.

"No," Vendir answered. "That was outlawed centuries ago. The Low Elves here... well, their magic hasn't evolved as much as yours because of the extended use of those bracelets. A former empress banned them in an effort to make their magic come back so that the bracelets could be used much more effectively later, but then she died and no one ever picked up the practice."

"So how did Anron get his hands on them?"

"Like I said, the empress at the time planned on eventually starting it back up again, so stashes of them still exist in the Palace of the Never Setting Sun."

"This all seems a bit too good to be true," Mordren said from my other side. His eyes were locked on Vendir as he flicked a wrist to indicate the street around us. "Are we supposed to believe that our two species live in perfect harmony? Based on the actions of your dear friend Anron, I find that very hard to believe."

"You're right." Vendir brushed a stray petal from his armor. "I said that a lot has changed in the millennia since your ancestors left, but I didn't say that things are perfect now. There are still groups of High Elves who believe themselves to be your betters."

"Let me guess, Lester and Danser are part of that group too?" I chimed in.

"Yes. That's why it's so important that you keep a low prof–"

"Captain Vendir!" a strong voice called across the street.

Alarm flashed in Vendir's eyes as he checked that the black bracelet around his wrist was fully covered before he whirled around to face the source of the voice. Mordren and I edged a step towards the wall while turning as well.

My heart leaped into my throat.

A pair of High Elf soldiers in gleaming bronze armor came striding straight towards us.

CHAPTER 3

"Thank me," Vendir hissed under his breath.

I flicked my gaze between him and the approaching soldiers. "What?"

"Thank me for showing you the way." He turned towards us and gave us a pleasant smile that didn't reach his eyes. Nodding as if to a question, he raised a hand and pointed at the building behind us. "And go inside. Now."

"Thank you for your help." I gave him a, in my opinion, much more convincing smile in return and then turned to Mordren. "Shall we?"

He gave Vendir a businesslike nod. "Yes."

Sunlight glinted off bronze breastplates just two steps from us when Mordren placed a hand on my back and steered us away. There was a wooden door set into the building that Vendir had pointed at, and it was the closest one to us, so we walked towards it with purpose even though we had no idea what was behind it. A sign above the door said 'White Fire'.

"Captain Vendir," one of the soldiers said behind us. "We

didn't know you were back. Last we heard, you left with High Commander Anron to–"

His words were cut off as Mordren pulled open the door for us and we stepped into the room beyond. Coming from the bright sunlight outside, the space inside felt dark and gloomy. I blinked a few times while surveying the area.

Tables and chairs made of dark wood were positioned across the floor in a haphazard fashion, a worn counter filled with mugs took up half of the wall to our left, and a thin white haze filled the air. It smelled like herbs. And spilled alcohol.

Both High Elves and Low Elves occupied the seats and a buzz of conversation hung over the room. I turned to Mordren right as someone else called out to us from the bar.

"What can I get you?" The High Elf behind the counter, who presumably owned this White Fire tavern, looked at us inquiringly.

Mordren opened his mouth to reply, but then sudden realization flashed in his eyes. The same realization that had just shot through my mind as well. We didn't have any money.

"The rest of our party isn't here yet, so we'll just wait for them to get here before we start ordering," I lied smoothly. A grin slid across my mouth as I winked at him. "Would be rude to start without them. But thanks, though."

Before the owner could protest, I grabbed Mordren's arm and steered us towards a spot by the wall where we could see Captain Vendir through the window. Wood scraped against wood as we pulled out a couple of chairs and sat down at an empty table. Leaning back, I caught the slight scowl on Mordren's brow.

"Not used to being broke, huh?" I said.

"No." He straightened the sleeves on his shirt before fixing me with a serious look. "It is very… inconvenient."

I chuckled and shook my head in reply, but then the worry crept back in. Drumming my fingers against the stained tabletop, I swept my gaze around the room before casting another glance at Vendir. He was standing right outside with the two soldiers. They looked to be engaged in a friendly conversation rather than plotting to betray us. But I could be wrong.

"He won't sell us out, right?"

Mordren looked out through the window and was silent for a while before answering. "I don't know."

Shifting in my seat, I checked to make sure that no one was watching before I discreetly cracked open the window a tiny bit. Warm air smelling of flowers and baking bread blew inside and made the haze of white smoke around us swirl in lazy arcs. It also brought with it words from outside.

"I can't believe you weren't there to see it, Captain," the soldier from before said as if he had just finished a long tale of some extraordinary adventure.

Captain Vendir smiled, and this time it truly reached his eyes. "I'm sorry I missed it."

"When's the rest of the legion coming back?"

"I don't know." Vendir shrugged helplessly. "Like I said, High Commander Anron sent me back because he needs to consult the emperor on a sensitive subject. Until I speak with him, I won't know how long we'll be gone."

Surprise flashed through me. He was covering for us. And he was doing it very convincingly too.

"He is an excellent liar," Mordren said, as if he had been thinking the same thing.

I nodded. "Yeah."

Furniture crashed to our right. Both Mordren and I whipped towards the sound to find three High Elves in sweat-stained shirts. They looked like regulars at this establishment. The leader had banged his fist against the table and then shot up from his chair, which had made the worn piece of furniture topple backwards. His two companions stood up as well.

"What a waste!" the leader bellowed. His copper-colored hair rippled as he flicked it behind his shoulder before stabbing a hand towards a Low Elf seated at the table next to us. "Is this how you waste the drop of magic you have?"

"Yeah, you tell him, Tundir," one of his companions chimed in.

The Low Elf, a gangly male with short white hair and a merry twinkle in his pale blue eyes, blinked in surprise as he whirled towards them. He had been smoking a beautifully carved pipe and had been creating tiny figures in the thick white smoke that he blew out. The remnants of a jumping hare evaporated and blended with the rest of the pale cloud.

"I just..." he began, but the angry High Elf, Tundir, was already stalking towards him.

"You don't deserve to have magic at all, *Low Elf*." Tundir spat the words as if they tasted foul. "None of your kind do. The Great Current that runs through us is sacred."

"I don't use the Great Current. I was born with the ability to–"

Wood clattered against the floor as Tundir slapped the male's pipe away. Grabbing him by the collar, he yanked the Low Elf from his seat and growled in his face, "It's still our magic. Have you seen the White Tower and the physical manifestations of magic in there? No? Well, I have. I have seen it." He threw the white-haired elf aside. "And you are not worthy of it."

The Low Elf stumbled and crashed into another table

before being able to catch himself. His pale blue eyes were filled with fear as he snatched up his pipe from the floor and then scrambled out the door. I watched him.

So, that trio was part of the group of High Elves who believed themselves superior to everyone else. Oh how I wished I could throw a fireball at them just to shut them up.

"And what do you think you're looking at?" Tundir snapped.

I turned to find him glaring at us.

"Nothing," Mordren replied in a neutral voice.

His gaze flicked down to our empty table before he narrowed his eyes at us again. "What are you? Freeloaders? If you wanna sit here, you gotta buy something."

"We're just waiting for the rest of our party," I added.

"Right," Tundir snorted. Shaking his head, he stalked towards us while his two companions did the same. "I'm so sick of you people."

Mordren and I pushed to our feet. I cast a quick glance out the window. Captain Vendir was still talking with the two soldiers, but I could no longer hear what they were saying over the noise that the angry High Elf trio was making.

"We were just about to–" Mordren began and took a step forward.

"No." Tundir planted his palm square against Mordren's chest and shoved him backwards into the wall. "You think you can come in here and just sit for free?"

Mordren's silver eyes flashed like lightning as he stared down at the large hand pressed against his impeccable black shirt. The other two High Elves came to a halt next to their leader. All three of them towered over us.

I opened my mouth to say that we were just leaving, but

before I could get a single word out, Tundir's blond companion shoved me back against the wall as well.

"Who gave you permission to speak?" he growled.

My knife was in my hand before he had even finished his sentence. In one smooth motion, I had it positioned against his side.

"I suggest you take that hand off her," Mordren said, and slid his eyes to the blond male in front of me. "Before she pushes that blade through your ribs." He shifted his attention back to Tundir and then cast a pointed look down at his own hand. A blade gleamed in his grip as well. "The same applies to you."

Tundir's hand shot up from Mordren's chest and wrapped around his throat instead. "You think you can threaten me? You are vermin. Leeches. Our ancestors should never have given you freedom. It has made you arrogant and lazy." He flicked a dismissive glance up and down Mordren's body. "Look at you. You're half the male I am."

His grip tightened around Mordren's throat. The Prince of Shadows flexed his fingers on the blade but only looked back at the High Elf with cold eyes. I shifted the grip on my own knife as well, but with the blond male's forearm pushing me against the wall, there was nothing more I could do. Unless I killed him.

Without even meeting his gaze, I knew that Mordren was considering it too. But killing three High Elves in the middle of a crowded tavern would certainly attract attention. And we were supposed to be laying low. Mordren clenched his jaw.

"Someone needs to teach you some–" Tundir continued.

"What is the meaning of this?" a stern voice demanded.

Glancing towards the door, I found Captain Vendir

striding into the tavern. He scowled while stalking towards us.

"Nothing to concern yourself with, soldier," Tundir said. "We were just–"

"*Soldier?*" Vendir's voice dripped with authority and threat. "I would choose my next words carefully, if I were you."

The dark-haired elf on Tundir's other side, who had been silent until now, scrambled back a step while hissing to his companions, "He's a Wielder. That's Captain Vendir."

Tundir and his blond companion released us and retreated as well.

"M-my apologies, Captain Vendir," Tundir stammered as the three of them bowed. "If I had known who–"

"What seems to be the problem?" Vendir cut him off and flicked his wrist between them and the two of us by the wall.

"These two have just been sitting here without actually paying for anything. So we just wanted to–"

"Is that right?" Captain Vendir whirled to face us. "Disrespectfulness is never tolerated. Bow and apologize."

Disbelief shot through me. I opened my mouth, but before I could say anything, he took a threatening step forward and leveled a hard stare at us.

"Now," he ordered.

Mordren held his gaze for another second. Then he dropped his eyes to the floor and inclined his head. I did the same.

"Apologies," the Prince of Shadows pressed out.

"I'm sorry," I said as well.

"Good." Vendir shifted his attention back to the three High Elves. "And you, if you ever disturb the peace inside this tavern again, you and I are going to have problems. Am I making myself clear?"

"Yes, Great Wielder," Tundir said and dipped his head.

"Sit back down." Captain Vendir jerked his chin towards their previous table before turning to me and Mordren. Grabbing a hold of Mordren's arm, he shoved him towards the door while twitching his fingers at me. "And you two... outside."

The other patrons watched in silence as Tundir and his companions shuffled back to their table and sat down while we were marched out the door. Only once we were halfway out on the street did the buzz of conversation start back up again.

Clear summer winds blew away the lingering white smoke that had clung to everything inside the tavern. I drew in a deep breath as we emerged onto the street and shut the door behind us.

"Oh you enjoyed that, didn't you?" I said as I looked up at Captain Vendir while Mordren straightened his shirt.

Smug amusement tugged at the edge of Vendir's lips and he didn't even bother to deny it. We had been bossing him around for two and a half weeks. Of course he had enjoyed making us bow and apologize.

"I leave you alone for five minutes," he said instead. "Five minutes. And you still manage to get into a fight."

"We did not start it," Mordren pointed out while we moved towards the next street.

"Why do I find that hard to believe?" He shook his head and blew out a long sigh. "I don't even want to think about what kind of trouble the other six of you have managed to start while I wasn't there. Well, I suppose it will be interesting to see how many of you are still alive when those three hours are up."

I wanted to tell him that he was exaggerating, but in the end I couldn't.

Between me and Mordren, Valerie and Theo, Hadeon and… well, actually, every one of our friends, it would be almost impossible to get through an entire day without someone stirring up some kind of trouble.

A small smile tugged at my lips as I swerved around some tables and chairs that belonged to a café.

But we also specialized in trouble, so we would be able to handle it.

Whatever it was.

Hopefully.

CHAPTER 4

"You're late."

"Don't look at me," Hadeon said as he stepped into the living room after having taken the stairs two at a time. Lifting a muscled arm, he hiked a thumb over his shoulder. "She found a smithy a few streets away and, well, let's just say that we haven't seen much of the city beyond that."

Ellyda became visible at the top of the stairs as Hadeon moved towards one of the couches and threw himself down on it. She was wearing her usual brown pants and loose shirt, with her long brown hair pulled into a messy bun, but her eyes were now clear and bright. And there was a... glow around her whole being.

"They use such interesting techniques," she said as she came to a halt a few steps into the room. "And there were some tools and materials that I've never seen before." Her violet eyes sparkled as she turned to Vendir. "That pale blue substance, with what looked like the texture of molten lava, what is it?"

"Oh, uhm, I don't know." He gave her a helpless look. "I don't really know all that much about forging."

"It looked like they used it to coat the blade in between. If it does what I think it does, I might have an idea. But I need to know what it is for sure."

A small smile drifted over Vendir's lips. "If we still haven't heard back from the palace by tonight, I could take you there so that you can ask them, if you want? If I'm there with you, they'll answer any questions you ask."

Leather creaked. Captain Vendir blinked as if remembering himself and then flicked his gaze towards the other side of the room. Mordren and Idra were standing by the wall with their arms crossed, and both of them had their eyes locked on Vendir. On the couch next to them, Eilan was spinning a knife in his left hand while Hadeon sat forward and cracked his knuckles.

"I, uhm…" Vendir began.

"I would like that," Ellyda replied before he could finish. She gave him one of her rare smiles and moved towards one of the armchairs. "I would like that very much."

Curling up in the dark blue armchair, she pulled out a pen and began sketching something in a notebook. The rest of the room looked between her and Vendir, but Ellyda's attention was now focused solely on the paper before her. Vendir rubbed his wrist and cleared his throat a bit self-consciously.

Thankfully, Idra saved him from having to answer by instead saying, "Did you notice that worldwalking doesn't work here?"

"Yeah," I said. Mordren and I had tried to use it to get back to this inn, but it hadn't worked so the three of us had to walk all the way back instead. "It feels as if something is blocking it. Like the air is pushing back."

"It might be the Great Current." Captain Vendir swept his gaze around the room. "As you might have noticed, no High Elves are able to *worldwalk*, as you call it. And if it feels like there is something in the air pushing back, then it might be that the Great Current is too strong here since this city is the source of it."

"That actually makes a lot of sense, and…" Eilan began, but he trailed off when footsteps sounded from the stairwell.

Everyone except Ellyda turned towards the opening. Whoever was coming up the stairs wasn't in a hurry, so we all waited in silence while boots thudded rhythmically on the steps. I shifted my weight on the sofa that Valerie and I were currently occupying.

At long last, the elf who owned this inn appeared in the doorway.

"Captain Vendir," he said as he closed the distance to the High Elf. Lifting a hand, he held out an envelope with an intricate seal made of golden wax. "A message just arrived for you."

A ripple of anticipation went through the room. I sat forward.

"Thank you," Vendir said as he took the envelope.

We all stared at the innkeeper, waiting for him to disappear before anyone dared say anything. If he felt our impatience, he didn't let it show as he descended the stairs again with unhurried steps.

"Is that…?" Valerie blurted out once the echo of the innkeeper's footsteps had faded.

"Yes," Captain Vendir confirmed.

The room sucked in a collective breath. Then Vendir cracked the seal and pulled out the letter.

"What does it say?" Valerie asked even though the captain had probably only had time to read the greeting so far.

His brown eyes swept back and forth across the page. Once he reached the end, he looked up. Whatever feelings he had were hidden behind a carefully constructed mask of neutrality.

"Our request has been accepted." He held out the letter for us to verify. "The Emperor and Empress of Valdanar expect our presence in the Palace of the Never Setting Sun tomorrow at midday."

Standing up, I took the offered letter and skimmed it to make sure that it truly said what Vendir had claimed before I handed it to Mordren, who did the same.

"Alright." Valerie jumped up from the couch and executed a dramatic bow. "Time to practice our polite bows and our best smiles."

"We're all going?" Theo asked.

"Of course we are."

Hadeon stood up and motioned towards Theo. "Actually, I think he's got a point. Sending everyone into a heavily guarded palace that we know nothing about is not a strategic move. What if it's a trap?"

Idra's dark eyes slid to Hadeon. "I agree."

"Me too." Nodding, I swept my gaze around the room. "Vendir and I will go in alone in case something goes wrong."

The room erupted in protests. People talked over each other as everyone except Ellyda shot to their feet and motioned towards each other.

"Absolutely not," Idra snapped from her position by the wall. "No one is going in alone. Least of all you."

"What do you mean *least of all me*?" I threw my arms out. "Need I remind you all that I am the only one here capable of actually walking through walls? I have, by far, the best chance of getting out if something happens."

"Excuse me?" Valerie called and raised her eyebrows while flapping a hand between her and Theo. "We are thieves. We specialize in getting in and out of places without people noticing."

"No." Eilan shook his head at her. "You two are not going."

"Why not?"

"Because you're human."

Irritation flashed across Valerie's face. "So? Are you saying that we're less than you because we're human?"

"No!" He jerked back as if she had slapped him. "That's not what I'm saying. You two shouldn't go because even though you are good, really good, at what you do, you will stand out too much. If something goes wrong, how are you supposed to remain undetected when you are literally *the only two members of your entire species* on this whole continent?"

"Oh." She blinked at him for a second. Then she shook her head. "But I still have a better chance at getting out than most of you."

"No, I should go," Eilan said firmly. "I have the best chance of making it out unnoticed if things go sideways."

Valerie let out a confused huff. "You? What kind of sneaky abilities do you have that would be better than mine?"

Hesitation flickered in Eilan's pale green eyes. Only half of the present company knew that he was a shapeshifter, and Valerie was currently not among them. For a moment, it looked like he was going to tell her. But then he only raked a hand through his long black hair and expelled a sigh.

"It's not–"

"Enough," Ellyda snapped from the couch. Lowering her notebook, she shifted her sharp gaze from person to person.

"Most of you are right, so I don't understand what it is that you are arguing about. Let me summarize it for you. Idra is right, no one is going in alone."

From her position by the wall, Idra shot me an I-told-you-so look. I rolled my eyes at her.

"Here is what's going to happen," Ellyda continued. "Mordren, Eilan, Kenna, and Valerie… you will be going with Vendir to the palace. Between the four of you, you have a wide range of skills that involve getting in and out unseen, as well as powerful battle magic. Hadeon, Idra, Theo, and I will be staying here because we have the best chance of helping you escape from the outside if we need to. Theo knows how to break into places, Hadeon and Idra can take on whatever forces we might need to fight…" She shook her head. "And I am apparently the only one here with decent observational skills."

Ringing silence filled the cramped living room. From outside the window, faint sounds of a bustling city drifted in along with warm summer air. Ellyda raised her eyebrows expectantly. The rest of us exchanged glances.

"Well, you heard her," Hadeon finally declared into the silence.

Nods and murmurs of agreement spread through the room. Everyone seemed more or less satisfied with their roles, so no one protested. Or perhaps no one dared disagree with Ellyda.

"You are awfully quiet," Mordren observed as he locked eyes with Captain Vendir.

"Yes." He shrugged. "Because this is not my problem. I will get you through the door and give you a chance to plead your case. That was the deal. Whatever happens after that, and whatever the emperor and empress decide, is up to you and them."

"You do not sound very guilt-ridden for someone who is about to betray his High Commander."

"Perhaps I don't always agree with everything High Commander Anron does." Vendir raised his hand and shook it, making the black bracelet shift around his wrist. A hint of challenge crept into his eyes. "Or perhaps you just didn't give me much of a choice."

Mordren gave him a smile that was laced with both amusement and threats. Shaking my head, I blew out a sigh.

"Regardless," Eilan said before either of them could speak up again, "our deal involved you giving us a chance to speak to your rulers. That means you need to teach us how the protocol works for this kind of visit."

Captain Vendir tore his gaze from Mordren. After rolling his shoulders, he nodded at Eilan. "True. Well, listen up then."

Fabric rustled as the eight of us settled down on the couches and armchairs again and got ready for a crash course on how to behave around royalty in this land. Because tomorrow, we would at last be going to the Palace of the Never Setting Sun to meet the Empress and Emperor of Valdanar.

What could possibly go wrong?

CHAPTER 5

A gigantic palace stared down at us. Arches and twisting spires reached for the clear blue heavens, grand fountains sent streams of water washing down into artful pools around the courtyard, and immaculately trimmed hedges and flowers swayed in the breeze. The whole palace was made of some kind of pale mirror-like material. It caused the bright summer sun to reflect off the surface, making it look like the whole castle radiated sunlight. The Palace of the Never Setting Sun, indeed.

My heart pattered against my ribs as I mapped every courtyard we passed for potential escape routes and hiding places. Without even looking, I knew that Mordren, Eilan, and Valerie were doing the same thing.

Captain Vendir was walking a couple of steps in front of us, but behind the dark-haired High Elf who acted as our escort. I flicked my gaze up and down Vendir's body. He didn't look nervous. Or worried. His armor was polished to perfection and his posture was confident, as if he had done this a million times. While he had kept his word when we ran into those soldiers in town, I still couldn't help thinking that this would be the perfect time for him to betray us.

Instead of giving us a chance to tell the empress and emperor about Anron's plans, Vendir could just as easily tell them that we were the villains of the story. That we had tried to stop Anron's noble quest and taken him prisoner in order to force him to betray his High Commander. Then we would be left in an impenetrable castle with the two most powerful beings on this whole continent and very little chance of escape.

But it was a risk we would have to take. This was our best chance, our *only* chance, to save our homeland from Anron and Syrene's wicked plans. So all we could do was hope that Vendir would be true to his word.

After crossing yet another open courtyard, we reached a long hallway that ended with the most imposing doors I had ever seen. I had to tilt my head back to even see the top of them.

Our guide paused in front of the doors.

The rest of us trailed to a halt behind him as well. A hand brushed my side. Glancing sideways, I found Valerie mouthing '*east courtyard*' at me before she shifted her gaze and did the same to Eilan and Mordren. I nodded. We would escape to the east courtyard if Vendir betrayed us.

Then, as if on some invisible signal, our escort pushed open the doors and motioned for us to step inside.

They swung open a lot easier than doors of that size should have, and also without making any sound.

I swallowed. My hand brushed over my empty thigh even though I knew that my knife wasn't there. Bringing weapons into the palace was forbidden.

"Let's go," Captain Vendir said.

And then he strode into the grand hall beyond.

We followed.

Our steps echoed against the polished floor as we moved into what looked like a throne room. While the hallway we had left behind had been covered in shadows, this space almost looked like it was outdoors because sunlight streamed in from what could only be a glass roof. It made the walls and floor radiate sunlight in the same way that the outside of the palace did. Glancing up, I tried to spot the ceiling above us, but it was so high up that I couldn't make out where it ended and where the sky began.

Banners depicting a bright sun on top of a rich blue background hung from the walls along the room. At the end of the rectangular hall were two tall thrones made of the same mirror-like material as the rest of the castle.

"Remember what I said," Vendir whispered out of the corner of his mouth, not taking his eyes off the twin thrones ahead. "Bow deeply, don't speak until they tell you to, and don't look them directly in the eye."

There was a faint crackling sound coming from up ahead.

I forced myself to keep breathing normally as we closed the distance to the raised thrones. No one spoke.

Once we reached the space below the shining steps, I finally saw what the source of that crackling sound was.

Magic.

The Emperor and Empress of Valdanar were covered in magic.

On the right, the emperor sat straight-backed on his throne. He wore regal armor that looked to be as expensive and ornate as it was functional. The signature sun was emblazoned on his chest, and a rich blue cape fell down from his shoulders. Fire covered the entire cape. Magical flames of bright yellow crackled and burned continuously along the beautiful fabric and ended atop his shoulders like fiery spikes. Small flames flickered down the length of his long blond hair as well.

The empress, seated on the throne beside him, wore a breathtaking dress in black and silver. Her long dark brown hair tumbled down her back, but her face was covered by a beautiful veil made of black lace that only hinted at the features underneath. Apparently, it was meant as a reminder to anyone who would dare cross her that she would make widows of them all. Though, according to Vendir, some whispered that she wore it to cover the scars from where her husband had accidentally burned her in a fit of rage. But no one knew for certain.

I dared another glance up at her.

Lightning crackled down her arms. Not once or twice. Just like the emperor, the magic clung to her like it was part of her clothes.

A spike of fear shot through me. These two people could draw on the magic of every single High Elf throughout their whole continent. They had access to so much magic that they could keep a constant reminder of it on their skin as a show of strength. Dread settled like a stone in my stomach. If Vendir was about to sell us out, there was no way we would be able to escape.

Captain Vendir bowed at the waist.

The rest of us followed suit.

We stayed like that until a commanding voice at last cut through the silence.

"Captain Vendir," the emperor said.

"Your Imperial Majesties," Vendir replied before finally straightening.

"Who are these people that you have brought?"

Vendir stepped aside so that his rulers could see all four of us clearly. I kept my back straight and my chin raised, but let my eyes rest on the emperor's chest so that he wouldn't catch me looking directly into his face.

"May I present Prince Mordren Darkbringer from the Court of Shadows," Captain Vendir said as he motioned towards the two black-haired elves on my left. "And his brother Eilan Voidcaller, also from the Court of Shadows." His hand moved towards me and Valerie. "And Lady Kenna Firesoul from the Court of Fire. And her advisor Valerie of the Hands."

Even without looking at her, I could almost see the chuckle building in Valerie's throat. I wasn't sure if it was because of the very grand title 'of the Hands' or the fact that he had called her an advisor rather than the perhaps more accurate job description of spymaster, thief, and gang leader. But thankfully, she held it together.

"And may I present to you," Captain Vendir continued with a sweeping gesture towards the twin thrones. "Their Imperial Majesties Emperor Lanseyo and Empress Elswyth of Valdanar."

We all bowed once more, just as we had been instructed beforehand.

"Why have you brought these strangers here, Captain Vendir?" Emperor Lanseyo asked while we straightened again.

My pulse sped up. If Vendir was going to betray us, he would do it now.

"I shall explain the details of how this situation came about soon, but the short version is that they have traveled here from their homeland to share information with you."

Tension fell across the room. He hadn't betrayed us. Yet.

Since we had been instructed not to say anything until they gave us permission, the four of us only continued standing there in silence.

"Well then," Empress Elswyth said. She had a rather musical voice, but the authority in her tone suggested that she was used to people obeying her every command. "Speak."

According to Vendir, the emperor was in charge of all military matters in their realm while the empress handled all the political aspects. Since Anron was a leader in the military, but who also tried to get political power, we would need to convince both of them if this desperate gamble was going to work.

"We have come before you to tell you about a sinister plot to usurp your thrones," Mordren said in a calm and clear voice. "Allow me to explain from the beginning."

We had already decided that Mordren would do the initial talking since he had the most experience in dealing with royalty. I shifted my gaze between the empress and emperor while Mordren explained what Anron had done on our island and what he planned to do here. Even though I didn't dare look up into their faces, I could tell that they showed no outward emotions. No shock. No anger. No nothing. I wasn't sure if that was good or bad.

Oppressive silence fell across the high-ceilinged hall once Mordren finished. I drew in a calming breath that did nothing to actually calm me down. Next to me, Valerie brushed her hand against mine as if to simply remind me that we were all here for each other no matter what.

"You expect me to believe that High Commander Anron, a war hero and one of the best military leaders under my command, is plotting to overthrow us?" the emperor said at last, breaking the silence.

"Yes," Mordren replied. "Why else would we risk coming here if we were not telling the truth?"

Silence fell across the throne room once more. I could feel the weight of their stares as the emperor and empress studied us from atop their shining thrones. Since I still didn't dare look up into their faces, I watched the way the light sparkled off Empress Elswyth's dress before I shifted my gaze to the sun across the emperor's chest. Without being able to see their facial expressions, it was incredibly difficult to guess what they were thinking, but I tried to read them based on their posture.

Nothing.

Whatever they were thinking, I wouldn't know until they actually spoke up and proclaimed their judgement.

Blood pounded in my ears. I forced shallow breaths into my lungs and tried to dispel the nerves wreaking havoc in my chest.

The Emperor of Valdanar drew in a deep breath.

I held mine.

This was it.

"I see." His voice cut through the silence like a knife. "So it is true."

A lightning bolt hit me straight in the chest.

CHAPTER 6

*E*nergy crackled through my body. I was vaguely aware of air rushing in my ears as I flew backwards before crashing down on the hard floor. Dull pain pulsed from my shoulder and down my arm as I landed and then rolled over and over again until I finally stopped. Lying on my back, I stared up at the blue sky and the bright sun visible beyond the impossibly high glass roof. My limbs twitched.

While still trying to figure out what had happened, I rolled over on my side and pushed myself up on shaking arms.

Mordren was climbing to his feet a short distance away from me while Eilan crouched in front of Valerie, who lay unconscious on the floor. Terror washed over me.

Another bolt of lightning shot towards Mordren. He threw up a shadow shield right at the same time as I raised a shield of fire in front of him as well. The lightning cut through our shields like a knife through soft butter, but Mordren at least managed to dive to the side.

My flame shield only served to draw attention to me.

The Emperor and Empress of Valdanar were striding

down the steps from their thrones. They walked leisurely, unhurriedly, and their entire bodies radiated power.

Mordren called up another shield of darkness.

Without breaking a stride, or even so much as blinking, Emperor Lanseyo sent a wave of fire that burned through Mordren's shadows as if they had been nothing more than a thin sheet of paper. Shock flashed across Mordren's face as another lightning bolt came out of nowhere and sent him flying backwards.

I raised a wall of fire before me, but just like Mordren's defense, it was wiped away as if it was nothing. A wave of water washed over my flames and extinguished every ember right before another flash of lightning connected with my chest as well.

The throne room spun around me as I once more flew through the air. My breath rushed out of my lungs as I slammed into the shining floor a few strides away from Mordren. Lying on my side, I could just barely make out Eilan and Valerie on the other side. He was still crouched in front of her with his arms out, as if to stop any attacks. The emperor and empress apparently didn't deem them enough of a threat because they ignored them completely as they descended the final steps to the floor.

Captain Vendir had backed away and was staring between the two of them and the four of us. Shock and confusion bounced across his face.

To my left, Mordren tried to push himself up.

Lightning crackled through the air.

It hit him in the shoulder, making him flip over, right before another bolt took him in the side.

"Stop," I called, but I could barely hear myself over the ringing in my ears.

Mordren's body spasmed uncontrollably.

"Please stop," I pleaded again.

I tried to stand up but I couldn't get my muscles to obey me.

The emperor and empress stopped a couple of strides before us. Cocking his head, Lanseyo studied Mordren. Then he sent another lightning bolt at him. Fear and hopelessness threatened to drown me as Mordren continued twitching on the floor. Against these beings, we were like helpless children.

"Stop," I rasped again. "Please."

Emperor Lanseyo let out a vicious laugh. "If you come over here and lick my boots, I will stop."

No longer caring about proper etiquette, I flicked my gaze to his face.

Malice shone in the emperor's blue eyes and a wicked smile, the smile of a bully, curled his lips.

Ellyda's words from back in King Aldrich's castle clanged through me. Suddenly, I understood exactly why High Commander Lester was terrified of his emperor. He really did have a cruel streak and enjoyed making people feel powerless.

"Well?" he goaded.

I swallowed my pride. Since I couldn't get my legs to work properly yet, I was forced to crawl over to the emperor. Stopping before his shining black boots, I closed my eyes briefly. Then I licked the side of his boot.

Smug laughter echoed through the sunlit hall.

A hand shot down and grabbed the front of my shirt. I sucked in a breath as Emperor Lanseyo yanked me up before depositing me onto my knees. With my head still ringing, I glanced over my shoulder.

Mordren's body had stopped spasming. He rolled over on his side. And then he threw up. Again. And again.

The empress let out a disgusted noise and then flicked a hand. Fire incinerated the puddles on the floor, leaving nothing in its wake. I closed my eyes. We were never going to survive this. And I didn't even understand what had gone wrong.

"Why?" I whispered pathetically as I opened my eyes again. "We warned you about a threat to your rule. Why are you doing this to us?"

"Because you are desperate liars who would do anything to undermine me and the work I do for our sacred emperor and empress."

I whipped my head to the side. The move made my vision sway and I had to blink several times before the view came back into focus again. When it did, I found three tall figures striding towards us across the floor.

"Anron," Eilan hissed from his position next to Valerie.

Captain Vendir stumbled a step back. "High Commander?"

Bronze breastplates gleamed in the bright sunlight as High Commanders Anron, Lester, and Danser strode across the throne room. They bowed deeply to their leaders before turning to us. Anron's sharp blue eyes glittered in the sun.

"We figured out your nefarious plan quickly," he said. "But luckily, we got here before you did so that we could explain what was really going on." A cold smile spread across his lips as he turned towards Vendir. "So that we could explain that one of our own had betrayed us and sided with the enemy."

Captain Vendir jerked back as if someone had struck him. "What?"

"I blame myself, really." Anron placed a hand on his own chest and shook his head. "If I had known that he would fall for the Low Elf Ellyda Steelsinger during all those long nights working in the forge, I would never have allowed him to watch her. Never had I believed that his infatuation would make him go to these extremes. But that is the way of love, I suppose."

"N-no," Vendir stammered. Utter confusion swirled in his brown eyes as he glanced between Anron and the emperor. "Please. High Commander, what are you saying? I would never willingly betray you." Raising his hand, he showed them the black bracelet around his wrist. "I was coerced into flying them here. They threatened me." He shook the bracelet again. "With *this*."

A lightning bolt struck Vendir straight in the chest. He flew through the air and tumbled down on the floor while Anron lowered his hand after the shot.

"Do not disrespect your emperor and empress by continuing to lie," he growled at the captain who was now struggling to his feet a short distance away. "I put that bracelet on you so that I could bring you home to face justice for your crimes after you helped these outlaws set up that ambush at the bank. The least you can do is take responsibility for your betrayal."

"He's lying!" I called. "We did kidnap Captain Vendir and threaten–"

Lightning exploded into my chest again.

It threw me off my knees and I slammed back first down into the cold hard floor. Energy shot up and down my limbs, making them spasm uncontrollably.

"Enough," Empress Elswyth snapped somewhere above me. "Lock them up."

I wanted to fight. To scream. To do something. Anything. But all I could do was lie there on the floor until someone in bronze armor picked me up and threw me over their shoulder like a sack of grain. My vision went in and out of focus.

"No, please," Captain Vendir called from what sounded very far away. "Don't do this. Please. Emperor Lanseyo, you know me. I have served faithfully for decades. I have always been loyal. I'm telling the truth. *They're* telling the truth. Please."

Lifting my head, I saw more soldiers pour into the throne room.

They picked up all of my friends and grabbed Vendir by the arms even as he tried to fight back.

And then they dragged us away.

CHAPTER 7

I didn't know what it was like to be hit by real lightning, but repeatedly getting struck by magical lightning was not something that I would recommend. Ever. Bolts of energy still shot up and down my body at random intervals and I couldn't for the life of me make any of my muscles obey me.

Metal clanked somewhere around me and a dull jolt shot through my thighs as someone sat me down against a wall.

"No, not her." Anron's commanding voice cut through the fog in my brain as a flash of fear took its place. "She can walk through walls."

Blinking, I tried to clear my vision while someone grabbed me by the shoulders and dragged me towards the middle of the stone floor instead. A moment later, cold metal appeared around my wrists and ankles. Chains clattered.

When my vision had finally cleared enough for me to see my surroundings, I found myself sitting in the middle of what could only be a prison cell. Thick stone walls boxed in the empty space and the only illumination came from a barred window high up on the wall, as well as from the solid metal door that was currently open. Manacles locked my wrists and ankles together. I glanced down at the sturdy chain running from my restraints to a metal ring that was buried in the stone floor. There would be no walking through walls with this on.

"There is nothing underneath the floor," High Commander Anron said as if he could hear my thoughts. "Only solid rock. So there will be no escape for you."

Since I couldn't muster enough energy to both move my head and speak, I had to settle for simply tipping my head back to glare at Anron. His blue eyes glinted as he answered with a smug smirk.

"What is she?" another voice said.

With great effort, I managed to turn my head to truly take in the rest of the room. Another wave of terror washed over me.

Mordren, Eilan, Valerie, and Captain Vendir were sitting with their backs against the walls. One at each wall. A long metal bar with cuffs at each end trapped their hands against the stone wall above their heads.

"She's a human," Anron answered. "They're an even weaker species than Low Elves."

My gaze snapped to Valerie.

The High Elf soldier who had locked her into the contraption by the wall had grabbed a fistful of her hair and tilted her head so that he could look at her ears. Valerie's head lolled to the side like a broken doll.

"Don't touch her," Eilan growled from the opposite wall.

Anron arched an eyebrow at him. Then he shot a lightning bolt straight into Eilan's chest.

"No!" Mordren shouted from the other side.

Eilan's body spasmed against the wall for a few seconds before he stopped moving. Unconscious. His head rested against his chest, but the restraints kept his body in a sitting position.

"I will kill you for this," Mordren promised in a deadly whisper.

He was unnaturally pale and it looked like he was having trouble focusing his eyes, but the Prince of Shadows glared at Anron as if he could make the High Commander drop dead on the spot. If he had been able to concentrate enough to use his pain magic, he probably could have.

"I sincerely doubt that," Anron said.

Metallic clanking echoed throughout the cell as the two soldiers by the wall opposite Mordren finally finished locking Captain Vendir's wrists into the bar as well.

"Don't do this," Captain Vendir pleaded as they stepped back and gave him a clear view of his High Commander.

Anron flicked his wrist. The other soldiers in the cell dipped their chins and then filed out the door. Only when their footsteps had gone silent did Anron speak again. Anger flickered in his eyes as he leveled a hard stare on Vendir.

"You were going to betray me," he said.

"I knew about your plans from the start and I never betrayed you." Captain Vendir yanked uselessly against his restraints. "And I never would have if they hadn't forced me."

"Yes, and that's the problem, isn't it? You're *weak*. You always were weak. I knew that from the start but I thought that I could mold you into someone better. But then you allowed a bunch of Low Elves and humans to force you into selling me out."

"Please, I–"

"And I have no room for weaklings and turncoats."

"Don't–"

"I should have let you drown that day."

Captain Vendir rocked back as if Anron had hit him. The words he had been about to say died on his tongue as he stared up at the High Commander. I could almost see his heart cracking.

Whirling around, Anron started towards the door.

"The empress said she had questions about your elemental magic," he said and kicked my thigh as he passed me. "And since you are always so secretive about your magic, I assume that she will come here and interrogate you directly after she is finished questioning me."

When I didn't answer, he paused with his hand on the door and turned back to sweep his gaze over the five of us. "Did Vendir tell you why she wears that black veil? It's because she makes widows of everyone who defies her."

"Please," Captain Vendir whispered. His voice cracked slightly. "I beg you."

Disgust flashed over Anron's features. He raised his hand. Lightning appeared along the length of his arm.

I raised my chin and forced a vicious smile onto my lips. "If she makes widows of the ones who defy her, then I look forward to seeing what she does to you when she–"

A crack split the air.

And the last thing I saw was a flash of blinding white light.

CHAPTER 8

Water splashed across my face. I jerked up and coughed to get the liquid out of my mouth and nose. Blinking, I tried to clear my vision enough to see my surroundings.

"I did try only a few drops at first," said a voice that was both musical and full of authority, "but you must have said something truly provocative for Anron to render you so firmly unconscious."

An elegantly embroidered hemline became visible a few strides away. I glanced up the length of the dress.

"Empress Elswyth," I said carefully.

She was wearing the same black and silver-colored dress as before, and lightning still danced up and down her arms. My gaze stopped at her collarbones, but I could tell that she wore the same black lace veil over her face as well.

"Stand up," she said.

With a glance down my own body, I found that I wasn't restrained in any way. And I wasn't in the cell either.

Placing my palms against the floor, I maneuvered myself

onto my knees and then slowly got to my feet. While taking my time to stand, I surveyed the room.

It was a circular space. There were no windows at all, which made the white stone walls look dark and foreboding. A discreet glance over my shoulder confirmed that the only door in the round room was positioned a short distance behind me. But strangely enough, that wasn't the part of the room that commanded almost all of my attention. It was the section behind the empress.

A dozen pedestals were arranged in a semi-circle along the far half of the room, and atop each pedestal was a wide metal bowl. Fire burned in one of the bowls while water twisted above another. Dark shadows swirled up from yet another. Lightning crackled in a fourth one. Then stone. And wood. And several other. My heart skipped a beat as I stared at the contents. The whole room hummed with magic. Because that was what it was. Magic.

Finally straightening, I tore my gaze from the bowls of magic and instead shifted my attention to the empress.

Silence fell.

I wiped the remaining water from my face and smoothened back my messy hair, but didn't dare break the quiet. Once I let my arms drop back down, I only continued looking at the black and silver dress before me.

"Are you not going to try to escape?" Empress Elswyth asked at last.

"No," I said.

"Why not?"

"Because you could mop the floor with me without even lifting a finger."

Silence descended on the room once more. I remained motionless.

Then she laughed. It was more of an amused huff of air than a real laugh, but it still dispelled some of the tension that had been building inside me. I drew in a soft breath.

"Wise choice," the empress said, a hint of amusement still in her voice. "You are an intelligent one, I see. I like that."

Since I wasn't sure how to respond to that, I only inclined my head in acknowledgement.

"Do you know where we are?" She raised a lightning-covered arm and motioned at the room around us.

"No."

"This is the White Tower. It is where we keep a manifestation of the magic that the gods have bestowed upon the High Elves. A symbol of when the gods granted the first Empress and Emperor of Valdanar the right to rule."

My eyes swept over the pedestals again. The multitude of elemental magic cast shifting colors on the white stone walls and made the whole room shine even though there were no windows.

When the pause stretched on, I assumed that she was waiting for an answer so I said, "It's spectacular."

"Indeed." The veil in front of her face rippled slightly as she cocked her head. "In the throne room, I saw that you can use fire magic."

"Yes."

"And your friend, Mordren Darkbringer, can use shadow magic."

"Yes."

"Low Elves on our continent do not have access to unrestricted elemental magic in that way."

"So I have been told."

"Anron informed me that you did not have access to fire magic the whole time. In fact, you only recently acquired it when you became the ruler of your court. He said that you drank the fire out of a bowl."

"That's right."

Only the faint crackling and swishing of magic, both in the bowls and along her arms, broke the silence. I already knew where this conversation was heading, but I didn't want to give away more than I had to so I only remained standing there. If she had a question, she was going to have to ask me outright.

Light from the multitude of magical sources made the silver details of her dress sparkle. I studied the way the lightning along her arms highlighted the silver threads woven into her sleeves. The silence continued.

"Your ancestors must have stolen magic from this room before they fled," the Empress of Valdanar finally said.

They probably had, and I saw no reason to defend them, so I simply said, "Yes, I believe so too."

Another brief pause filled the room, as if she had been expecting me to deny it. Then she brushed a hand down her dress and squared her shoulders. "We want it back."

"I guessed as much." I kept my gaze on her collarbones. "But I'm afraid that won't be possible."

She let out a cold huff of laughter that was more threat than amusement. "I could make you do anything I want."

"I know. But we still wouldn't be able to give the magic back."

"Why not?"

"Because there is nothing to give back. All we have is one small bowl of magic for each prince. During the coronation ceremony, the new elven prince drinks the elemental magic connected to their court. And when they die, the magic is returned to the bowl and the process is repeated. Or that's how it should be, anyway. Now, we will be the last of the princes."

"Why is that?"

"Because Anron unwittingly destroyed the bowls. They were kept locked away in a secret temple under our king's mountain. Your High Commander made a deal with an elf called Princess Syrene. In exchange for him breaking her out of prison, she would help Anron kill our king."

"Why is this relevant?"

"The prison was built as a barrier to protect the temple."

"And?"

"And Anron blew up the prison to get Princess Syrene out."

Empress Elswyth clenched her left hand in a distinctly annoyed gesture.

"That whole section of the mountain collapsed, destroying the bowls with it. Now when we die, there is nowhere for the magic to go. So we will be the last of the princes able to wield elemental magic."

"I see." She paused as she took a step closer to me. "Then perhaps I should simply kill you right now to once and for all free the magic that your ancestors stole."

A spike of fear shot up my spine. I swallowed. Dozens of plans flashed through my brain as I tried to figure out how to manipulate her into keeping me alive. None of them seemed good enough.

"Please don't," I whispered, trying to stall for time.

Lightning crackled along her embroidered sleeves and the hem of her dress rustled against the stone floor as she took another step closer to me. My heart pounded in my chest. I would never make it to the door in time, and I had no idea what was beneath the floor so I couldn't phase through it either.

"Why not?" she asked, as if she was genuinely curious about what kind of reason I would give for why my life should be spared.

Blood pounded in my ears and I still didn't have a plan. I was out of time.

"Because I don't want to die."

She stopped.

Standing two strides away, I barely dared to breathe.

Empress Elswyth let out another amused huff of laughter. "A sincere answer? How refreshing." Her dress rippled as she started walking again. This time, right past me towards the door. "Follow."

Jolted out of my near-death moment, I cast one last glance at the magic before me and then hurried to catch up with the empress. My heart still thumped in my chest.

"So, you are both an intelligent and an honest one?" she continued. "I like that. Perhaps there is no reason to kill you right this very night."

"Thank you," I blurted out.

With my pulse still thrumming in my ears, I poured all of my energy into rebuilding the mask of sincerity and trustworthiness that I had kept firmly on my face until the moment she almost killed me. While forcing the lingering panic down, I desperately hoped that she wouldn't realize that I had been lying through my teeth during most of our conversation.

There wasn't just one bowl per element. There were two. One for each reigning prince, and then one for the king as well. Otherwise, how would both Prince Edric and King Aldrich have been able to wield their stone magic? Since the king came from a different court each time, or at least usually, there needed to be two bowls of every element. And right now, since the king was dead, all of the extra ones were filled.

While it was true that the bowls were kept in a secret temple, they certainly weren't kept anywhere near the prison. That had just been my way of trying to get back at Anron. If the empress believed that he was responsible for the destruction of the bowls, he would lose some of her favor. But the bowls still existed, and they were currently being protected by Prince Edric and his most trusted people.

Empress Elswyth flicked a hand.

The metal door swung open soundlessly without her even touching it. A starlit sky became visible above us as we stepped onto a narrow bridge outside the door. It was made of the same white stone as the tower we had just exited. Two High Elf soldiers fell in beside me as we started back across the bridge. The metal door banged shut behind me, and then a click sounded, like a lock snapping shut. A few moments later, a third guard took up position behind my back.

"I shall consider whether or not killing you and your friends is the best course of action politically and strategically," Empress Elswyth said. "But for tonight, I will let you live."

"Thank you," I said while my gaze swept back and forth across the surrounding area, committing every detail to memory.

What I saw did not inspire hope. We appeared to be walking towards a heavily guarded part of the massive palace. Since there were guards around me, I also couldn't turn around to see what was behind the tower and the bridge we were on. But at least I would be able to map out part of the castle on the way back.

"I expect to have reached a decision tomorrow," the empress said.

My stomach dropped. We only had until tomorrow to figure out a way to escape? That would make an already impossible mission so much harder.

I scanned the area as we finally stepped off the bridge.

But this walk might at least provide me with an escape route. Flicking my gaze back and forth, I tried to take it all in while also not looking too suspicious.

Black fabric appeared before my eyes.

It took all of my self-control not to scream in frustration as the guard behind me tied a blindfold firmly over my eyes. A second later, the two soldiers at my sides grabbed my arms and started steering me forward as we continued walking.

No escape route. No clues. No plan. And worst of all, no time.

And it was all my fault.

CHAPTER 9

Manacles clicked shut around my wrists and ankles. Sitting on the cold stone floor of the cell, I watched the High Elf soldier as he strode back towards the door. Four pairs of eyes watched me in turn, but no one said anything. At last, the metal door banged shut.

"We need to leave," I said into the oppressive silence.

"Yes, we do," Eilan said from my right. He glanced up at the lone window high up on the wall. "Based on the moonlight, it's the middle of the night. Ellyda, Hadeon, Idra, and Theo will have figured out that something is wrong by now and they're probably making a plan for how to get us out right at this very moment."

"No, you don't understand. We need to get out. *Now*. We can't wait for them."

Mordren met my gaze from across the room. "What happened?"

"I made a mistake." My hands shook slightly so I reached up and raked my fingers through my hair so that the others wouldn't see it. The movement made my chains rattle, but at least it gave my hands something to do. "I was just trying to… I didn't think she would…"

"Kenna," Mordren interrupted, his voice calm. "What happened?"

Blowing out a breath, I let my hands drop back down into my lap. Panic and guilt wouldn't help me fix this, so I forced the feelings aside and inhaled again. With my mind at least a little calmer, I cast a glance at Captain Vendir from over my shoulder. His brown eyes studied me intently.

If he learned the truth, there was a risk that he would try to sell us out in exchange for his own life. But we would also need him if we were to stand any chance of escaping. Maybe a bit of trust went a long way. Besides, High Commander Anron had made it very clear that sacrificing Captain Vendir to make sure that his own secrets never saw the light of day was an acceptable outcome.

I swept my gaze over the rest of them. "She wanted to know about the magic. More specifically, how we acquire our elemental magic and how it can be returned to the High Elves since our ancestors apparently stole it from their sacred tower before they left. I told her that there was only one bowl for each element and that the bowls had been destroyed when Anron blew up the prison. So there is no way to give the magic back because there are no bowls for it to return to when we die."

"And she believed that?" Eilan asked.

"Yes."

Valerie squinted at me from opposite him. "I don't get it. Why is that bad?"

Mordren and Eilan's dark brows were creased as well

when they looked back at me. I was just about to answer when another voice cut through the silence.

"Because now she wants to kill you and Mordren so that the magic will at least be free." Vendir arched a pale brow at me. "Am I right?"

"Yeah." Dragging a hand through my hair again, I tipped my head back and heaved a sigh before turning to meet his gaze once more. "How did you know?"

"It's how she thinks."

"I thought… I thought she would be satisfied that no one would be able to get the magic again. I didn't think she would want to kill us just to speed up the process." I met each of their gazes. "I'm sorry. I bought us time until tomorrow while she considers whether killing us really is the best course of action, but mercy doesn't seem like her kind of thing so we really need to get out tonight."

Mordren nodded. "Agreed." His eyes slid to Vendir. "Are you with us?"

Captain Vendir was silent for a few seconds, as if considering whether throwing his lot in with us really was his best shot. Then the shadows in his eyes cleared and he gave us a decisive nod. "Yes."

"Alright, then we have several problems we need to solve," Valerie said. "Problem one." She yanked against the metal bar that kept her arms pinned to the wall above her head. "We need to figure out a way to get out of these restraints. If I could only reach my lockpicks, and the actual lock, I'd be able to get us all out. But with my hands like this, I can't do either of those."

"I, uhm…" Eilan's pale green eyes were full of hesitation as his gaze flicked back and forth across the room. "I can, uhm… take care of that."

Valerie blinked at him in surprise. "Seriously? How?"

"We'll get back to that." He cleared his throat a bit awkwardly. "So once we're out of the restraints, then what? The lock is on the outside of the door."

"I can walk through it," I said. "But I need to know where the guards outside are posted."

"There will be one at that wall," Vendir explained, and nodded towards a spot halfway between Mordren and Eilan. "He will have the key to the door."

"Alright, I'll go out, get the key, and unlock the door. But how do we get out of the palace?"

"I know the way," Vendir said. "But I won't be able to just walk us all out like this."

"I can hide us with shadows, if need be," Mordren offered.

"And I can walk through any locked doors and open them from the inside," I filled in.

"I'm a cat burglar," Valerie added, as if that was explanation enough. Which I suppose it was.

Eilan nodded. "Yeah, I think I can do something to help us look less suspicious too."

We all turned to Captain Vendir. For a moment, he only stared back at us with raised eyebrows. Then he shook his head.

"Okay." He blew out a sigh. "You make sure we stay invisible and I will lead us out."

"I still don't get what kind of magic trick you've got up your sleeve that will get us out of these restraints," Valerie said as she turned and raised her eyebrows at Eilan.

He shifted his gaze between her and Vendir. I had guessed what he was going to do the moment he spoke up, and I assumed Mordren had as well. We all watched him in silence.

A hint of pain crept into his eyes. After our conversation at my birthday party, I understood what this was going to cost him. Not only would he have to reveal to two more people that he was a shapeshifter, he would also have to reveal it to *Valerie*. I knew that he liked her. Even though they had never gone beyond the friends stage, I knew that they cared for each other. And once Eilan had told the person that he was a shapeshifter, all of his other relationships had fallen through because they couldn't accept all parts of him.

But if we didn't get out of this cell right now, we were all going to die.

He knew that.

We all knew that.

So in the end, he simply drew in a deep breath. I could almost see the curtain of steel that fell over his features as he braced himself for reactions he didn't want to see.

"I can explain more once we're out," Eilan began. "So for now, just..." He shrugged as if he didn't know how to finish that sentence.

Valerie and Captain Vendir watched him curiously.

Eilan closed his eyes briefly. Then the edges of his body began to blur. From across the room, Valerie sat up straighter and leaned forward as much as her restraints would allow.

Gasps echoed between the pale stone walls.

Where Eilan had been sitting a few seconds before, a young elf now sat. He had the same black hair and green eyes as Eilan, but he was short and skinny and looked to be no older than six or seven. With hands and wrists that were several sizes smaller than they had been before, he effortlessly slid his hands out of the restraints.

From their positions by the wall, Valerie and Captain Vendir gaped at him in utter shock.

That emotionless curtain of steel still covered Eilan's

features as he straightened and brushed himself off before shapeshifting back into his regular size.

"You're a shapeshifter," Valerie finally blurted out.

"Yes." Even his voice was carefully devoid of all emotion. He patted his clothes and then started towards Valerie. "I seem to have lost my own lockpicks when they dragged us here. Where are yours?"

"Why didn't you tell me?"

"Valerie." His voice stayed calm and detached as he came to a halt in front of her. "The lockpicks?"

"In my bra." She, on the other hand, sounded very distracted.

Eilan blinked in surprise and his movements faltered as he glanced between her face and her chest.

"Why didn't you tell me that you were a shapeshifter?" Valerie repeated while Eilan presumably tried to figure out how he was supposed to get the lockpicks from her bra in a respectful manner. "*That*," she nodded towards the wall where he had been sitting earlier, "was the coolest thing I have ever seen! Here I thought Kenna had the most awesome power of all, and then *bam*! You can shapeshift." She laughed and shook her head. "Imagine all the sneaky shit we could pull off together."

Eilan's brain seemed to be completely malfunctioning because all he did was stand there in front of her and stare down at her grinning face.

"Brother," Mordren said from the wall on his right. "The lockpicks, if you please."

"Right." He cleared his throat and gave his head a couple of short shakes before motioning awkwardly towards Valerie's chest. "May I…? Is it okay if I…?"

"Oh. Yeah, of course. Go ahead."

I swore that I could see a slight shade of red on Eilan's cheeks as he crouched down and gently moved the V-shaped neckline of Valerie's shirt sideways, exposing her skin. His eyes flicked up to hers again.

"The left one," she said, a smile tugging at her lips. "My left."

He nodded and then cleared his throat again before his fingers trailed downwards. Now the red color on his cheeks was unmistakable. Valerie studied every line of his face while his hand slid down over her breast.

"Right," she said. "More."

His gaze shot up to hers.

"To the right," she clarified, a wicked grin on her face. "More to the right."

Despite the dangerous situation we were in, I couldn't help the smile that spread across my lips. I had never seen anyone capable of continuously throwing the usually so smooth Eilan completely off his game in this way. No one except this grinning little thief. It was like watching a master musician compose a symphony of blunt flirtation mixed with subtle maneuvering.

The blush had spread down Eilan's cheeks and now covered his neck too, but he made an admirable effort to seem unaffected as his fingers slid over her breast and prodded it for the hidden lockpicks.

"There you are," Valerie said as Eilan finally pulled out a pair of thin metal picks. "I knew those clever fingers of yours would eventually find the right... spot."

By the wall on their left, Captain Vendir let out a groan and muttered something about the gods.

Eilan raked an embarrassed hand through his long dark

hair and mumbled something under his breath while moving towards the lock at the side of the metal bar.

A spark of hope fluttered its tiny wings in my chest as the lock clicked open and Valerie straightened on the floor as well.

One problem solved.

Only ten more to go.

CHAPTER 10

"That's it. If we can get through that door, we're in the clear."

Mordren and I stole a glance around the corner. We were somewhere on the far side of the palace, and the small door before us seemed to be some kind of servants' entrance. Two guards were posted by it, but they looked more bored than anything. I turned back to Captain Vendir.

"Would they recognize you?" I asked.

"Yes," he replied without hesitation.

"So how do we–"

"Incoming!" Valerie hissed as she skidded around the other corner behind us.

We darted towards her and threw ourselves into the small nook in the wall. Mordren's body pushed me up against the cold surface while Captain Vendir squeezed in next to us. At the edge of the small space, Eilan drew himself up against the wall and yanked Valerie in as well. She slammed into his chest with a thud.

A moment later, Mordren threw up a wall of shadows in front of the opening.

My heart pattered in my chest.

For a while, only the sound of night winds making lazy circles through the shining palace broke the silence. Then, the soft thumping of boots came around the corner. We all held our breath.

Two High Elf soldiers strode past the opening.

Mordren's muscles shifted slightly against my body, but other than that, no one moved. I resisted the urge to close my eyes. Instead, I watched through the murky shadows as the two soldiers in bronze armor disappeared from view. Still no one moved.

Once we had estimated that enough time had passed, Eilan and Valerie edged out onto the street again. Mordren, Vendir, and I followed.

"We need to get past those guards," Vendir whispered as he motioned towards the door set into the outer wall.

"I can take care of that," Eilan replied after casting a quick glance at them. He turned back to Vendir. "Who would they believe most, a messenger or a soldier?"

"Soldier."

Eilan nodded. "I'm on it. Mordren, get ready to hide everyone with your shadows."

The edges of his body blurred once more. And then a tall High Elf in gleaming bronze armor was standing next to us instead.

Valerie tilted her head back and stared up at him. "I'll never get tired of that."

"I'll never get *used to* that," Captain Vendir muttered under his breath.

After one last nod to his brother, Eilan strode around the

corner with quick steps. Mordren motioned for us to get back into the nook. Another wall of shadows sprang up.

One minute passed.

Then the sound of thudding feet came from the direction of the door. A moment later, the two guards ran past in the other direction. I raised my eyebrows at Mordren. He shrugged. Whatever Eilan had said must have been very convincing.

Valerie, who had been standing closest to the edge, flashed us a grin. "Well then, shall we?"

The shadow wall disappeared. We kept our eyes alert as we snuck around the corner and approached the door.

A High Elf soldier was standing close to it and it looked like he was trying to pick the lock.

"Valerie?" Eilan's High Elf persona said in an unfamiliar voice as he straightened from the uncooperative lock. "A little help picking it?"

"No need." She grinned at him and lifted a metal ring filled with keys. "I swiped this when they ran past."

Despite myself, I let out a soft chuckle as she deftly inserted one of the keys and unlocked the door. We slipped out. And then we ran.

I couldn't believe that we had actually pulled it off. But between the five of us, I supposed we possessed enough sneaky skills to manage an escape like this.

It had taken far longer than I would have liked, though. Panic had continuously bounced around inside me and my mind had been convinced that an army of High Elves was breathing down our necks the entire time. But we had made it out.

As we ran through the darkened streets, I tried to dispel the lingering dread and fear that had crawled back up my spine the moment I stepped through that cell wall. I had almost gotten my friends killed tonight with my insufficient lies. That could never happen again. I had to do better. Be better. I had to be perfect every single time. In a game with stakes as high as these, there were no do-overs. Feelings of inadequacy spread through my chest like cold poison. Who was I to think that I could take on someone like High Commander Anron, let alone the Empress and Emperor of Valdanar, and win?

"Your legs are too long," Valerie suddenly blurted out between breaths. "Gods damn it, can we just…"

It snapped me out of my churning mind. Looking around, I found that we were finally getting close to the inn we were staying at. A dark night sky still hung above us and the only light came from the bright summer moon.

Valerie trailed to a walk. She was breathing heavily by now. Even though we had only jogged most of the way, it was quite far between the palace and the edge of the city.

Slowing to a walk as well, I looked over at Valerie. I was panting, but she was outright gasping for air. As I studied the difference in height between her and the rest of us, I realized that she had probably been all-out running the entire way. My eyebrows shot up. Her level of endurance had to be better than all of ours put together.

Eilan shapeshifted back to his original form as he fell in beside Valerie.

For a few minutes, only the sound of our heavy breathing filled the silent streets.

"Why your bra?" Eilan's befuddled voice cut through the stillness. When he realized that we had all turned to look at him, he cleared his throat and met Valerie's gaze while repeating a bit more quietly, "Why do you keep your lockpicks in your bra?"

I shifted my attention back to the street ahead. As did Mordren and Vendir. But all three of us continued eavesdropping anyway.

"Because it's good to have them spread out," Valerie replied.

"What do you mean?"

"I have a pair in my boots, and my belt, and one in my sleeve too."

"What?" Eilan sounded very flustered. "Then why didn't you tell me to get the ones in your boot instead?"

I glanced over just in time to see Valerie wiggle her eyebrows. A darker color spread across Eilan's cheeks.

On their other side, Vendir massaged his forehead.

To Eilan's relief, our inn became visible at the end of the street before he had to form a reply. We scraped together our final bits of energy and jogged up to the door.

Since we were the only customers, the building was dark and still when we walked inside. However, that changed the farther up the stairs we got. Muffled voices came from the living room on the top floor. They sounded angry.

"No," Ellyda snapped. "We can't just go charging in there without knowing where they are."

"And how are we supposed to figure that out if we don't go inside?" Hadeon retorted.

"I could–" Theo began before being cut off.

"No. Like I said…" Ellyda trailed off.

We crested the stairs and poured into the living room to find a pair of sharp violet eyes staring straight at us. Three more people whirled around to face us.

Relief washed over the entire room.

"You're okay," Theo called as he ran over to embrace Valerie.

Hadeon and Ellyda cornered Mordren and Eilan to interrogate them. Or yell at them. Or hug them. It was a bit hard to tell, so maybe all of the above. Meanwhile, Captain Vendir hovered awkwardly by the wall.

"Where the hell have you been?" Idra snapped at me as she drew herself up in front of me and crossed her arms.

"Hello, Idra." A tired smile tugged at the corner of my lips. "Nice to see you too."

Her pale brows were furrowed and she glared at me as if she was angry with me for getting beaten up and thrown in prison. But no matter how much she tried to hide it, I could see the worry and relief swirling in her dark eyes.

"I hate to cut the reunion short," Captain Vendir interrupted from his position by the wall. "But we need to go. The letter they sent to invite us to the palace was addressed here, so they know that this is where we are staying. As soon as they figure out that we're gone, this is the first place they will look."

"He's right," Ellyda said. "We need to leave right now."

"Alright, everybody," Hadeon boomed across the room. "Grab your gear. We're out the door in ten."

Murmurs rippled through the room as we all lurched into motion and started towards our rooms to pack everything up. Only the glittering canopy of stars watched us from the open windows as we hurried back and forth across the floor.

Seven minutes later, we were disappearing down the stairs and into the darkness.

Hunted once more.

CHAPTER 11

A small garden filled with what looked like all kinds of junk spread out before a dark two-story house. We paused on the messy lawn and stared skeptically at the building before us.

"What is this place?" Hadeon asked.

Vendir continued studying the house in silence for another few seconds before he started towards the door. "It's the home of someone who can help."

Raising a hand, he pulled on the rope that hung outside the door. A clanking noise came from inside. The rest of us exchanged a glance where we stood in a half-circle behind Vendir, but no one said anything.

After a while, thudding came from somewhere inside the house. It was followed by more clanking and clicking right on the other side of the door. Then the door was shoved open.

"Do you have any idea what time it is?" A male High Elf stuck his face through the crack in the door and glared out at us. "Why would you…"

He trailed off. His gray eyes widened as they fell on

Captain Vendir, and for a moment, he seemed entirely lost for words. Then he shook his head forcefully.

"No!" He raised a finger and shook his whole hand in the air. "No. You do not get to just waltz back here after you abandoned me to run off with the army. The *army*. After all the plans we had. The futures we dreamed of. I haven't seen you in decades. *Decades*. And you think you can just come back here and ring the doorbell in the middle of the night and expect me to–"

"Heldan," Captain Vendir interrupted. He raised his hand as well, but not to shake it in his face. Instead, he showed him the black bracelet that was still wrapped around his wrist. "Please."

Heldan stopped talking. Narrowing his eyes, he scowled down at the bracelet before finally looking up again. He jerked back as if realizing for the first time that there were eight other people standing behind Vendir as well. Shifting his gaze back to the captain, he frowned in silent question.

"It's a long story," Vendir said.

"Bah. Aren't all stories." Then he shoved open the door even more and stepped aside. "Well, don't just stand there. Get in."

"Thank you."

"Don't thank me yet." He hiked a thumb over his shoulder while we began filing through the door. "In the kitchen. And don't touch anything."

Candlelight flared to life as Heldan lit the candelabra in the hallway. I swept my gaze over the corridor and glanced into the rooms we passed. The floor was clear, more or less anyway, but every tabletop and shelf I saw was filled with tools and materials and scrap metal and things that I didn't even know how to classify. Whatever Heldan did for a living, it involved making a mess.

Almost my entire life, these kinds of chaotic and messy environments had made my stress levels spike. But interestingly enough, ever since I became the Lady of Fire, it hadn't bothered me as much. It was as if the fact that I was finally in control of my own life had decreased my need to control everything else around me.

"By all the tools in the shed, Vendir, where did you find this lot?" Heldan said as he stalked into the gigantic kitchen that we had ended up in. He nodded towards Valerie and Theo. "And those two? They're not High Elves or Low Elves. What have you gotten yourself into?"

Captain Vendir spread his arms in an apologetic gesture. "Like I said, it's a long story."

"Well, I'd best put on some tea then." He flapped his arms towards the long table to our left. "Don't just stand there. Sit down. You're stressing me out."

Wood scraped against stone as the nine of us pulled out chairs and sat down. The table seated twelve people, so there was more than enough room, but the eight of us still sat close to each other. Captain Vendir dropped into a chair and tipped his head back to blow out a deep sigh.

Pots clanked and water sloshed as Heldan got the tea started. I took the opportunity to scan the room again.

While all other rooms we had passed had been filled with clutter, the kitchen was a neat and tidy place. But it was also warm and inviting. Wood panels lined the walls and a multicolored rug covered most of the floor in the middle of the room. Shelves filled with plates, cups, and pots, as well as jars of spices and herbs filled the space above the wooden counters.

"So, what's this about then, Vendir?" Heldan asked once he had put the kettle on the fire.

"I'm not sure where to start."

"How about you start with why you abandoned me to join the army all those decades ago."

"I…" Hesitation flooded Vendir's warm brown eyes as he flicked his gaze over the rest of us. "Do we have to…?"

Steel crept into Heldan's eyes as he tied back his long brown hair. "Either tell me the whole story or get out."

Ellyda watched Vendir curiously. In fact, we all did. He cleared his throat and pulled at his collar.

"I'm a Wielder," he finally said.

"So I heard." Heldan began passing out mugs painted with different kinds of flowers. "Eventually."

"I know. I didn't get a chance to tell you because… Well, everything happened so quickly and…"

"You were my best friend," he said, a hint of acid in his voice. "And you just left without even bothering to tell me."

Hurt bloomed in Vendir's eyes. It made the carefully constructed mask he always hid behind crack a little, and more emotions started flooding into his eyes. They were quickly replaced by anger, as if he shoved them out by force.

"I didn't just leave." Captain Vendir banged his fist down on the table. "Do you want to know what really happened? Fine. Here you go." Anger still burned in his eyes as he locked eyes with Heldan. "I found out that I was a Wielder and I was *devastated*. Because you know what that means. All Wielders have to report to the army. And I didn't want to. I didn't want to train to kill and destroy and conquer. I wanted the life we talked about. But because I was born with this ability that I never asked for, I would be forced to spend the rest of my life destroying things when all I wanted to do was the exact opposite."

Ringing silence filled the room. I stared at Captain Vendir, but he held his friend's gaze like they were the only two people in the room. Maybe in the world. Vendir had pushed to his feet and was bracing himself against the table with his fists. Tears rose in his eyes.

"I couldn't bear it. I couldn't bear to face a future like that." He swallowed thickly. "So I tried to end it. In White Water Bay."

Heldan's mouth slid open, but no sound escaped. He only stared back at Vendir with horror in his gray eyes.

"I immediately regretted it." Bitterness laced Vendir's words. "But it was too late. High Commander Anron flew past right when I thought I was going to drown, and he pulled me up. I was grateful at first. But then he told me to report to the army first thing the next morning, and since I owed him a life debt, there was no way out of it." He let out a mirthless laugh and slumped back into his seat. "So here I am, decades later, living the life I tried so hard to escape."

"Vendir." Pain swirled in Heldan's eyes. "I'm so sorry."

"Yeah. Me too."

The kettle whistled from behind him. After giving his friend a look of regret, Heldan stood up and went to retrieve it. I shifted my attention back to Vendir.

By all the gods and spirits, I had no idea that he had been carrying around all of that this whole time. But I supposed that was the thing. Everyone was fighting a battle that most people knew nothing about.

From across the table, Ellyda watched Vendir as if she could see into his very soul. For a while, he only stared after

Heldan, but then he seemed to remember that the rest of us were present too.

A hint of panic flashed across his face as he blinked at us. Then he reached up and wiped the budding tears from his eyes with two embarrassed swipes. He cleared his throat.

I didn't know what to say since he probably hadn't wanted to share all of that with us. And neither did the rest of my friends, apparently, because we all just slid our gazes to each other instead.

Thankfully, Heldan returned with the tea before the silence became too drawn out. The scent of flowers and herbs filled the room as he poured the tea into our mugs. I drew my fingers through the steam that made lazy patterns in the air.

"So how did you end up here?" Heldan nodded towards the bracelet and then towards the eight of us. "With that? And them?"

Captain Vendir sipped at his tea. "You might want to sit down for this."

Once Heldan had taken a seat at the table again, Vendir launched into the rather complicated story of how we had gotten to this point. Heldan scowled at us when he reached the part where we had blackmailed Captain Vendir into this mission, and at least most of us had the good grace to look a bit sheepish. Mordren, Idra, and Hadeon, however, only looked back at him unapologetically while Ellyda stared at Vendir as if he were a riddle she was trying to solve.

"Then we escaped and now we're here," Captain Vendir finished.

"Ah. Well, that certainly explains a lot." The chair scraped against the floor as Heldan pushed to his feet. "Vendir, can I talk to you alone for a second?"

"Of course."

Vendir swept his gaze around the table as if waiting to see if any of us would protest. When no one did, he followed his friend into another room without a second look back.

"Did you know that…?" Theo asked into the silence that fell.

"No," I said.

Another tense silence descended on the room. I traced my finger along the rim of my mug before lifting it to take a sip. It tasted of both sweet flowers and savory herbs and it smelled like a summer garden.

"We should remove the bracelet," Ellyda announced.

"I agree," Eilan said.

A thoughtful look passed over Mordren's face. "We cannot afford to lose his help."

Ellyda met his gaze head on. "He held up his end of the bargain."

"Yes. However–"

"Save your breath," Captain Vendir interrupted as he strode back into the kitchen with Heldan behind him. "It's already done."

Several pairs of eyes shot towards his wrist. The black bracelet was gone. I blinked in surprise and looked back up at Vendir and his friend.

Heldan shrugged. "I'm an inventor. It's what I do."

The rest of us pushed to our feet while uneasiness fluttered through the room.

Shadows twisted around the cuffs of Mordren's suit jacket as if he was expecting an attack now that Captain Vendir had access to the Great Current once more.

"I have held up my end of the bargain," Vendir said as he raised his chin. "I flew you here and I arranged an audience with our emperor and empress. That was the deal."

"And now what?" Mordren said. "You will crawl back to Anron?"

"No." His careful mask slipped again and pain surged into his eyes before he forced it out once more. "He pinned it all on me and left me to be executed with you. My life debt to him is paid."

"We still need help," I said gently.

"I know. But honestly, I don't care anymore." At that, his stoic mask shattered completely and I could see the full force of the heartbreak that bled from his eyes. "I helped you, and because of it, I lost *everything*. I'm a fugitive in my own land." He shifted his gaze to Mordren. "And I know that against all eight of you, even with my magic back, I would lose. I know that you could force me to help you. But I am asking you." His voice cracked slightly. "Please, just leave me alone."

"We–"

"Mordren," Ellyda's voice cut through the room like a knife. She locked sharp eyes on the Prince of Shadows before starting towards the door. "Let's go."

Surprise pulsed through the room. Both Vendir and Heldan blinked at Ellyda as she stalked towards the doorway. Then Hadeon blew out a sigh and shook his head, but he started after her. Theo and Valerie followed.

"I'm sorry the circumstances turned out like this," Ellyda said to Captain Vendir as she passed him.

Before he could reply, she had already disappeared into the hallway beyond.

Idra met my gaze from across the table. I shrugged and followed the others as well. The footsteps behind me informed me that Idra, Mordren, and Eilan did the same.

From their positions by the wall, Vendir and Heldan looked like they couldn't believe that we had actually agreed to leave without a fight. I briefly met Captain Vendir's gaze and gave him a nod before I moved into the hallway.

He was right. Our scheme had cost him enough, and he had held up his end of the bargain.

Whatever happened next, we would have to figure it out in the same way we had solved all of our other problems before.

On our own.

CHAPTER 12

The first light of dawn stretched its pale tendrils over the eastern horizon. A flash of panic rippled through me as I watched the dark blue of night give way to the bright morning. Soon, people would start flooding the streets. We needed to find a safe house before that happened.

"We should've stayed at Heldan's place," Hadeon grumbled. "At least this one day. Randomly searching the streets for somewhere to stay when it's this close to dawn is risky."

Idra slid her gaze to Hadeon. "I agree."

"They didn't want us to stay," Theo pointed out.

Mordren gave a nonchalant shrug. "We could have made them."

"No." Ellyda had been studying the sky visible between the buildings while we walked, but now she tore her gaze from the color-shifting heavens and fixed it on Mordren. "He helped us. More than he had to. And in exchange, we ruined his life. We don't need to endanger his friend as well by forcing them to let us stay there."

"She has a point," Theo said.

"Yes, but that still doesn't—"

"Oh. Oh!" Valerie interrupted. Jumping from foot to foot, she rubbed her hands together and then slapped Theo on the arm. "Theo, are you seeing what I'm seeing?"

The blond thief followed her line of sight and narrowed his eyes at a building on our left. A smile lit his gray eyes. "Indeed."

"Ha! Told you we'd find one." With a sweeping gesture, Valerie flung a dramatic arm towards the house. "This is it. Welcome to our temporary safe house."

The rest of us frowned at the two-story building before us. It was made of both wood and stone, the windows were dark, and a few evergreens had been planted in ceramic pots on the tiny porch. It looked exactly like every other house on this street.

"I don't get it," Idra announced.

Eilan shot an apologetic glance at Valerie. "Yeah, I don't see it either. How do you know that no one is living here right now?"

"Amateurs." She chuckled and then nodded towards the house again. "Look at the porch. You can tell by the patterns of sand that the door hasn't been opened in days. And the windows. People only leave them like that if they're going to be away for a while."

We all squinted at the building again.

"Nope, I don't see it," Hadeon said.

Valerie let out a groan. Jerking her chin at Theo, she took off towards the side of the building. He followed. The rest of us watched from the ground as the two thieves scaled the wall and then disappeared into a window to make sure that the house really was empty.

A cart rumbling down a stone street sounded from behind

the row of buildings on our right. I flicked a glance up and down our road. No movement yet. But the sun was climbing farther over the horizon with every minute. We needed to get off the street.

The evergreens rustled slightly as a morning wind whirled down between the buildings. A few loose strands of hair blew in front of my face. I hooked them behind my ears while trying to stave off the tiredness that threatened to wash over me.

Yesterday, we had not only met with the Empress and Emperor of Valdanar, we had also been hit by multiple lightning strikes, been thrown in prison, I had almost sped up our execution, and then we had somehow managed to flee before being thrown out on the street by the only person who we could trust to help us navigate this strange land. My body ached and my nerves were raw. In truth, I was exhausted. And overwhelmed.

"I still don't understand exactly how you managed to escape," Idra said, as if she could follow my train of thought. "Vendir glossed over a lot of parts."

"Yeah, uhm…" My gaze slid to Eilan.

"We will explain everything after we have gotten some sleep," he filled in. "We also need to make a new plan. But right now, I think everyone is too exhausted to be thinking about that."

"I second that," I said.

Idra narrowed her eyes at us, as if she could tell that we were holding something back, but in the end she only nodded.

The door cracked open and a head of loose brown curls popped out.

"Come on then," Valerie called. "Meet your new lodgings."

A tired chuckle rippled through our group. Mordren held

out a hand, motioning for me to go first. I drew my fingers over his arm as I passed him and then continued into the house that we would be staying in.

"See? Told you it was empty." Valerie wiggled her eyebrows at me as I walked towards where she was standing by the stairs. "I thought you were a spy."

"Shut up," I huffed, a smile tugging at my lips.

The soft thudding of boots and rustling of clothing filled the hallway as the rest of our group entered as well. Wooden walls looked down at us with disinterest as we crowded together below the stairs.

"There are only four bedrooms, though," Valerie said once the front door was firmly shut behind us. "So we're gonna have to partner up."

Twisting around, I met Mordren's gaze. He gave me a sly smile in reply.

"Idra," Ellyda said.

The white-haired warrior blinked in surprise, but turned and met her gaze. When Ellyda said nothing else, Idra took that to mean that she had been claimed as a partner, and simply nodded in acknowledgement.

"Hadeon, we should probably…" Eilan began.

"Yeah," he confirmed.

A hint of disappointment blew across Valerie's face. Rolling her eyes, she turned to Theo. "I guess that leaves you and me."

"Don't sound too excited," he teased.

"Alright," I interrupted before she could retort. "Let's all get some sleep first and then we'll make a new plan."

Murmurs of agreement echoed between the wooden walls. With one final nod, I turned and followed Theo and Valerie up the stairs. The others did the same. Once the two thieves had pointed out the four bedrooms, I just picked one at random and strode inside.

It was a relatively small one. The bed was more a one and a half bed than a double bed, but at least the linen looked fresh. A desk and chair, along with a drawer, lined the room. I swept my gaze over the walls. They had been painted in a bright yellow color that actually helped lift my spirits a little.

After dumping my backpack and gear in one of the corners, I stripped out of my clothes and immediately started towards the bed. Mordren walked through the door right as I rolled up with my back against the wall and pulled the cover over me.

He swept his gaze over the room in the same way that I had. "What an… optimistic-looking color."

I chuckled. "That's what I thought too."

His silver eyes slid to me where I lay on my side, watching him from the bed. Reaching up, he started loosening his tie. It slid over his collarbone as he pulled it off along with his suit jacket. Then he started on his shirt. Even after everything we had just gone through, his crisp dark clothes were only slightly rumpled. The thought was so absurd that I let out a soft laugh.

Mordren paused with his fingers on the final button. "What is it?"

"Nothing." I smiled at him. "I was just thinking that whoever makes those suits of yours is very good at what they do."

"Yes." He let out an amused huff while undoing the final button on his shirt. "I quite agree."

I studied the way the pale light of dawn painted shifting shapes over his muscled body as he draped his suit jacket and shirt over the nearby chair. Unbidden, the memory of him twitching uncontrollably on the floor of the throne room flashed into my mind. Out of all of us, he had been hit the most with those magical lightning attacks.

"Are you okay?" I asked softly.

After taking off his shoes, he met my gaze briefly before starting on his pants. "To be honest, it took a few hours before I regained complete feeling in my hands." His eyes shot back up to me. "But don't tell Eilan that."

"I promise."

He nodded. While he turned and hung his pants over the chair as well, I studied his body for any signs of injury. As far as I could tell, there were none.

"And now?" I asked. "You're okay now?"

"Yes."

Sweeping his long dark hair over his shoulder, he closed the distance to the bed. I held open the cover as he climbed down next to me. The wooden frame creaked faintly as he maneuvered himself onto his back and then wrapped one arm around me where I lay on my side next to him. I placed the cover over both of us before resting my arm on his chest.

"And I'm sorry," he said.

"For what?"

He tilted his head so that he met my gaze. "That you had to lick the emperor's boots to stop him from hurting me."

"You saw that, huh?" Glancing down, I began tracing circles over his chest instead. "I was hoping you didn't."

"I saw it."

Not sure what to say, I only continued drawing my fingers over his heated skin.

"Hey." He placed his other hand on my chin and tilted my head back, forcing me to meet his gaze. "I am sorry. I never wanted you to have to grovel before anyone ever again. But also… thank you. If you hadn't stopped him, I think…" He drew in a shuddering breath. "I think there would have been permanent damage if he had continued with the lightning strikes."

Fear surged up inside me.

"There is no permanent damage now," Mordren assured me, as if he could read the unspoken worry in my eyes. "I promise you. But we cannot go up against them like that again. Even with all eight of us, we would lose."

"Yeah." I blew out a tired chuckle. "Blackmail and underhanded manipulation it is."

Mordren stroked his thumb along my jaw before leaning down to steal a kiss from my lips.

"Good thing we specialize in that," he breathed against my mouth.

A dark laugh escaped my lips. "Indeed."

Mordren tightened his hold on me. I relished the feeling of his hands on my body. His lips against mine. Drawing my fingers over his abs, I pulled his hard body more firmly against mine. And then I made a vow.

One day.

One day, we would create a world where neither of us had to bow and grovel before anyone else. Ever again.

CHAPTER 13

The scent of fried mushrooms and garlic lingered like an aromatic cloud over the kitchen. To everyone's surprise, Theo and Valerie had somehow found the time to go out and steal some food. After they had dumped two dozen eggs, along with some garlic, mushrooms and herbs, on the kitchen counter, Eilan had taken it upon himself to make omelets for us. Closing my eyes, I savored the final mouthful before setting my fork down. I could barely remember the last time I ate something.

"I didn't know you could cook," Valerie said as she smacked her lips contentedly before shifting her attention from her now empty plate to the elf who had made the food.

Eilan gave her a sly smile. "I am a person of many mysteries."

"Oh don't I know it."

Idra's observant eyes slid to Eilan. He cleared his throat.

"So, now what?" Theo asked from the other side of the table.

We were all crammed in around the wooden table in the

kitchen. It was only large enough for six people, so we had dragged in a couple of chairs from the living room in order to fit all of us. Ellyda's capacity for social interactions had run dry about halfway through the meal, and she had retreated into a random book she had grabbed off one of the shelves in the study. But everyone else glanced around the kitchen, as if checking to see if anyone had any bright ideas on what to do now.

Eilan cleared his throat again. "First, there's something you need to know."

"Are you sure?" Mordren asked.

"Yes. If we are going to survive this, I can't continue to keep it a secret. And besides, almost everyone already knows."

Mordren nodded. As did Hadeon. I studied Idra, while Valerie glanced over at Theo. The two of them, who were the only ones still in the dark about Eilan's secret, furrowed their brows as they sat forward slightly. Paper rustled faintly as Ellyda turned the page in her book.

"It's probably easier if I show you," Eilan said.

His chair scraped against the floor as he pushed to his feet and took up position between the table and the wall. Since he was now standing almost directly behind Idra, she had to move her chair sideways and twist around to watch him. He drew in a soft breath and raked a hand through his long black hair.

Golden light from the afternoon sun fell in through the kitchen window and illuminated his face.

Then the edges of his body began to blur.

Idra sat up straighter.

From across the table, Theo rubbed his eyes as if he thought there was something wrong with his own vision. Abruptly, he stopped. Pausing with his hand hovering next to his face, he stared at the elf that was now standing in the kitchen.

Gone were the pale green eyes and the black hair. Instead, an elf with short brown hair, gray eyes, and bland features had taken Eilan's place. The Void.

Silence rang like a bell through the cozy kitchen.

For a moment, no one moved or made a sound. Idra's dark eyes were wide as she stared in disbelief at the person who was no longer Eilan.

"You're a shapeshifter," she finally said. She said the words slowly. As if her mind was still trying to process it.

"Yes," Eilan answered in the Void's voice.

Mordren lifted his shoulders in a casual shrug. "How do you think we know so much about the other courts?"

Sudden realization flashed in Idra's eyes. She cast a quick glance at Mordren's nonchalant expression before her gaze locked on to Eilan again.

"You've spied inside the Court of Fire." Her words were more statement than question.

"Yes," the Void confirmed.

His features blurred again. This time, an elf with blond hair and red eyes appeared on the kitchen floor. There was an air of smugness over this version of Eilan. A cocky tilt of the chin, and a calculating gleam in the eyes.

He gave Idra a quick rise and fall of his eyebrows. "Remember me?"

Idra stared at him, dumbfounded, for a few seconds before finally pressing out, "You? I thought he... *you* were dead."

"I am. Well, this version of me anyway."

Chaos erupted. Wooden clattering echoed between the walls as Idra shot to her feet, knocking over her chair as she flew forward. Moving like a lightning strike, she slammed the blond spy up against the wall. Furniture scraped as everyone but Ellyda leaped to their feet as well, but Idra had already locked him in a death grip.

With one hand wrapped around his throat, she leaned forward. Anger flashed over her features.

"You bastard," she growled in his face, her voice cold and deadly. "You tried to kill me."

The arrogance that seemed to be a permanent part of this version of Eilan didn't falter as he looked back at her and flashed her a cocky grin. "Well, to be fair, we tried to kill everyone in Volkan's inner circle. You were just one of the few smart enough to actually survive."

"I thought you were one of us. I trusted you."

"A horrible decision really."

Her hand tightened around his throat. "You–"

She slammed into the wall next to Eilan's blond persona. In one fluid motion, Hadeon had yanked Idra away from him, spun her around, and shoved her back first into the wall. He kept her pinned against the smooth wooden surface with a hand on each of her shoulders.

Shock bounced across her features. She stared, her mouth slightly open, between Hadeon's hands and his face as if she couldn't quite believe what he had done.

"Alright, calm down," Hadeon said while Idra's mind was still trying to catch up. "You already knew that we were the ones who took out most of Volkan's inner circle."

The sound of his voice snapped her out of her shock. She yanked up her arms and then rammed them down in the crook of Hadeon's elbows. While his arms shot downwards, she twisted with the motion and shoved him face first into the wall.

With one hand forcing Hadeon's arm up his back, Idra

stabbed her other hand towards Eilan's blond shapeshifter form. "I didn't know that Eilan and... *him* were the same person." She narrowed her eyes at him. "When this is all over, you and I have some scores to settle."

"I look forward to it," the blond spy said, and flashed her another smug grin.

With her attention on Eilan's shapeshifter persona, she missed the elbow Hadeon rammed into the side of her ribs. Stumbling sideways, she lost her grip and Hadeon flashed around to face her. His large hand closed around her throat at the same time as she placed her lethal palm against his chest.

For a moment, the two warriors only stared at each other.

I glanced towards Mordren. He shrugged as if to say that trying to get involved would be pointless. On the other side of the table, Theo flicked his gaze between the two of them, while Valerie studied Eilan.

"Well," Idra began. A sharp smirk slid across her lips. "At least now I won't have to feel bad that I sent that girl to assassinate you."

Hadeon frowned. "What girl?"

"Blond. Beautiful silver eyes."

His mouth dropped open. "You're the one who sent her?"

"Yes."

"She tried to slit my throat while we were having sex!"

"I know." There was a dangerous glint in her eyes as she met his furious gaze. "That was my idea."

"Idra," Ellyda's voice cut through the kitchen like a blade. Lowering her book, she locked sharp violet eyes on the white-haired warrior across the room. "You tried to kill my brother?"

Idra's gaze slid to Ellyda. "Yes."

Silence fell over the crowded room. Mordren and I

exchanged another glance. When I first met Ellyda, she had threatened to cut my heart from my chest and crush it with her hammer if I ever hurt Hadeon or the others. Hearing that Idra had almost succeeded in assassinating her brother was sure to make her see red. Even the blond spy that was Eilan looked a bit worried now and he took a step towards Ellyda right as I was about to open my mouth too.

"But you also saved his life by worldwalking him away from that battlefield," Ellyda announced, cutting off my intervention. "And we did try to kill you too."

Another tense silence fell as Ellyda and Idra continued watching each other.

"Yes," Idra said once more.

Ellyda cocked her head. "So we'll consider it even."

With one final decisive nod at the warrior, she lifted her book again and continued reading.

A short burst of laughter escaped my throat. It rippled through the room and drew chuckles from a few of the others as well. Idra slid her gaze back to Hadeon and arched an expectant eyebrow.

"The hell we will!" he blurted out. Lowering his hand, he moved it from its position around her throat to the top of her leather armor. With a firm grip on her collar, he yanked her face closer to his. "When all this is over, you and I are gonna settle up too."

Idra tilted her chin in a smug gesture. With a wicked smile on her lips, she took her hand from his chest and instead reached up and patted Hadeon's cheek. "Come try it anytime, lover boy."

Hadeon had been about to reply, but the *lover boy* taunt apparently threw him off his game, and all he did was blink at her while his mouth was stuck on the first word.

"Wow," a voice cut through the room.

We all turned towards the source of the voice. Theo was standing behind the table, his pale brows raised, shaking his head at us in complete disbelief.

"Thanks, guys," he continued. "My own life suddenly doesn't seem all that messy anymore." He turned to Valerie while motioning at us. "Can you believe what an absolute mess these people are?"

"Such a mess," she agreed with a serious nod. But the mirth in her sparkling brown eyes couldn't be hidden as she looked around the room. "Good thing we're the ones in charge."

Mordren raised his eyebrows at her.

She winked and flashed him a grin. "Oh you know I'm right."

"Well, you heard the boss," Theo said. "Come sit down. We still have a plan to make."

Another laugh slipped my lips. Shaking my head, I lowered myself into my chair again. Idra and Hadeon locked eyes for another few seconds before he reluctantly let go of her collar. She brushed her hands over it while the two of them returned to their seats. By the wall, Eilan shapeshifted back into himself before taking a seat next to Mordren.

"So, now that we've gotten the threatening and the reality-shifting truth bombs out of the way," Theo continued once everyone was seated, "do you realize that you've actually solved our problem?"

A spark of hope rippled through the room.

Hadeon sat forward. "How?"

"Eilan is a shapeshifter."

"So?"

"So, he can just shapeshift into Anron and confess his sins to the empress and emperor." Theo's gray eyes gleamed with excitement as he threw his arms out. "Or even better, he can shapeshift into the empress or emperor! And then he can just sentence Anron to death himself without us having to persuade the real empress and emperor."

The hope that had bloomed in Eilan, Hadeon, and Mordren's eyes died out. Eilan blew out a dejected sigh and shook his head.

Confusion drifted across Theo's face. "What?"

"I can't shapeshift into people who already exist," he said, and spread his hands in an apologetic gesture. "It's one of the limitations of my power."

"Oh. So no shapeshifting into Empress Elswyth and Emperor Lanseyo and just…" Theo snapped his fingers, "giving a couple of orders that would've solved all of our problems in a single afternoon then?"

"No, I'm afraid not."

"Well." He let out something between a sigh and a chuckle. "Why would anything ever be easy?"

The room seemed to blow out a collective disappointed breath. Sitting back in his chair again, Theo drew a hand through his short blond hair and glanced up at the ceiling. The curtains behind him fluttered as a warm summer breeze snuck in through the small gap that we had left open in the window.

"Well, now that you're all looking sufficiently defeated," Valerie said with a wide grin on her face, "are you ready to hear the absolutely brilliant plan that *I've* come up with?"

"You have another plan?" I said, unable to hide my surprise.

"Of course I do." She shook her head as if that should have been obvious. "Told you. I'm the boss. And the boss always has a plan." A few good-natured groans and eye rolls spread through the room, but she only winked and plowed ahead. "So, I was thinking. What is it that we're good at?"

"Tricking people?" Eilan offered when it became apparent that it hadn't been a rhetorical question.

"Yes, and?" She swept her gaze around the room.

I shrugged. "Blackmailing people?"

"Yes!" She flicked a hand between her and Theo. "And…?"

"Stealing stuff," I filled in.

"An–"

"Get to the point already," Idra interrupted as she turned to scowl at the grinning thief.

Valerie's smile only widened. "We might not be able to make the emperor and empress kill Anron for us, but we can at least make them cut their support to him by doing what we do best." Her warm brown eyes glittered in the golden afternoon sunlight as she leaned forward and rubbed her hands together. "We find our way back to that tower the empress took Kenna to. Then we steal one of their precious magic sources and then we use that to blackmail–"

"Persuade," Theo cut in.

"And then we use that to *persuade* the empress and emperor to cut off Anron's support," Valerie amended. "And *boom*, we can kill him without having all of Valdanar descending on our heads."

"That's…" I began.

"Insane," Hadeon finished.

"And brilliant," Eilan added.

Mordren studied the excited thief. "Could we really make that work?"

"Yes."

We all jumped at the sound of Ellyda's voice. Clothes rustled and furniture creaked as we turned to stare at her. She had apparently stopped reading once Valerie had started talking, and now she lowered her book to the table while she swept sharp eyes over the rest of us.

"Yes, we can," she repeated. "I can make something that would allow us to transport the magic." Her gaze stopped on Theo and Valerie. "You might need to steal me some supplies first, though."

I massaged my brows. "And we need to figure out how to actually get to that tower."

"Kenna." Mordren waited until I met his gaze. "Do you remember that... *encounter* we had in the White Fire tavern?"

For a few seconds, I only frowned at him. It felt like years had passed since Captain Vendir showed us the city for the first time. What had been so special about...? Realization hit me like a lightning bolt.

"Oh," I said.

"Care to share with the rest of the class?" Eilan quipped.

"We might know some people who know how to get to the tower," I said.

"They might need some *persuading*, though," Mordren added.

"Yeah." I shifted my attention to Hadeon and Idra. "You're with us."

Before they could protest, Valerie leaped up from her seat. "Alright, and we'll go steal... whatever it is that we're supposed to steal."

Eilan blew out a sigh before motioning towards the two thieves. "I'll make sure they don't get into trouble."

"Ahem," Valerie huffed with mock affront.

"I'll make sure they don't get into *too much* trouble," he amended.

"You're welcome to try."

"I–"

"Stay out of sight," Mordren interrupted, his voice full of authority. "Remember that we are wanted fugitives now."

A sobering silence spread through the room as we all nodded.

He was right. We could no longer walk the street openly. Without even knowing how the justice system worked in this city, we had no idea how much the general population knew about escaped prisoners and how quickly we might be recognized. But we still had to somehow make our plan work.

Schemes spun in my mind as Mordren, Idra, Hadeon, and I drifted towards the living room to plan out our mission. As soon as night fell, we would be leaving.

We had some High Elves to threaten.

CHAPTER 14

Shadows swirled around us. Standing with our backs pressed against the cool stone wall, we peered in through the window while Mordren's mass of twisting darkness continued to hide us from view. Night had fallen. And with it, the White Fire tavern had become packed with patrons.

"We need to lure him outside," Mordren said.

My gaze slid to the High Elves crowded around a table at the back of the tavern. A male with copper-colored hair took a swig from his mug before he called something to his companions. Tundir. The High Elf who had picked a fight with us last time we were here. He had also thrown out another elf who had been using his magic to make smoke figures, saying that Low Elves didn't deserve magic. He had *also* boasted that he had seen the magic inside the White Tower. Time to see if there was some truth to his claim.

"I can get him outside," Idra announced.

"You?" Hadeon twisted so that he could scowl down at her.

"You couldn't even charm your way past a bunny if your life depended on it."

"I never said I was going to charm him. There are other ways to make people do what you want."

"Yeah, but this needs to be done discreetly."

Idra lifted one shoulder in a nonchalant shrug while a sharp smile spread across her lips. "Just because you are unable to threaten people discreetly doesn't mean I am."

"That–"

"I will do it," I interrupted before their argument could get even worse. "I can get in through the wall instead of the front door so it will look like I have been there for a while. And I can both charm him and threaten him, or whatever I need to do to get him outside. Discreetly."

Mordren nodded towards the left side of the building. "Try to get him to that side alley."

"Yeah." I scanned the tavern again until I found a spot by the wall where I could enter without anyone noticing. "I'll go in over there. Check that no one is looking."

The shadows followed me as I snuck a bit farther down the building. Once I reached the spot I'd mentally marked, I looked back at the others. They signaled that it was clear. I stepped through the wall.

Chatting and laughing washed over me as I left the silent street behind and materialized inside the busy tavern. The clear night air was replaced with a mist of white smoke that smelled of herbs. Breathing through my nose, I took a few moments to reorient myself.

Across the room, Tundir bellowed something that made his friends roar with laughter. Ale sloshed over the edges of their mugs as they slapped the table. I swept my gaze over the rather sizeable group around him. Getting Tundir alone would be difficult. Not to mention that there was a considerable risk that someone else in the tavern might know that I was a fugitive.

Desperately hoping that my face wasn't plastered across wanted posters throughout the entire city, I blew out a steadying breath and started towards Tundir's table. I hadn't really decided how to play it yet, because I wasn't sure if he would recognize me from our earlier encounter or not. With different schemes still swirling in my head, I weaved between the final two groups.

"I'm sorry to bother you, but–" I began in a soft voice as I stopped next to Tundir.

"You," he interrupted, recognition flashing in his eyes.

Shit. He remembered me. Adjusting my plan, I transformed my face into a mask of innocent surprise.

"You," I said, as if I had only just recognized him as well. "Oh. I, uhm…"

"I thought I told you that you had to pay if you wanna take up space here."

"Yes, but–"

"So you haven't paid?"

"Uhm…" I flicked my gaze around the room as if looking for a way out.

Tundir pushed to his feet. Like all High Elves, he towered over me. Around the table, his friends let out an expectant *ohh* before brazen laughs echoed between them.

From what I had observed during our first encounter, Tundir was a person who got off on making people feel helpless. He believed himself to be superior to most people, and to Low Elves in particular, and he enjoyed intimidating others because it made him feel powerful. So I did what I knew he wanted me to do. I edged a step back as if I was afraid of him.

"What were you gonna do?" he demanded. "If you weren't gonna pay for your own drinks?"

Flicking another desperate glance around the rest of the room filled with patrons, who paid us no mind, I made a show of swallowing nervously.

"Answer," he snapped.

I flinched. "I was hoping to get someone else to buy me drinks."

"You wanted me to pay for your drinks?"

"Yes." I dropped my gaze. "I'm sorry."

His hand shot out. Grabbing my chin, he forced my face back so that he could look me in the eye. A malicious grin spread across his mouth as he eyed the knife strapped to my thigh. Then he arched an eyebrow at me. "Not so tough when you're all alone, huh?"

I raised my hands the tiniest bit, to show that I wasn't planning on drawing the blade.

"Finally learning your place," he said.

"I'm sorry," I repeated. "I'll just leave."

"Oh, I don't think so. You still haven't paid."

"But I don't have any money," I whispered in a frightened voice, trying to lead him the final bit down the path I had so carefully laid.

His grin widened. "Then you're going to have to beg me instead. Get down on your knees right here and beg me."

The other High Elves hooted and whistled behind him. I tried to back away again but his fingers tightened on my chin. While keeping the scared look on my face, I swept my gaze over his friends as if not wanting to do it in front of everyone.

"Outside?" I pleaded. "Please."

"No. Right here."

"We will disrupt the peace," I bargained. "And that Captain Vendir fellow said that he would be angry if we did that again."

Tundir sucked his teeth. I knew that he remembered that part vividly. Vendir had pulled rank and made them back off and sit down like trained dogs. Hopefully, the memory of that was enough to convince him to do what I wanted.

"Fine." He released my chin and instead took my arm in an iron grip. "But if you'd done it in here, I'd have settled for some light begging. Now, I'm gonna make you truly grovel."

"Yeah, you show her!" a few of his friends called after us as he marched me towards the front door. "Make her learn her place."

It took all my self-control not to roll my eyes. Instead, I kept the frightened look on my face as I was dragged out into the night again.

Clean air filled my lungs as we left the room filled with white smoke behind and stepped out onto the street. Tundir walked me another few steps away from the door before he let go of my arm. I backed away another step.

"Don't even think about it," he warned.

I bolted.

Whirling around, I darted towards the side alley.

Curses split the air behind me as Tundir took off after me. I would never have been able to outrun him in a real chase. But thankfully, I wasn't trying to.

His hands snatched at my clothes, but I managed to round the corner without him grabbing me. Swerving quickly, I avoided crashing straight into Mordren where he was standing a few strides in.

Tundir sprinted into the alley after me.

He hadn't even made it two steps in when he stopped

abruptly. Not of his own volition. Shadows that blended into the darkness had shot out and wrapped around his ankles, which froze him in his tracks. The sudden stop made him almost topple over and he spun his arms to try and stop the momentum still carrying him forwards. Idra and Hadeon helped gravity along by delivering well-aimed kicks at the back of his knees. He crashed down onto the street.

Before he could open his mouth to scream, Hadeon pressed the edge of his sword across his throat from behind.

Tundir stopped moving.

On his knees in a dark alley, with a sword against his throat, he blinked like a stunned fish at the two Low Elves he could see.

I gave him a quick rise and fall of my eyebrows before hiking a thumb in Mordren's direction. "You remember my partner?" With a jerk of my chin, I indicated Hadeon and Idra who were standing behind him. "We brought some friends too."

Hadeon pushed the sword higher up under Tundir's chin.

"What?" I taunted, a wicked smile on my lips. "Not so tough when you're all alone, huh?"

His eyes flashed at his own insult being thrown back in his face, but he said nothing.

"Now, we have some questions," I said. "And I would recommend prompt answers."

"About what?" he grumbled.

"Last time, you boasted that you've been to the White Tower and seen the magic in there."

"Yeah, so?"

"Is it true? Think carefully before you answer because if you lie, this evening is going to become very unpleasant for you."

"Of course it's true!" He puffed up his chest. "I was a guard in the Palace of the Never Setting Sun."

A knowing smirk slid home on Mordren's lips. "Until there was an unfortunate misunderstanding about your work ethic?"

"You insolent little..." Tundir trailed off when Hadeon pressed the edge of the sword harder against his skin. "It *was* a misunderstanding."

"Do you know how to get there?" I asked, trying to bring the conversation back on track.

"Yeah, I–"

"Tundir, what's taking–" a voice called from around the corner.

"Here!" he bellowed before we could stop him.

Feet pounded against stone.

"Shit," I swore.

And then several things happened all at once.

Hadeon shoved Tundir towards us while Mordren's shadows shot out to catch him and I drew my knife. Black tendrils wrapped around Tundir's limbs and kept him on one knee until I could get my knife in place against his throat. At the mouth of the alley, Idra and Hadeon whirled around to face the High Elves who skidded around the corner.

Stunned shock bounced across their features as they took in the scene.

Idra and Hadeon didn't give them a chance to recover. Darting forward, Idra drove her fist into the closest elf's stomach while Hadeon rammed the butt of his sword into another's. Screams of surprise echoed between the buildings but then the remaining High Elves finally got their act together and charged. They were unarmed and drunk. But there were a lot of them.

"Kenna, make sure he doesn't escape." Hadeon barked the order over his shoulder while ramming his sword back into its sheath. The world probably wouldn't miss this particular group of people, but a bloodbath would draw a lot of unwanted attention. "Mordren, run interference."

Without waiting for confirmation, he leaped into the fight. Tundir had been about to call something, but I pushed the knife high up, forcing him to shut his mouth again. While keeping some of his shadows around our captive, Mordren shifted his position so that he could see the assailants before us more clearly.

Idra and Hadeon fought back to back against the drunk High Elves. They were a lot bigger than our two friends, but Hadeon and Idra had both the speed and the skills. And they fought together seamlessly.

A dark-haired High Elf charged at Idra, but right before he could swing at her, Hadeon rammed an elbow into his side. It made him stumble, which created the opening Idra needed to knock him out. The fighter behind him lost his balance as Mordren's shadows slithered across the street and yanked at his ankle. Hadeon used the opportunity to plant a knee into his groin. As he howled in pain and bent forwards, Idra ended it all with a well-placed strike to the side of his neck, while Hadeon took care of the elf that had been about to kick her from behind.

Another few of the assailants stumbled as Mordren's pain magic flickered through the night, followed by more inconvenient shadows. Hadeon crouched down right as Idra started running, and gave her a boost that sent her flying straight into the final High Elf.

An *oof* echoed over the now silent street as his breath was driven from his lungs and he collapsed on the ground.

Idra and Hadeon scanned the alley to make sure that no one else was coming. Then they looked at each other.

Even in the dark, with only the moon to illuminate the area, I swore I could read the thoughts in Idra's eyes. She was impressed. And so was Hadeon. They stared at each other as if they couldn't quite believe that the other had managed to keep up with them.

Then Idra shut down.

The impassive mask she usually wore descended on her face like a curtain of iron and she turned away. Stalking towards us, she instead fixed her gaze on Tundir. I opened my mouth to say something, but before I could, she drove her fist into his solar plexus.

His body spasmed underneath me and I had to yanked the knife away to stop him from accidentally slitting his own throat. Dull thuds rang out as he hit the street unconscious.

"Let's go," Idra announced, and bent down to drape Tundir's limp arm over her shoulder. "Before more of his friends come looking for him."

"Uh…" I began very eloquently.

"She's right," Hadeon said as he grabbed Tundir's other arm so that they shared his weight between them. "We can finish questioning him back at the safe house."

Mordren nodded as he fell in behind them. "I agree."

A thin mist of shadows sprang up around us. It would keep prying eyes from seeing us from afar, but it wouldn't stop someone if they passed us directly. I jogged ahead and peered around the next corner. Empty.

Now, we just had to hope that we could get him all the way back to our safe house without anyone spotting us.

CHAPTER 15

Muffled yells echoed through the root cellar. A few disgruntled turnips glared in annoyance at the writhing High Elf as he disrupted their peaceful surroundings with more screams. I leaned back against the door, my arms crossed, and watched as Mordren sent another wave of pain magic over Tundir.

"Do all High Elves truly have a pain threshold that is this pathetically low?" Mordren cast an incredulous glance at me over his shoulder before looking back at our captive. "I thought Vendir was an exception. But apparently not."

Tundir growled something unintelligible from behind his gag, which only made Mordren ramp up the flares of pain. More muffled screams followed. Idra, Hadeon, and I watched him impassively.

Bending down slightly, Mordren snapped his fingers in front of Tundir's face. "Hey. Eyes on me." Once Tundir had finished blinking and was once more focused on the Prince of Shadows, Mordren continued. "Pull yourself together. We haven't even gotten started yet."

Fear bloomed in the High Elf's eyes.

"Unless you want to tell us how to get to the White Tower," I said from my place by the door.

He flicked his gaze between the four of us. Then he slowly nodded.

Mordren smiled. "Excellent."

As if on some hidden signal, Idra and Hadeon closed in on Tundir. Grabbing him by the front of his clothes, Hadeon yanked him to his feet. Idra removed the gag but kept the rope that bound his wrists behind his back.

"So?" I prompted.

Tundir worked his jaw a couple of times and cleared his throat before answering. "You get to the White Tower through the Palace of the Never Setting Sun. It's at the end of a heavily guarded path at the back of the palace grounds."

That was not what I had wanted to hear. Sneaking through the entire palace to reach the tower and then sneaking back out again without anyone noticing would be next to impossible.

"Is that the only way?" I asked.

"Yes," he replied.

Idra's dark gaze raked across his face. "He's lying."

"Are you now?" Mordren took a step forward, a cold smile dripping with threats on his face. "Perhaps you need a bit more… encouragement."

"N-no." Tundir tried to back away, but slammed into Hadeon's immovable body. "Alright, alright. Yes, there's another way. You can get to it if you go through Poisonwood Forest." He shook his head. "But no one goes into that forest!"

"Why not?" I asked.

"Because it's full of savages."

"What?"

Tundir swallowed and glanced around the root cellar as if those savages might be lurking behind a pile of potatoes. "It's a... cult. A cult of wild Low Elves. They were banished there as a form of punishment for trying to rebel, and they can't leave because they've got these anklets that bind them to that part of the forest. The forest is full of poisonous and hallucinogenic shit, and staying in there for so long without being able to leave has made them all kinds of crazy."

I frowned at him. "That sounds like a story made up to frighten children so they won't wander into the woods and get lost."

"It's the truth. I swear. It's true."

"If we were to take that route, how would we find the tower?"

"North. You just go in and keep heading north until you're on the other side. That's where the tower is. The White Tower is guarded by the palace walls on all other sides, but there's a ramp to get in and out from the forest. That's guarded too, but you know, not really anything I can do about that."

I shifted my gaze to Idra. She nodded. As far as we could tell, he wasn't lying.

"Alright, then," I said.

Tundir glanced between me and Mordren. "So you'll let me go now?"

"No." Mordren cocked his head. "You will be staying here until we have returned from the tower. So, if your information is in any way incorrect, now would be the time to say so."

"It's the truth," Tundir growled.

"Then you do not have to fear starving to death in here. As

soon as we have returned safely, you will be free to leave. Agreed?"

Tundir drew his eyebrows down but grumbled, "Agreed."

"Excellent. Now, back towards the wall."

Hadeon stepped aside to allow Tundir to take the final few steps to the wall. Mordren watched him with dark amusement in his eyes. Once our captive was standing in front of a crate, he stopped and simply stared back at us.

For a moment, no one said anything. It felt almost like Mordren was daring Tundir to do something, and I was pretty sure this was his way of getting back at the High Elf for how he had treated us earlier.

"Sit," Mordren commanded.

Fury flashed in Tundir's eyes, and for a second, it looked like he might lunge at the Prince of Shadows. But then he simply lowered himself to his knees. Slowly. Without breaking eye contact. Until he was kneeling in front of the crate.

Mordren smiled like a villain. "Good boy."

The rage in Tundir's eyes flared to life again and he ground his teeth together so hard I was certain they would crack.

With his gaze still locked on the High Elf, Mordren spoke up again. "Hadeon, if you please."

Hadeon lumbered over and tied Tundir's already bound hands to the crate behind him. Once his hands were firmly fastened, we all gave him a mocking onceover and then strode out the door. Idra locked it behind us before we started back up the steps to the kitchen.

"I'll stay and guard him," Hadeon offered.

"*We* will stay and guard him," Idra corrected.

"I am perfectly capable of guarding him myself."

"Of course you are," she sniped back. "But you still need to sleep at some point."

With Hadeon muttering reluctant agreement, we finally crested the stairs and poured into the kitchen. Eilan and our two thieves were still out stealing supplies for Ellyda, who was lost in a mountain of paper and sketches, so we just glanced around at each other.

"Get some sleep," Hadeon said as he pulled up a chair and took a seat at the table next to his distracted sister. He waved a large hand towards the stairs to the root cellar. "I'll take first watch."

Idra gave him a curt nod before stalking off. After a decidedly more appreciative nod, Mordren and I disappeared towards our bedroom as well.

Once the door had clicked shut behind us, I turned and stabbed a hand towards Mordren. "Okay, *that* was unnecessarily hot."

A surprised chuckle escaped his lips. "What?"

Crossing my arms, I raised my eyebrows at him and mimicked his dark commanding voice. *"Back towards the wall. Sit. Good boy."*

Mordren let out a husky laugh and gave me a quick rise and fall of his eyebrows. "Oh you thought so, huh?"

"Hmm."

"Well, what should we do about that?"

"I might have a few ideas."

"So do I." He advanced on me. Once he was standing so close that I had to tilt my head back to meet his gaze, he lifted a hand and pointed towards the desk. "Sit."

A dark chuckle slipped my lips. Shaking my head, I held his gaze, but I still backed towards the desk. It produced a soft thud as the back of my thighs connected with it. After placing my palms on the edge, I drew myself up on the tabletop so that my legs dangled over the side. Mordren closed the distance between us.

Placing his hands on my thighs, he spread my legs and stepped in between them. While his palms traveled from my thighs to my hips, he leaned down and placed his lips next to my ear. "Good girl."

A shudder of dark desire coursed through my body. Grabbing the collar of his shirt, I pulled his lips to mine. He tightened his grip on my hips while stealing a hungry kiss from my mouth. I drew my hands down over his chest and abs until I reached the hem of his dark shirt. My fingers brushed the skin right above his pants.

He moaned into my mouth.

Smiling against his lips, I traced my fingers back up his chest and then began unbuttoning his shirt. He answered by grabbing the hem of my own shirt and pushing it up my stomach.

Bolts of lightning shot across my skin when his hands brushed my ribs. My concentration wavered and my fingers fumbled with the buttons as Mordren massaged my breasts on his way up my chest. Renewing my efforts, I finally got the final button loose.

Dark fabric whispered against my wrists as I slid my hands inside his shirt and traced them over his heated skin. His body shuddered under my touch. Temporarily taking his hands off me, he shrugged out of his shirt. It fluttered through the air before landing on the wooden floor behind him. I raked my eyes over his body.

The lean muscles on his chest and arms flexed as he leaned forward and grabbed the shirt that was still sitting halfway up my chest.

"Arms," he commanded. "Up."

I raised my arms above my head.

With a decisive pull, he yanked the shirt over my head and then dropped it on top of his own on the floor. My skin prickled at the sudden exposure.

Mordren placed his hands on either side of my face and then leaned down to steal a savage kiss from my lips. I dragged my fingers over his ribs and around his back, pulling him tighter against me. His tongue tasted mine while his fingers trailed down my throat. Pleasure coursed through my body. I tightened my hold on him as his hands continued down my sides and then towards my ass. With a firm grip, he lifted me off the desk.

I wrapped my legs around his waist as he carried me towards the wall instead. Pushing my back against the cool wood, he gently put me down on the floor while he continued stealing the breath from my lungs. Another pleasant shudder went through my body as he drew his hands up over my ass and towards the front of my pants.

A dark moan slipped my lips as he started undoing the fastenings. I returned the favor by drawing my fingers over his stomach until I reached his belt, but before I could start unbuckling it, something cool and silken slid around my wrists.

"No," Mordren said in between kisses while his shadows moved my hands until they rested against the wall above my head. "Keep them there."

His shadows withdrew.

Mordren paused. For a moment, he only watched me with raised eyebrows, daring me to move my hands. I narrowed my eyes but kept my arms against the wall. A wicked smile spread across Mordren's lips. Then he started on my pants again.

The fastenings came loose. I drew in a breath as Mordren began easing my pants down my legs. Once they reached my mid-thighs, he knelt down in front of me instead.

My heart skipped a beat as Mordren's lips brushed my thigh. Arching my back, I tried to suppress a shudder as he kissed his way down my leg while he continued to strip me of my pants.

A dark moan escaped my throat as his lips moved towards the inside of my thigh. Still keeping my hands against the wall above my head, I flexed my fingers and threw my head back.

My body trembled as Mordren continued his sweet torture.

After unlacing my boots, slowly, one at a time, he finally freed me from the rest of my clothes. Closing my eyes, I curled my fingers as Mordren started kissing his way back up my legs again.

His hand made its way up my calf while his lips brushed the skin on the inside of my thigh. Another moan tore from my throat as he brushed a sensitive spot high up. With a firm grip on my left leg, Mordren lifted it and draped it over his shoulder where he still knelt before me. I sucked in a shuddering breath as his tongue teased my throbbing entrance. His fingers tightened on my thigh, keeping my other leg immovable.

Arching my back, I heaved in deep breaths while Mordren's tongue continued exploring. My knees trembled as I could feel the climax building. Clenching and unclenching my hands, I tried to keep myself from moving. Unbearable desire pulsed through me as I neared the edge. He blew softly on my throbbing areas. I sucked in a ragged breath. A dark moan vibrated in my chest as his tongue started up the mind-numbing torture again. My vision flashed black and white behind my closed eyelids. Tremors racked my body.

A gasp ripped from my lips as Mordren's tongue flicked a sensitive spot.

My hands shot down. I raked my fingers through his hair before taking it in a firm grip.

Mordren stopped moving.

I drew in a shuddering breath, trying to force my eyes to focus again.

Slowly, the Prince of Shadows stood back up.

My hands moved from his hair and down to his chest as he rose. When my vision cleared again, I noticed the wicked glint in his silver eyes as he stared down at me. Reaching out, he took my chin in a firm grip and forced my head back.

"What did I say about moving your hands?" he demanded in a dark voice.

"Did you say something about it?" I answered, breathless. "I can't seem to remember."

His hand slid down my throat before he steered me away from the wall and towards the bed instead. "Well, I suppose that means we will have to start all over again." Once we were standing right next to the wooden frame, he released me and jerked his chin towards the bed. "Lie down."

I let out a dark chuckle and shook my head at him, but then maneuvered myself onto the bed while Mordren stripped out of his own pants.

He arched an expectant brow at me. "Hands above your head."

Narrowing my eyes at him, I complied and placed my arms against the mattress where he had instructed.

The bed creaked as Mordren climbed onto it and straddled

me. He raked his eyes over my body, ending on the hands I kept above my head. A satisfied smirk slid across his lips.

Placing his palms on either side of me, he leaned down and stole a single kiss from my lips before a dark whisper caressed my mouth.

"Good girl."

CHAPTER 16

*P*oisonwood Forest loomed like a dark barrier before us. Tilting my head back, I gazed up at the top of the gigantic trees. My heart pattered in my chest. This was probably a really bad idea.

It had taken Ellyda two days to finish making the container that now sat waiting in my backpack. Tundir had stayed locked up with the vegetables in the basement the whole time, but thankfully, no one had tracked him to our safe house. Yet. Idra and Hadeon, along with Ellyda and Theo, had agreed to stay behind in case trouble did come knocking. Between the four of them, I was certain they could survive anything. I glanced at the three people who were with me. The four of us, on the other hand, I was a bit more worried about.

"So…" Valerie began, drawing out the word. "Poisonwood Forest is filled with all kinds of dangerous stuff and also a wild cult of elves who suffer from some sort of mental breakdown?"

"That's what they say," I replied.

"Fabulous." She glanced down at the compass she had stolen on our way across town. Looking back up, she stabbed an arm straight ahead. "That's north. Let's go!"

"I have a bad feeling about this," I murmured, but started after the excited thief.

Eilan met my gaze briefly. "You're not the only one."

"Keep your eyes and ears open." Mordren's hand shot out and grabbed the back of Valerie's shirt before she could get too far ahead. "And stay together."

She swatted at his hand until he let go, and then flapped her arms in an impatient gesture. "Fine. Fine. Stay together and all that." Straightening her shirt again, she grinned and marched forward once more. "Keep up then."

Mordren and Eilan let out a ridiculously synchronized groan and massaged their brows. I wiped a hand over my mouth to hide the smile visible there. How she did it was a mystery to me, but somehow Valerie always managed to do just the thing that would lighten a tense situation.

Suppressing the urge to hold my breath, I followed the confident thief into the forest.

As soon as we left the open grasslands behind, the light grew darker. The trees were so high and the canopy so thick that they blotted out most of the sunlight even though it was a bright summer morning. I swept my gaze over the thick tree trunks as we walked.

Everything was eerily silent and still.

We were in a forest in the middle of summer. There should have been insects humming in the grass and birds singing in the trees. Maybe the soft snap of branches as a larger animal moved through the underbrush. But there was just... nothing.

Even the wind was suspiciously absent.

Pulling at the collar of my shirt, I tried to persuade myself that I was just imagining that it was difficult to breathe. Yes. That was it. My mind was just playing tricks on me.

As if the sullen forest had rubbed off on us, we also walked in complete silence.

The farther in we got, the more the landscape changed. At the edge of the forest, the trees had been relatively straight. But now, what I estimated to be an hour into our walk, they had become weird and utterly foreign. It looked like someone had taken the trunk and the branches and just twisted them in all directions before grabbing a different part of the tree and doing the same. Dark purple moss hung like curtains from the gnarled branches.

Sweat beaded on my forehead.

I dragged my fingers through my hair to remove the few loose strands that stuck to my face. When it barely seemed to work, I retied the string that held up my long red curls. It was getting uncomfortably warm in here. Forcing a deep breath into my lungs, I pulled at my collar again and then rolled up my sleeves.

"I don't think the air is moving at all in here," Eilan said.

His voice shattered the long silence like an explosion and I jumped at the sound. To my surprise, so did Mordren and Valerie. I cleared my throat.

Valerie gave her head a short shake as if to clear it. "I don't think anything moves in here."

"Are you certain that this is north?" Mordren asked.

She glanced down at her stolen compass again. "Yes."

He gave her a distracted nod before going back to scanning the forest around us.

Pale blue mushrooms started appearing on the trunks as we continued through the woods. And then pink flowers began dotting the ground as well. A few minutes later, bright yellow lichen covered every stone and boulder in sight. Between the green grass and canopy above, the brown trunks, the purple hanging moss, the blue mushrooms, the pink flowers, and the yellow lichen, it was like walking through a rainbow.

Something nagged at the corner of my mind. Then realization hit. We had walked for what had to be an hour or two, and we still hadn't seen a single animal.

A dark shadow flashed at the edge of my vision.

I sucked in a gasp. "Something's here. A dark shadow."

The others crowded in around me and whipped their heads from side to side.

"Where?" Mordren asked.

My gaze flicked back and forth across the trees.

The dark shape darted past on my right.

"There!" I yelled.

Eilan stabbed a hand in the opposite direction. "There was one there too."

"Shit," I hissed.

Black shadows shot past on all sides. This time, Mordren and Valerie pointed at them too. We backed away together. Primal fear surged inside me. I couldn't remember the last time I had been this afraid. My mind was trying to reason with me that we didn't even know what it was, but all I could think was that we were going to die horribly if we stayed here.

"Run!" Mordren snapped, as if he felt the same.

We bolted.

Barely even looking where we were going, we hurtled through the woods. Leaping over boulders and fallen trees, we tried desperately to escape the nameless horror that we were sure hunted us.

The colorful forest blurred around me like water on paint.

My lungs burned. Sucking in desperate breaths, I crashed through a dark green bush and stumbled over a branch. The world tilted around me and I slammed into the grass. Earth and crushed flowers clung to my body as I rolled over and over until I came to a halt next to a stone covered in yellow lichen. The canopy high above my head seemed to be moving. Rippling. Like waves.

"Stop!" Eilan screamed.

With great effort, I rolled over on my side and pushed myself back to my feet.

"Where are we?" Eilan panted.

Mordren and Valerie had screeched to a halt a short distance away, and now we all looked between each other.

"I don't know," Valerie finally said.

Mordren pressed a hand to the side of his head as if to stop it from spinning. "Which way is north?"

She looked down at the compass. Blinked. Rubbed her eyes. Then she squinted at it again. Panic flashed across her features.

"I don't know," she breathed.

"What do you mean you don't know?"

"The compass. It won't stop spinning."

Mordren stalked over to her and grabbed her wrist. Moving the compass closer to him, he stared down at it as well. He also blinked. And rubbed his eyes. I looked up at the canopy again. The green leaves whirled around like a maelstrom.

"It won't stop spinning," Mordren said.

"That's what I said," Valerie pressed out before she yanked at her collar. "Why is it so warm in here?"

Eilan pulled at his shirt as well. "I can't breathe."

His words sent a spike of panic up my spine. I couldn't breathe either. Fumbling for the hem of my shirt, I yanked it over my head and threw it on the ground. Valerie quickly did the same thing.

Warm air seemed to press against my body from all sides and clung to my limbs like fog. I felt claustrophobic. My hands shook as I threw off my pants as well and then sat down against a boulder. The cold stone was like a kiss against my back.

"It's cold," I said.

Mordren, Eilan, and Valerie, who were all half-naked as well, rushed over and crowded down next to me. Pressing our backs against the stone, we all forced out a collective breath.

Our clothes were scattered across the forest floor and we were sitting in our underwear just to feel the touch of a boulder. Deep in my mind, I knew that something was terribly wrong, but I couldn't make my brain form any rational thoughts. Instead, I blurted out one of my deepest darkest secrets.

"I don't know what I'm doing." I stared at the trees in shock but my mouth kept talking. "I've spent my whole life under someone else's control, and now I finally have power but I feel like I don't know what I'm doing half of the time. I'm responsible for everyone else's safety and I have to be perfect every minute of every day to make sure that no one gets hurt and I'm terrified that I'm going to make a wrong move and fuck up so badly that there's no coming back from it."

Mordren turned to stare at me. It looked like he was trying very hard to process what I was saying. "I'm scared that my luck will eventually run out." He blinked as if he was surprised at which words had actually come out of his mouth, but he kept talking. "I've been scheming my way out of impossible situations for years, and now I'm terrified that my luck is going to run out soon. That I will go up against something that I can't beat and that everything I've built and everyone I'm trying to protect will be destroyed because I can't come up with a clever enough scheme."

"I'm terrified of being alone," Eilan blurted out. He cast a quick glance at me. "You're scared of fucking things up so badly that there's no coming back from it? I'm afraid that *I* am so badly fucked up that there is no fixing me. I'm hundreds of people, all crammed into one. What kind of person does that make me?" His pale green eyes were wide and desperate as he turned to stare at Valerie. "And then you say or do something that makes me… feel, and I think there might be hope for me yet. But then I remember that you've only met one part of me and you still haven't met the torturers and the murderers and the cruel vicious people that I also am sometimes and then I realize that I really am fucked up."

Valerie looked back at him in silence for a few moments. Or minutes. It was getting increasingly difficult to estimate how much time had passed.

"I was really hurt that you didn't trust me enough to tell me that you were a shapeshifter until you literally had to choose between dying and telling me," she finally said.

Eilan looked like she had stabbed him.

Tearing her gaze from him, she blew out a deep breath and looked up at the leaves above instead. Thoughts pounded against my skull, but all I did was tilt my head up and stare at the canopy as well.

Silence fell.

Nothing moved. No wind. No animals. Not even the sun. Or did it? Blinking, I squinted at what I thought were the tiny patches of sky that were visible between the branches. Did it look darker than it had before?

I leaned my head against the boulder again. Who cared about the sky?

Sharp thoughts hammered against my brain once more. Something was wrong. Very wrong. I shook my head to stop the blaring alarm inside me, but it only grew louder.

"Leave me alone," I mumbled.

Mordren tilted his head towards me. "What?"

Bells clanged inside my mind. *Something is wrong. Something is wrong.*

"Leave me alone!" I screamed and sent a ring of fire pulsing out around us.

Logical thoughts snapped into my brain again. Why were we sitting half-naked by a boulder? What time was it? Why were the woods suddenly so dark? Which way was north? We had to go.

The others shook their heads and looked around as if they too were just waking up from a daze. I flicked my gaze around the area.

Colorful moss and mushrooms and flowers stared back at me. Dread crawled up my spine.

"There's something in the air." I struggled to my feet and sent another small ring of fire pulsing out around us. "Some kind of hallucinogenic. Or something. We've been breathing it in."

"Get dressed," Mordren said, his voice suddenly clear and sharp again. "Kenna, keep burning whatever it is out of the air."

While sending intermittent pulses of flames to clear the air around us, I awkwardly pulled my pants and shirt back on before hefting my backpack. The others looked equally embarrassed.

"If it's a hallucinogenic," Eilan began. "How much of what's happened today has been real?"

I thought back to the dark shapes chasing us. The spinning compass and the whirling trees. The soul-baring truths we spilled. Had all that really happened?

"I don't know," I replied.

We all finished getting dressed. I sent more flames to purify the air and then stopped to look at the others. Awkward glances bounced between the four of us.

"Uhm…" Valerie began.

Eilan cleared his throat. "We, uhm…"

"This never happened," Mordren announced. "Agreed?"

Relief washed over everyone's faces.

"Yeah."

"Agreed."

"Sold."

After one final embarrassed look at one another, we cleared our throats and pulled ourselves together.

Then we continued deeper into Poisonwood Forest.

CHAPTER 17

Darkness hung heavy over the forest. Those hallucinations had warped our perception of time and made us lose most of the day. We must have run for longer than we thought too, because we had gotten far off track. Sunset was close, and we still hadn't made it out of the forest.

"Are you sure that this is north?" Mordren asked for the fifth time.

Valerie looked down at the compass. "Yes."

"Then why are we not out yet?"

"How should I know?"

Silence fell.

We trudged on. I kept a ball of flames above us to light the way, and sent sporadic bursts around us to clear the air. But the continuous use of magic in this way was draining me faster than I wanted to admit.

"Guys." Valerie's voice was sharp and full of alarm. "Did you see that?"

"See what?" Eilan asked.

Mordren glanced over at me.

I shook my head. "I've been purifying the air this whole time. We shouldn't be hallucinating."

Branches rustled. The sound was so unexpected that I jumped, making the flames above us splutter. After spending an entire day in a forest where nothing moved, I wasn't sure if hearing branches rustle was a good thing or not. I strengthened the firelight and swept my gaze around the area.

"There," Valerie hissed.

That time I saw it too. Sleek dark shadows moved along the large branches around us. Alarm rippled through our small group.

Without speaking, we quickly formed up in a defensive position with our backs to each other. The twisted trees watched us impassively. For a moment, nothing else happened. Then a few curtains of purple hanging moss swayed gently as something snuck past.

I sucked in a gasp.

A large cat-like animal stepped out of the shadows. Its short black fur was shiny and striped with patches of deep red. Sharp teeth, and two long fangs that went past its lower jaw, glinted in the firelight as the beast let out a rumbling growl.

My heart pounded in my chest.

Behind me, Valerie sucked in a sharp breath as well.

And then more animals prowled towards us. They jumped between the branches, and some leaped down to the forest floor. We tightened our circle.

"Who are you?" a voice cut through the dark forest.

I whipped my head towards the sound.

Behind the black and red animals, other figures appeared. My eyes widened as a mass of elves stepped into the light.

They were Low Elves. Dressed in the colors of the forest, they were almost invisible in the dusky woods until they came into range of my firelight. Their clothes looked to have been made from various elements that could be found in the forest, and their hair was artfully braided and decorated with leaves, feathers, and very poisonous-looking flowers. Red anklets gleamed around their feet.

But that was not what drew most of my attention.

It was the bows that they held, arrows drawn and pointed at us.

"I guess we're about to meet the wild elf cult," Valerie whispered.

"Who are you?" the leader called again.

He was tall and wiry, with long black hair pulled back from his face by a series of braids. A crown of what looked like spiky red branches encircled his forehead. His observant brown eyes assessed us as he continued training an arrow on my chest.

"We are only passing through," Mordren called back.

"No one passes through here." He shifted his attention to the Prince of Shadows. "Everyone in this land knows not to go into Poisonwood Forest."

"We are not from this land."

"Liar."

"He's not lying," Valerie said. She lifted a hand and stepped forward as she spoke. "Look, I'm–"

An arrow sped through the air. Panic flared up my spine and I threw up a wall of fire in front of her. The arrow looked to have been aimed at the ground before her feet, but it was incinerated as it struck the flaming barrier.

Shouts rang through the forest.

Wood creaked as bows were drawn taut. Mordren raised a

shadow wall next to my fire as the elves started shouting threats and warnings. The black and red beasts snarled and circled closer. Whipping my head from side to side, I tried to keep them all in view at the same time to anticipate where the next attack would come from.

"Hold," the leader snapped.

The other elves fell silent and the animals stopped moving. My heart was slamming so hard against my ribs that I feared they would crack any second. If they attacked, we would not survive.

"You can wield fire," the leader said. It was more of a statement than a question. His brown eyes slid to Mordren. "And shadows? But you're not High Elves, so you shouldn't be able to do that."

"Like I said," Mordren began, "we are not from here."

"I'm not even an elf," Valerie called.

A ripple of surprise went through our ambushers. They all glanced to their leader. He narrowed his eyes at Valerie and then lowered his bow. After returning the arrow to his quiver, he twitched two fingers at Valerie.

She started towards him without hesitation.

Eilan's hand shot out and grabbed her sleeve. "Wait."

"I'll be fine." She slipped out of his grip and patted his arm before continuing on her way. "It's not like I haven't done this before. Well, I mean, I haven't. But you know what I mean."

The red-striped felines turned their heads and watched Valerie as she strolled across the grass. Several of the elves shifted their aim and tracked her movements. After leaping down from the branch he had been standing on, the leader crossed his arms and waited for Valerie to close the final distance.

"See." She lifted her hair to show her ears. "Not an elf."

He studied her whole face, and then raked his gaze up and down her body too, before finally saying, "What are you then?"

"I'm a human."

"Human." He rolled the word over his tongue as if tasting it. "And can you do magic too, human?"

"That depends on your definition of magic."

A grin flashed across her face as she held up what looked like a small wooden pipe. Warning shouts echoed between the trees and half of our ambushers swung around to point their arrows at Valerie while the leader patted his clothes. Shock danced across his features as he looked between his clothes and the pipe that Valerie had apparently pickpocketed.

I would have facepalmed if I hadn't been so worried that they were actually going to shoot her.

With that wide grin on her face, she handed the pipe back. "No, I can't do magic. Not your kind, anyway." She gave him a dramatic bow. "I'm Valerie, by the way. Nice to meet you."

For a moment, the black-haired elf only stared back at her in stunned silence, as if he couldn't quite figure out what to do with this strange creature. To be fair, I wouldn't have known what to do either. But then he cleared his throat and put the pipe back in his pocket.

"I'm Mendar," he said while giving her another assessing look. "Why are you here, Valerie the Human?"

"It's just Valerie. No fancy last name or title. And we," she swept her arm to indicate the three of us as well, "are here because we're planning to steal some of the magic from the White Tower and use it to blackmail the Empress and Emperor of Valdanar into cutting High Commander Anron loose so that we can kill him without fear of retribution so that he won't take over our home and give it to a power-hungry princess."

Ringing silence echoed between the trees. The other elves flicked their gaze between their leader and the weird thief.

"You're going to steal their magic and blackmail them?" Mendar said at last. He snorted. "Good luck with that."

"It will work. We just need to find the tower first." She motioned towards the compass. "We keep heading north but we never seem to get there."

Laughter blew across the woods.

"That's because the magnetic fields in here mess with compasses," he explained. With a flick of his wrist, he motioned for his people to withdraw. "Well, good luck then."

Purple moss swung and branches rustled as the elves and their fanged animals started to leave. The four of us exchanged a panicked look. If the compass didn't work, we would never find our way out again.

"Wait!" I called. "Do you know how to get to the tower?"

Mendar paused and looked back at me. "Of course we do. But we're not getting involved in your crazy plans."

"Ellyda," Eilan whispered.

It only took a second for my mind to catch up.

"What about a deal?" I blurted out. "We can get those anklets off you."

Everyone froze. A hushed sense of shock spread through the trees. Then, as one, the elves all turned to stare at me.

"As you already know, we're magically skilled," I elaborated. "And one of our friends back in town can forge magical objects. She can make something that would break those anklets."

Their eyes shifted to Mendar.

"In exchange for…?" he asked.

"Showing us the way to and from the White Tower."

"That's it?"

"That's it."

I held my breath, waiting for his answer. And so did everyone else, apparently. Mendar swept his gaze over his people. Hope sparkled in a lot of eyes.

He ran a hand over his jaw. "It's an... intriguing offer. Come. Let's discuss it over dinner." Jerking his chin, he motioned for us to follow. "Crossing the forest in the dark is a bad idea anyway. The tower can wait until morning."

Mordren and I exchanged a glance before letting our shields of magic drop. With an enthusiastic wave, Valerie urged us on while she marched after the leader of the elves. Eilan shook his head in exasperation, but fell in beside us as we walked.

Elves with bows and black felines with long fangs and blood red stripes formed a formidable escort around us as Mendar led us all towards the heart of the wild cult's camp.

CHAPTER 18

Light and music filled the woods up ahead. I swept my gaze over our armed escort to see how they reacted to coming back home. Smiles lit up their faces as a few other elves came running to greet them. When they saw us, the newcomers trailed to a halt, but their friends pulled them away while pointing towards us and whispering in a conspiratorial manner. The black and red felines began branching off as well. Some prowled into the darkness and others went straight into camp.

Eilan's eyes tracked them as they slunk away. "What are they?"

"Blood panthers," Mendar answered.

Valerie smacked her lips. "Well, that doesn't sound ominous at all."

He chuckled and reached out to stroke one of the blood panthers along the back as it passed. It looked up at him, and he scratched it under the chin. A low rumble came from the animal. After nudging Mendar's hand with its nose, the blood panther prowled ahead.

"And about the hallucinations…?" I began as we neared their camp.

"Ah, yes. That's from the blue mushrooms. There aren't too many of them in this area, so you'll make it to dinner." When I frowned in confusion, he went on. "Eating the mushroom makes you more or less immune to the hallucinogenic spores they emit."

"You know, out of all the things I thought someone was going to say today, that was not one of them," Valerie announced.

"When I woke up, I would never have guessed that I would meet a human today either," Mendar replied and arched an amused eyebrow at the thief strolling along next to him.

The last barrier of twisting tree trunks disappeared and we stepped into their camp proper. I trailed to a halt.

We were standing in a wide clearing. Those huge twisting trees formed a barrier around it, like the walls of a house. Far above, a dark blue sky dusted with silver stars looked down on us. Cottages made of wood dotted the open meadow and a stream that glittered in the starlight ran through the middle of the settlement. Between the sturdy homes were fireplaces with logs positioned around them, as if those were the main gathering places for the elves who lived here. And they probably were, because all of them were packed with people.

Talking, laughing, and playing strange wooden instruments, the elves of Poisonwood Forest looked like a kind and friendly group. Not like the wild cult they had been described as.

Something colorful moved at the corner of my eye. I turned. And my mouth dropped open.

Not only were blood panthers making themselves at home around the camp, the whole area was filled with a range of animals I had never seen before. A bright orange animal, that looked like a cross between a squirrel and a rabbit, scuttled up the tree next to me. My gaze tracked it upwards until I noticed the cacophony of color that spread out along the branches. Birds of all manners of sizes and hues perched up in the trees.

I snapped my gaze down as a small fluffy ball ran past my feet. It looked like a pink cloud with legs, and big blue eyes. A large fox with fur that matched the dark blue and silver glitter of the night sky snuck between two houses up ahead.

"Uh..." I said.

Not exactly my sharpest assessment ever, but I had never seen so many strange animals before. I knew that there were magical animals in this land since we had flown here on a green winged serpent, but the sight of this camp still left me speechless.

"Just because we're forced to live in here doesn't mean we can't make the most of it," Mendar said. Raising a toned arm, he pointed towards an empty fireplace. "You can sit down over there while we discuss your offer. I would recommend not wandering off."

I wasn't sure if that last part was meant as a threat or a friendly warning, but I decided not to dwell on it and instead gave him a nod. The others did the same before we started towards the indicated logs and firepit.

A sharp whistle cut through the air.

"Meeting!" Mendar called as he strode towards a large cabin on our right.

Several male and female elves stopped what they were doing and started towards the same cabin.

Fire streaked past above me. I whipped my head back and looked up to see a gigantic bird speeding towards camp. Its coat of red, orange, and yellow fire looked to be made of actual flames. Embers whirled up into the air as it landed on the ground a short distance away. A female elf with long white hair slid off the firebird's back. Stroking her hand over the fiery plumage, she patted it goodbye before she jogged towards Mendar's cabin.

"Wow," I said as I slumped down on one of the logs by the fire.

"Yeah," Eilan said.

On some unspoken signal, we all took a log each so that we would be able to see in all directions and warn each other in case a threat presented itself. Mordren, who sat opposite me, searched my face until I gave him a tired smile.

"This has got to be the coolest place I've ever seen," Valerie announced as she plopped down on the log opposite Eilan. "Why don't we have animals like this back in our lands?"

"Most likely because there was not supposed to be any magic there," Mordren said.

"How boring."

I chuckled. "Yeah." Twisting to my left, I met her gaze. "Good job on convincing Mendar, by the way."

"Yes," Mordren added before arching a dark brow at her. "Though, in the future, may I suggest not pickpocketing the leader of the group who has arrows pointed at our heads?"

"*Tsk.*" She waved a hand in front of her face. "You know he was impressed with me."

"His people were also considering whether or not to shoot you."

"Insignificant details."

Mordren met my gaze while motioning towards the grinning thief. "Remind me again how she has managed to survive this long?"

I chuckled and shook my head. "Don't look at me. I have no idea either."

Valerie winked at me while Mordren blew out an amused huff. Then silence fell once more. It was a heavy silence. Despite our light banter and the wonder of seeing all of these extraordinary animals, we all knew that our survival would be decided by the elves in that cabin. And there was nothing more we could do about it. Only wait.

The rest of the elves in the camp watched us curiously from a distance, but no one approached. I supposed that they were also waiting for their leader's decision.

Wood popped in the fireplace. I tore my gaze from our distant audience and watched the way the flames licked the air above the pit. Tiredness, and hunger, rolled over me. Once again, we had gone through a very intense day with little food and rest. I wasn't sure how long I could keep doing this.

"It wasn't because I didn't trust you," Eilan said, breaking the tense silence that had settled.

We all looked up at him, but his pale green eyes were locked on Valerie.

"It wasn't because I didn't trust you that I didn't tell you that I'm a shapeshifter," he said. "I didn't want to tell you because I value our friendship and I didn't want to ruin it."

Valerie frowned at him, confusion swirling in her warm brown eyes. "Why would that ruin it?"

"I have told a few people throughout the years, and well…" His gaze dropped to the dancing flames. Blowing out a sigh, he dragged a self-conscious hand through his hair. "Let's just say that it has never worked out in the end."

"Why not?"

"No one ever looked at me the same once they knew. Once they had seen the versions of me that aren't all that pleasant."

He let out a bitter laugh. "You know, I could even see the exact moment that it changed. Second by second, how the way they looked at me irrevocably shifted. It's, uhm… It's not a fun experience." His eyes flicked up to Valerie's again. "And I didn't want to watch as that happened with you too."

Valerie stared back at him. A whole tangle of emotions blew across her face, but all she said was, "Oh."

The door to the cabin opened. My heart skipped a beat as I watched Mendar stride towards us. That had been a short meeting. Hopefully that meant good news.

We all sat up straighter as the leader of the Poisonwood Forest elves took a seat next to Valerie. Several of his senior council, or whatever the people who had gone to the meeting were, sat down as well. I scooted over as the white-haired female who had arrived on the firebird plopped down next to me.

"We accept your deal," Mendar said without preamble.

"Fantastic," I blurted out in reply while my heart started up an excited pattering.

"We will get you to and from the White Tower," he continued. "And then your friend will make something that can remove these anklets."

"Yes," Mordren confirmed as well. "She might need to come here and study the anklets before she can do it. But she is very good at what she does, so she will find a way."

Mendar nodded in acknowledgement.

Studying him, I watched the firelight cast dancing shadows over his face. He looked determined and calm, but not very hopeful. In fact, when I thought about it, I realized that he was agreeing to a deal that he had no way of enforcing. Once he had escorted us to and from the tower, and we left the forest, there was nothing stopping us from leaving our end of the bargain unfulfilled. Mendar and his people could never leave the forest, so they couldn't come looking for us afterwards. All he had was our word that we would come back.

"Why?" I asked, knowing that he would understand the full question embedded in that word.

His observant brown eyes slid to me before he lifted his shoulders in a shrug. "Because we have nothing left to lose."

My heart squeezed painfully at the look in his eyes. That steady expression of someone who had stopped hoping a long time ago and accepted that this was what life was like.

"We will come back," I said, holding his gaze. "And we will find a way."

He only nodded in response.

Before anyone could continue, a group of elves drifted over from another firepit. They were carrying wooden bowls that they proceeded to pass out to everyone. I looked down at the bowl that I was handed. It looked like a mix between grilled meat and different kinds of vegetables. Using the spoon that had accompanied the bowl, I shifted the pieces around until I found something blue.

"Is this the mushroom?" I asked while lifting it up on my spoon.

"Yes," the white-haired elf next to me answered. "We eat them with every meal. They give you temporary immunity to various kinds of mind-altering substances that fill the air in this forest."

"Huh." I nodded and then popped the piece of mushroom in my mouth.

It tasted a lot fresher than I had thought. Almost like mint. With an appreciative nod to the surprisingly tasty mushroom, I dug into the rest of the food. The grilled meat was so perfect that it almost melted in my mouth, and it was seasoned with some kind of green herb I had never tasted before. It complemented the fresh mint and the other crisp vegetables wonderfully.

As I savored the taste of the well-composed meal, I couldn't help but wonder how long it had taken these people to figure out that eating the mushrooms would stop the hallucinations. The few hours we had been trapped under its spell were enough to send lingering spikes of dread up my spine. I couldn't even imagine what it must have been like to be thrown into this forest without preparation, high on mushroom spores, and knowing that you would be trapped here forever. A shudder coursed through me. We would definitely hold up our end of the bargain. If we survived the visit to the tower, that is.

As if he could hear my thoughts, Mendar put down his now empty bowl and swept his gaze over the four of us. "We will get you there, but I have to warn you. I don't think your plan is going to work. As far as I know, no one has ever been able to take magic from the White Tower."

We exchanged a glance.

"From what we have been told, our ancestors apparently did," Mordren explained. Shadows twisted between his fingers as if to provide further evidence.

"I see. Then it might be possible." He sat back and stretched his legs out before crossing his ankles. "But I would still suggest that you form some kind of backup plan."

A backup plan? This *was* our backup plan.

"If this turns out to be impossible, what would you do?" he prompted.

Setting down my own empty bowl, I gave him a helpless shrug in reply. I knew that he was trying to strengthen his own odds of us coming back to help him, but the truth was that we didn't have another plan. We had to steal the magic and blackmail the emperor and empress into disowning Anron. It was a miracle that Valerie had even come up with this brilliantly insane plan, and I didn't have anything better to offer. We had to make this work.

"Alright, this might be news to you," Valerie began as a wicked grin spread across her mouth, "but I've always believed that rules are meant to be broken."

Eilan let out an amused snort. "Shocker."

Picking up a small piece of wood, she hurled it at him. He ducked it gracefully while she flashed him another smile that I knew only meant trouble. I massaged my brow.

With that scheming glint in her eyes, she swept her gaze over us and Mendar and the other elves. "You all seem so stuck on this view that some rules are absolute. But there are always loopholes. Hear me out. Say you want to buy something, yeah? But you don't have the money to buy it, and you're not really a skilled forger either, so you just copy the top side of the paper bill, pay with it, and then run like hell."

She paused and spread her arms while a satisfied expression beamed on her face, as if she had just shared some sort of brilliant advice. The rest of us frowned at her in confusion.

"What?" I said.

"Wouldn't you just go to a real forger and have them make passable bills instead?" Eilan added.

"Or, I don't know," Mendar cut in, "not take the thing if you can't pay for it?"

The white-haired elf next to me furrowed her pale brows. "What's a paper bill?"

"*Ugh*," Valerie groaned and threw her hands up in a show of exasperation. "It's like a pigeon."

"A pigeon?" Eilan stared at her in complete bafflement.

"Yes, a pigeon. And a dove." She hurled another piece of wood at him. "Now shush and let me finish."

While Valerie started up a convoluted explanation about pigeons and doves and badly forged paper bills, the white-haired elf nudged me in the side with her elbow.

"Look, uhm…" She trailed off and then looked me up and down. "What's your name?"

"Kenna," I replied.

She nodded. "I'm Endira." After another dubious glance at Valerie, she turned back to me. "Look, Kenna, Mendar is right. Stealing the magic will be next to impossible. Not only getting it out but also transporting it."

Smiling, I motioned towards the backpack leaning against the log. "That friend we told you about, the one who can make something that will break your anklets, she has made a container that will hold it."

"Oh." She blinked in surprise, but then shook her head as if getting her hopes up was foolish. "But you still need to get inside too. The High Elves won't just let a random bunch of *Low Elves*," she spoke the words with bitter irony, "saunter up to their precious tower and stroll inside. Trust me, they can be really cruel and vicious. Especially the ones who guard the White Tower."

My gaze drifted to Eilan. He was staring at Valerie, and his brows climbed higher up his forehead with every word that came out of her mouth. I smiled again.

"Yeah, I, uhm…" I watched Eilan's eyes sparkle with schemes as Valerie finished speaking. "I think we have a way around that."

Endira followed my gaze, but since she didn't know that Eilan was a shapeshifter, she only frowned in confusion again.

No, the High Elves would never let a bunch of Low Elves into the sacred White Tower. But if a High Elf soldier showed up with a wanted fugitive and told them that Empress Elswyth had sent them? A wicked smirk slid home on my lips. Then they might just let us walk right through the door.

CHAPTER 19

An open stretch of grass spread out before us. Great walls made of that strange mirror-like material rose up from the ground and cut off the bright green grass. Morning sunlight reflected off the defensive walls and lit up the white stone tower that was tucked in behind them. My gaze flicked between the archers posted on top of the walls that surrounded the tall tower and the two soldiers who were standing at the bottom of the ramp. Gates of twisted metal bars separated the ramp from the grasslands.

"I am telling you, this is not going to work," Mendar said.

We were standing at the edge of the forest. Just inside the tree line. It was as far as the anklets allowed them to go. Not that they had planned on following us to the tower anyway. And besides, we needed to stay unseen behind the trees for a little while longer before we got this crazy scheme started.

"The High Elves who guard this tower," Eilan began as he looked at Mendar. "What are they like?"

"What do you mean 'what are they like'?"

"Their personality. Are they especially loyal or calm or quiet? Or is it just a mix of personalities?"

"Cruel," Endira said. She raised her chin and swept her hair behind her shoulder as she stared out at the guards across the grass. "They are entitled. Guarding the magic is a great honor, which makes them think that they are better than everyone. Especially Low Elves, because we can't wield the elemental magic that they're so proudly guarding. And that makes them cruel."

Turning towards her, I raised my eyebrows in silent question.

She shrugged. "I was one of the people who attacked this part of the palace when we launched our resistance movement. They beat me up pretty badly and made me... *grovel* quite thoroughly when they captured me."

"I'm sorry," I said.

Endira just shrugged again as if it mattered little.

"Okay." Eilan's eyes were still fixed on the guards by the wall. "Cruel, entitled, physically violent, and think they're better than everyone else and Low Elves in particular."

Mendar and Endira, who were the only ones that had accompanied us here, frowned at him in confusion. The rest of us had already agreed on the plan. There was no way to do this without Endira and Mendar finding out, at least not if we wanted to get back out through the forest again, so I just turned to Eilan and shrugged.

"Ready when you are," I said.

A hint of pain crept into his eyes as he looked back at me. "If we are to really convince them, I might need to do things that..." He trailed off and flicked a glance at Valerie before meeting my gaze again. "That I normally wouldn't do. Things that will not be pleasant for you."

"I know." Reaching out, I gave his arm a squeeze to show him that I understood. "Don't worry about me. I can take it. Just do whatever you need to do to convince them and get us up that ramp."

"I'm sorry. In advance."

Drawing in a deep breath, he swept his gaze over the others. His eyes lingered a bit longer on Valerie than everyone else, but then he tore his gaze away and rolled his shoulders back.

The edges of his body blurred.

Mendar and Endira leaped back and stared in utter shock as a High Elf soldier in gleaming bronze armor appeared where Eilan had been standing only seconds before.

"*That's* how we're getting inside," I explained.

As soon as the High Elf's form was firmly in place, Eilan's entire demeanor changed. He stood straight-backed, his chin held high, and his whole body pulsed with power and arrogance. His normally so kind green eyes were now blue and looked down on the rest of us with cold distaste.

He snapped his fingers at Mordren. "Rope."

Mordren, who seemed entirely unfazed by his brother's changed personality, simply pulled out a length of rope from his backpack and offered it to him. Eilan snatched it up and then grabbed my arm.

With decisive movements, he yanked me around and forced my wrists together behind my back. I had to keep reminding myself that this was Eilan and not a real High Elf as he roughly tied my hands behind me.

Taking a firm grip on my arm again, he began pulling me towards the tree line. "Let's go."

"Wait," Endira said. She turned to Mordren. "Do you have any more rope?"

"Yes," he replied as he pulled out another length from his pack. "Why?"

I thought I could detect a hint of fear in her eyes as she turned to look at Eilan. Swallowing, she motioned between the rope and me. "Around her neck. Like a leash. That's how they do it."

Eilan stalked back to his brother and retrieved the rope before tying it like a noose around my neck. Once he was done, he grabbed the end of it and then yanked me forward again. As we started towards the open stretch of grass, I couldn't help thinking about the fact that Eilan had looked at everyone except Valerie. The moment he had shapeshifted into this High Elf, he had carefully avoided meeting her gaze. This was one of the versions of himself that he was afraid to show her. I could only hope that Valerie would share the sentiment I had concerning all of this, and not the one he feared. I understood that this was a role that Eilan had to play, and nothing he was about to do would change anything in our friendship.

Sunlight shone from the castle walls. It was bright enough that I wanted to shield my eyes, but since my hands were tied behind my back, I had to settle for an undignified squint.

The High Elf that was Eilan walked in complete silence as he marched me towards the two guards at the gate. Occasionally, he would yank on the rope as if to make me keep up. I stumbled slightly as he gave it a firm tug when we neared the entrance to the ramp.

The archers on the walls watched our approach, but since they could clearly see a High Elf in bronze armor, they hadn't nocked any arrows.

"Who's this?" the dark-haired guard on the right called.

"One of those foreigners," Eilan answered in a voice that

was a lot gruffer than his normal one. He gave the rope another savage pull that made me stumble forward. "Bitch tried to escape into the forest. Shows how much her intellect is lacking. Only morons would make a break for it to Poisonwood."

The two soldiers at the gate chuckled and nodded in agreement as we came to a halt in front of them. I flicked my gaze between the two of them. Based on the smug grins on their faces, they were buying Eilan's performance.

"Sorry, brother," the redhead on the left began, "what was your name again?"

"Gadrien," Eilan's High Elf persona answered.

"Right, of course," the soldier replied as if they had met at some point. "So what're you doing here with her?"

"Apparently, she can wield fire."

"Seriously?"

"Yeah." Gadrien nodded towards the tower. "Their ancestors stole it from here."

Indignant fury flashed on their faces. The dark-haired one took a threatening step towards me.

"You stole from our sacred tower?" he spat.

"No," I snapped back. "I haven't stolen anything–"

A hand cracked across my face. With a High Elf's strength behind it, Gadrien's backhand was enough to snap my head to the side and send my whole body crashing to the ground. Since my hands were tied, I wasn't able to catch myself. Pain flared up my shoulder as I hit the grass.

Before I could reorient myself, Gadrien placed his foot against my shoulder and pushed me over. I rolled over on my back right before he positioned his boot across my throat.

"Who gave you permission to speak?" he growled down at me.

My instincts were screaming at me. Keeping perfectly still, I reminded myself over and over again that this was really Eilan and that he would never actually crush my windpipe with his boot.

The two guards snickered above me.

Taking his boot from my throat, Gadrien turned back towards them. "So yeah, you gonna let us pass or what?"

"Sure, but what are you even gonna do up in the tower now?"

I rolled over on my side and maneuvered myself onto my knees while the three of them stared down at me. A lethal smile spread across Gadrien's lips.

Steel glinted in the morning sunlight as he pulled out a knife and spun it in his left hand. Then he stopped and abruptly pushed it up under my chin.

"Empress wants to see if there's a way to bleed the magic out of her," he said.

Approving laughter rumbled from their chests. Tilting his head back, the dark-haired one looked up at the archers on the walls and then blew a series of whistles while motioning with his hand. The metal gates swung open.

"Go on then," the redhead said and jerked his chin.

With a firm grip on the rope, Gadrien yanked me back to my feet. After a nod to the grinning guards, he started us forwards.

"Oh," the redhead called after him. "The empress gave you the key, right? Because we don't have any."

"Of course," Gadrien answered without hesitation.

Confidence pulsed from him like waves as he marched me up the shining ramp and towards the locked door at the top. I scanned the area. Once we reached the door, we would have the privacy we needed to get through it.

This was the reason that Eilan and I had to be the ones to actually complete the mission. He needed to use his shapeshifting powers to get us up the ramp without being shot, and I had to get us through the locked door without possessing the key.

When the door finally appeared before us, Gadrien quickly untied my hands and yanked the noose from my neck. "Hurry."

I walked right through the solid metal door.

Silk brushed against my skin. And then it was replaced by the powerful humming of magic.

Whipping around, I quickly unlocked the door and opened it to allow Gadrien inside.

As soon as both of his feet were past the threshold, it shut behind us with an ominous boom.

My pulse sped up.

After exchanging a glance, Gadrien and I turned around and faced the sacred magic sources of the White Tower.

CHAPTER 20

Before he took a single step forward, Eilan shapeshifted back into himself. Worry bloomed in his eyes as he placed gentle fingers on my jaw and turned it to inspect the red mark he had left there.

"I'm sorry, Kenna," he said.

"Oh, it's fine." I squeezed his arm before guiding his hand away. "I've been through a lot worse."

"I know. But you shouldn't have to." He held my gaze, and I realized that he was afraid that this had permanently damaged our friendship. "We can, uhm... You can settle the scores on this once we're back safely, if you want."

"You know what? I'll take you up on that." I flashed him a smile and winked. "You can cook me dinner, and then we're even."

A relieved laugh spilled from his lips. "Done."

"Now, let's see if we can steal some magic."

The dozen pedestals I had seen last time remained firmly placed in a semi-circle around the back of the room. A metal bowl containing a magic element rested atop each of the pedestals. The light from the twisting flames and crackling lightning cast the otherwise dusky room with dancing shadows. Eilan and I drifted towards the bowls on the right side of the room.

"I hope Edric and his court managed to get to the temple unnoticed," Eilan said as he looked down at the shifting mass of water floating above the closest bowl.

"Yeah." I resisted the urge to draw my fingers through the water and instead continued towards the next pedestal. "Imagine if Anron had figured out that he didn't actually need to capture all the princes to get access to our elemental magic."

"If he had found those bowls, and used that magic, he would have been unstoppable."

"And we would've had new gods."

I blew out a breath. "Yeah."

Fire burned in the next bowl. As I drew closer to it, the flames grew bigger and changed direction. Tendrils of orange and red licked the air as the fire reached towards me, almost touching my skin. It was as if it could feel a part of itself inside me. Feel the cupful of fire magic that I had drunk. The magic our ancestors had stolen millennia ago. I ran my fingers through the flames before giving the magic a wicked smile. I was not giving it back.

Pulling off my shirt, I unslung the special backpack I had been hiding underneath. "So which magic source should we steal?"

Eilan turned in a slow half-circle and looked from pedestal to pedestal while I put my shirt back on. "I'm thinking either fire or lightning, since those seem to be the elements that the emperor and empress favor."

"True." I looked between the fire that still reached towards me and the lightning a few strides away. "My vote is for lightning then."

"I agree. Even though the emperor is technically Anron's military leader, Empress Elswyth is the one in charge of all the political decisions, and in the end, this is a political decision. So she is the one we need to convince."

"Which means that she is the one we need to piss off."

"That too."

While walking towards the bowl of lightning, I shook out the backpack that Ellyda had lined with some kind of flexible metallic material. It didn't look like any material I had ever seen. Running a finger over it, I realized that it was smooth and almost soft. A faint blue glow shifted over it.

"Do you have any idea what this is?"

"Not a clue." He chuckled. "She tried to explain it to me but she lost me after like two sentences."

"Yeah, you know, sometimes I think I'm smart. But then I talk to Ellyda and get a reminder that I'm really not as clever as I think."

He huffed out a laugh and nodded in agreement as we came to a halt in front of the white stone pedestal. Flashing lightning lit up our faces as we stared down into the bowl.

"So..." I glanced between Eilan and the crackling magic. "How do you want to do this?"

"Maybe we just... pour it in?"

"Alright, let's try it."

Eilan moved into position next to the pedestal while I opened the mouth of the backpack as far as the metal inside would let me. After another uncertain look at one another, we shrugged and Eilan lifted the bowl from the white stone.

The lightning inside hissed and crackled, but nothing else happened.

It was a wide bowl. Perhaps twenty times as big as the tiny stone bowls that we kept our magic in back in that hidden temple. Placing one arm underneath it, and the other supporting the edge, Eilan tipped the bowl towards the backpack.

For a moment nothing happened.

I lifted the backpack higher, placing it right against the edge.

Eilan tilted the metal bowl even farther towards it.

Small bolts of lightning shot back and forth in the air. And then it finally started moving. White flashes fell from the bowl and into the backpack in my arms. I watched it with an incredulous look on my face.

"Of all the strange things I have done, pouring lightning into a backpack has got to rank among the top three," I said.

Eilan bit his lip in concentration while continuing to tilt the bowl. "At least in the top ten."

"Top *ten*?"

"Yeah."

With a soft laugh, I shook my head at him. "When you cook me that dinner, you're going to have to tell me about the other nine."

"Deal."

The last of the lightning slipped from the bowl and into the backpack. I yanked it closed so that it wouldn't escape again.

"Alright, keep that hidden underneath you." He met my gaze. "Ready?"

After shifting the backpack so that I held it close to my stomach, I nodded for him to proceed. We had already decided that the best way to get me out of the tower and into the forest again was to pretend that I had died while he was trying to bleed the magic out of me. Dumping my corpse in the forest was the only reasonable excuse we had been able to conjure for why both of us would go back to Poisonwood instead of heading towards the prison cells inside the palace.

The edges of his body shifted right before Gadrien, the High Elf soldier from before, appeared in front of me. That arrogant tilt of his chin was back, along with the whole air of smug superiority.

Crouching down, he grabbed me and hoisted me up so that my body was draped over his shoulder. The backpack stayed pressed between my stomach and his armor. I made my body limp.

With a firm grip around the back of my thighs, he started towards the door. It moved silently as he pushed down the handle and edged it open with his free hand. I watched the bowls of magic behind his back as he took a step across the threshold.

My stomach lurched.

The room spun around me as I was flung backwards. Limbs clad in bronze armor whipped through the air around me right before I crashed down on the floor with Gadrien. I rolled over and over until I came to an abrupt halt against a pedestal. Gadrien slammed into my chest.

Sucking in a desperate breath, I tried to push his huge High Elf body off me while at the same time trying to figure out what had happened.

The pressure disappeared as Eilan shapeshifted back into himself and rolled away from me. I blinked, trying to clear my head, while I struggled to my feet.

"By all the gods and spirits," I muttered as I ran a hand over my hip. Dull pain pulsed from it after the rough landing. "What happened?"

Eilan picked up the backpack that had landed on the white stone floor halfway between the door and the pedestals. His eyes darted between it and the door. Then he strode towards it again. I followed.

The gap in the door was still the same, and morning sunlight shone in through it.

I trailed behind him as he reached it. "Shouldn't you shapeshift back into–"

Air exploded from my lungs as Eilan flew backwards and slammed straight into me. My body took another pounding as we hit the stone floor a few strides away. A groan slipped my lips as I pushed Eilan off me and sat up. Rolling off me, he did the same.

For a few seconds, we sat there in silence on the cold stone floor and stared at the sunlit doorway.

"Shit," Eilan finally said.

"Yeah."

Pushing to his feet, he strode back to the door. This time, he left the backpack on the floor as he took a step across the threshold.

Nothing happened.

With eyes scanning the area outside the door, he snuck out into the sunlight. After successfully passing the threshold, he disappeared back into the tower again. Pushing the door shut once more, he walked back towards me. I rose from the floor while he picked up the backpack and then came to a halt in front of me.

"It's the magic," he said as he looked between the backpack and my face.

A few curls had slipped free from the hair tie, so I raked a hand through my hair and dragged them out of my face before dusting off my clothes. "Yeah. They must have added some extra security measures after our ancestors stole some of it all those years ago."

Eilan stared down at the container filled with lightning in his hands. "We can't take it with us."

"No."

We had threatened and kidnapped a High Elf to get information on how to get here, crossed a forest filled with hallucinogenic mushrooms, accidentally shared our darkest secrets with each other, been ambushed by a group of elves who had nothing left to lose, faked a guard and prisoner exchange that involved Eilan slapping the living daylights out of me... all to get here. And now we couldn't leave with the magic.

Tearing my gaze from the lightning-filled backpack, I met Eilan's eyes while blowing out a deep breath.

"So... new plan?"

He nodded. "New plan."

Shaking my head, I followed him back towards the empty metal bowl. We would just have to do something else to manipulate them into disowning High Commander Anron then.

It wasn't as if any of our other plans had ever worked on the first try anyway, so why should it have been any different this time? Backup plans upon backup plans seemed to be our new normal.

But still, it would have been nice to have things actually go our way.

Just this once.

CHAPTER 21

Starlight shone down from the dark blue heavens and joined the crescent moon in illuminating the rooftop terrace. I glanced up at Eilan while the two of us continued dragging the chairs into place.

"How are you feeling?"

He adjusted one of the lounge chairs before meeting my gaze. "Good. I'm really okay, Kenna. I promise."

I held his gaze for a few seconds before nodding and then casting a quick glance over my shoulder. Valerie was depositing a tray full of glasses on the table a short distance away.

"You're going to have to look her in the eye eventually," I said.

His gaze darted towards her briefly before he went back to repositioning chairs that no longer needed to be repositioned. "I know. But the longer I put it off, the longer I can remember the way she used to look at me."

Once we had left the White Tower and returned to the forest, we had all headed back to the city. Mendar and Endira had shown us the way. We had parted at the edge of Poisonwood with the promise to return soon with Ellyda so that we could figure out a way to break those anklets. Mendar hadn't looked particularly hopeful, but they had nodded before disappearing back into the forest on the backs of a couple of firebirds.

After skulking through the city, we had at last reached our temporary safe house and briefly filled the others in. Tundir had been knocked out and then released far from the house so that he wouldn't be able to find his way back. Some cooking and dragging furniture around later, we were getting a gathering together on the rooftop.

And during that whole time, every minute between leaving the White Tower and repositioning chairs atop the roof with me, Eilan had carefully avoided looking Valerie straight in the eye.

"How can you be so sure that she will look at you differently?" I asked. "I didn't."

"No, but you're... *you*."

"Thanks." I narrowed my eyes at him. "Or maybe *ouch*?"

Eilan chuckled. "What I mean is, you poisoned my brother and then made him get down on his knees while he was choking to death so that you could blackmail him into paying off your debt. You're just as bad as me and Mordren."

I arched an eyebrow at him while trying to hide the smile tugging at my lips. "Yeah, I'm still not sure whether to say thank you or ouch."

He huffed out another laugh and shook his head before turning serious again. "What I'm trying to say is that you've done some really bad things, so when you see *me* do some really bad things, it doesn't bother you." His eyes darted towards the brown-haired thief again. "But Valerie is not like that. She's kind and full of light. Like a ball of sunshine."

"Yeah, but she's also a thief. So she's not exactly unaccustomed to shady stuff."

"But stealing things and actually hurting people are two very different things." A hint of dread blew across his handsome face. "And now she has seen me tie you up, hit you, and press a boot against your throat."

"You were playing a part."

"I know. But now she has seen what I'm capable of. The cruel side of me. Yes, Valerie is a thief so her morals are not exactly scrupulous, but she's not a murderer or a torturer."

A memory flashed past in my mind of when Valerie stood next to me and watched as I tortured an assassin who had tried to kill me and Idra. Looking up, I gave Eilan a small smile. "I think Valerie is a lot more open-minded about morally complicated things than you give her credit for."

Hope flickered in his light green eyes for a moment, but then he stamped it out and raked a hand through his hair instead. With a noncommittal nod, he motioned for us to start back towards where everyone else had gathered by the table.

A few large plants with thick green leaves swayed in the gentle breeze before us. I swept my gaze across the rooftop. Mordren and Idra were talking quietly next to a bowl filled with peaches that Theo had stolen earlier that day. Said thief was busy uncorking a wine bottle that had presumably been procured in the same fashion. Ellyda was staring up at the silver-glittering stars and seemed to be explaining something to Hadeon, who gazed up at the sky with a smile on his face.

Eilan's step faltered and he began to turn around. "Maybe I should just…"

A yelp slipped his lips as a small figure materialize right in front of him as he turned. Valerie flashed him a grin while I pressed a hand to my chest, trying to calm my thundering heart.

"Valerie," he blurted out. They were staring straight at each other.

"The one and only." She raised her eyebrows at him. "I don't know why you're so surprised. I'm a thief. Sneaking up on people is literally what I do. Like, all the time."

Eilan only continued to stare at her. His mouth hung open a little as he searched her face.

"You're staring," she pointed out. Flicking her loose brown curls behind her shoulder, she gave him a devilish smile. "I mean, I know I'm pretty and all, but like... you're *really* staring."

Giving his head a few quick shakes, Eilan pulled himself together and snapped his mouth shut. Relief washed over his features like a tidal wave. He searched her face again, as if he couldn't quite believe what he was seeing.

When he still said nothing, Valerie turned to me and flapped her hand in the air. "So, yeah, are we gonna join the others and talk about that new plan or what?"

Eilan cleared his throat. "Right. Yes." With that intense relief still rolling off him, he motioned towards the table. "After you."

Valerie flashed him a satisfied smile and started towards the others.

Happiness sparkled inside my soul. *I knew it.*

As Eilan and I followed her, I bumped his shoulder with mine and whispered, "Told you."

The light in his eyes was answer enough.

Chairs scraped against the floor as we all took our seats at the table. With the lounge furniture out of the way, and a couple of extra chairs from the kitchen, we managed to fit all eight of us at the table. Glasses filled with red wine waited next to each plate, and platters filled with cold cut meat, fruits, cheese, and a couple of pies lined the middle of the table.

For a few minutes, only the clinking of silverware broke the silence as everyone helped themselves to some food. I took a sip of the wine while waiting for Mordren to finish cutting us a few pieces of pie. The wine was rich and fruity, with a pleasant aftertaste.

"So," Theo began around a mouthful of cheese, "we need to turn Anron and the empress and emperor against each other?"

"Yeah," I answered.

"But how exactly do we do that?"

Idra nodded from her seat next to him while she swirled the wine in her glass. "He's right. We know nothing about the empress and emperor. About who they are as people. What they like. What they can't stand. And if we don't know that, we don't know what to do to truly piss them off."

"Can't we spy on them?" Hadeon asked, and then waved a hand towards Eilan. "You know...?"

"That sounds like an incredibly ineffective way of learning the subtleties of their personalities," Idra said.

Hadeon knocked back his glass of wine. "Well, I don't see you sharing any bright ideas either."

"Exactly. If I don't have any sensible plans to share, I don't say anything."

"And how helpful is that if–"

"What about Vendir?" Mordren interrupted before their bickering could escalate into an actual swordfight.

Silence fell over the table. I stabbed a piece of pie and

popped it in my mouth. It tasted like buttered mushrooms and herbs. While savoring the bite, I considered Mordren's words.

"Huh," I said at last. "You're right. We need someone who knows them well, and Vendir does fit that bill."

"Yeah, just one tiny problem." Valerie waved her glass around, almost making the wine slosh over the edge. "He kind of kicked us out and told us he wants nothing to do with us."

Mordren lifted one shoulder in a casual shrug. "We could always convince him that helping us is in his best interest."

Whether that was by presenting logical arguments or torturing him was unclear, but no one asked him to elaborate.

Hadeon furrowed his brows as he turned to look at his sister. While pushing a piece of meat around her plate, Ellyda stared unseeing at the bowl of peaches.

"What is it?" Hadeon asked gently.

She continued chasing the piece of meat with her fork for another minute before she managed to stop and tear her gaze from the pile of fruit. Starlight glittered in her violet eyes as she blinked a few times before her gaze finally settled on Hadeon.

"Do we have to involve Vendir?" she asked.

Hadeon raised his eyebrows in surprise, and seemed to be temporarily lost for words. From his seat next to Mordren, Eilan blew out a soft breath.

"You care about him," Eilan said. It wasn't a question. Just a simple statement of fact.

Ellyda nodded. "Yes."

"Why?" Hadeon asked. He sounded genuinely curious.

"Because I see in his eyes the future that could have been mine." Her own eyes were clear and filled with emotion as she swept her gaze around the table. "He is what I would have become if I didn't have you."

"What do you mean?"

"I am magically gifted at creating weapons. My destiny on the battlefield was practically written in stone even though that is not what I want." She turned to look straight at Hadeon. "But by luck of circumstance, I got a brother like you." Her eyes slid to Mordren and Eilan. "And family like you. People who understand that I want to create things. Not destroy them."

A warm night wind blew across the rooftop. It made loose strands of hair escape her messy bun and fall across her face. She pushed them back behind her pointed ears and drew in a shaky breath before continuing.

"I know that I'm odd. I know that I say and do things in ways that seem strange sometimes. But you have always accepted that. Accepted my wishes and my decisions about my own future." She met each of our gazes in turn. "Vendir didn't have that. He was so terrified of having to spend his whole life destroying and conquering that he tried to end it. Only for Anron to save him and force him to do just that. And now Anron, the most important friendly relationship he has had for decades, has just told him that he wished he had let him drown. He is heartbroken and rootless." Ellyda dragged a self-conscious hand through her hair and shrugged. "And that could have so easily been me."

For a while, everyone only looked back at her in silence. Ellyda very rarely talked this openly about her feelings, and hearing how worried she had once been for her own future made my heart ache. It made me see Captain Vendir in a different light too.

"But wouldn't this actually help Vendir too?" Theo asked

gently. "If we manage to convince them that Anron was really planning to overthrow them, then that would clear Vendir's name too and he could stop hiding."

We all looked from the blond thief to Ellyda. She still looked hesitant.

"What if we just ask him?" Eilan suggested. When her gaze slid to him, he cleared his throat and added, "Ask him *nicely*. And if he says no, we just leave and try to come up with a different plan."

She held his gaze for a solid minute without saying anything. I could almost see the thoughts swirling in her eyes. Only the faint clinking of Valerie spearing a piece of pie with her fork broke the silence.

At last, Ellyda blinked and gave Eilan a firm nod.

The rest of the table exhaled softly and nodded as well. A smile spread across my lips. We had a plan.

Grabbing my wine glass, I held it out in front of me. "To backup plans of backup plans."

Laughter rippled around the table. Hadeon refilled his and Valerie's glasses before they raised them along with everyone else. Light from the moon and the candles along the table glittered in the eight goblets that were held aloft.

"To backup plans of backup plans!"

And I had a good feeling about this one. After all our ruined schemes, this one was actually going to work. It had to. Because I didn't think I had another backup plan in me.

This would work.

CHAPTER 22

The cluttered garden looked even messier in the bright morning sunlight than it had when we passed through it in the dark of night. I kept a close eye on the surrounding buildings while we snuck towards the front door.

Taking a running start, Theo and Valerie leaped onto the wall and silently climbed towards the upstairs windows. Valerie peeked into one of the windows before twisting over and motioning with her hand. *Two. In here.*

I nodded.

We couldn't risk a confrontation outside in case we were spotted, so we had to get inside Heldan's house before we began this rather awkward conversation. After exchanging a glance with Mordren, I walked right through the door.

The hallway inside was empty. Hopefully, that meant that Vendir and Heldan were the only two people here.

Turning around, I carefully unlocked the mass of locking mechanisms on the door and then edged it open. A pair of silver eyes looked down at me from outside. I jerked my chin to indicate that they all should enter.

Mordren slipped through the gap in the door, followed by Hadeon and Idra. Where Theo and Valerie had entered, I didn't know, but I assumed they were making their way into the building from somewhere upstairs. The last two people through the door were Eilan and Ellyda.

Once the door had clicked shut behind them, we all started down along the corridor.

Sounds of people talking came from upstairs. Tilting my head back, I tried to estimate what the layout would look like in the rooms above us. Sneaking up on them was a bit rude, but we didn't want to risk this turning into an all-out fight so we had to stack the odds in our favor. If we could just–

A wood panel slammed into the side of my ribs.

My breath exploded from my lungs and shock flashed through me as the hit sent me flying through the air and into the wide living room we had been passing. Worn furniture and a mass of strange inventions spun in my vision as I flew through the room before crashing into a table halfway down.

Pain shot up my hip as it connected with the sturdy slab of wood. Flipping over, I skidded along the tabletop and smacked into the chairs on the other side.

Shouts of surprise and grunts of pain rang through this room and the one across the hall. Dull thuds sounded from close by as two more people slammed into various pieces of inconveniently placed furniture. There was a whirring sound echoing inside my skull.

Shaking my head, I tried to clear it while I pushed the chairs off me in an effort to get to my feet. The whirring sound grew louder. I blinked as I finally freed myself from the tangle of wood and straightened.

Mordren snapped an order for Eilan to duck. I whipped my head towards the sound, but it was coming from the room on the other side of the corridor so I couldn't see what was happening.

Wood flashed in the corner of my eye.

My instincts screamed. Throwing myself backwards, I barely managed to duck the piece of wood that had been swung at my head. Disbelief washed over me, and for a moment, I was just uselessly backing away while trying to figure out exactly what was attacking me.

"Down!" Idra yelled somewhere to my right.

It snapped me out of my stupor and I whirled around to take in the rest of the room. Idra had grabbed a long metal pole that she hurled like a javelin towards the wooden monstrosity that had been about to bash Hadeon's head in. Diving behind a frayed green couch, Hadeon managed to avoid both the strike and Idra's projectile. In the second that it took her to throw, another mass of wood swung at her instead. It connected with her side and sent her stumbling across the carpet. Hadeon leaped up and drew the sword from his back right as something flashed in the corner of my vision once more.

Yanking out my sword and knife as well, I threw both of them up to meet the blow coming for me. A dull clang sounded as a thick wooden pole slammed into my intersecting blades. I stared at the thing before me.

It was a table. I was fighting a table. And a chair. Or maybe two and a half chairs. It looked like someone had taken the different pieces of furniture, chopped them up into random parts, and then just jammed them together in no logical order whatsoever. A flat part of the tabletop spun, making that whirring noise I had heard earlier, and I had to pull my blades free and jump backwards to avoid being hit by the armrest of a chair.

The illogical pile of wood spun and twisted like it was possessed. I slammed my sword into what I thought was some kind of joint, only for the damn thing to spin around and whack me across the shoulder blades with what looked like the leg from a table.

Footsteps pounded down the stairs, but all my attention was focused on not getting beaten to death by a pile of furniture. I didn't want to risk using my fire magic. Not now. And certainly not here. There were too many people who could get hurt if I couldn't control the attack properly. Not to mention that burning down a building would definitely draw the dangerous attention of soldiers patrolling the city.

The table part of the monster whirred again. Legs and armrests spun through the air as it sent another unpredictable attack towards me. I ducked the first, blocked the second with my knife, but the third smacked right into the back of my thighs.

A flare of pain pulsed up my legs. The force of the hit sent me crashing down on my knees and I had to roll with the motion to avoid being struck again. My shoulder blades ached from the previous hit as I tucked and rolled under the flying table leg. While coming up in a crouch, I swept my sword sideways.

It cleaved part of a joint in half and then got stuck.

The whirring noise grew louder as the wooden attacker tried to spin even though my blade was jamming some of its gears. A backrest from a chair sped towards me. From below, it almost looked like a giant trying to swat a fly. I had no intention of being flattened against the floor so I ripped out my sword and rolled away.

Whatever I had hit seemed to have done some critical damage to the violent mass of furniture and it jerked and whirred as if it was stuck. I leaped to my feet.

A blast of air took me straight in the chest.

For the second time in as many minutes, the air was forced from my lungs. I was just trying to suck in a breath when my back connected with the wall behind me and what little air I had managed to recover exploded from my lungs once more. The sudden stop bounced my elbow into the wall, making the sword fly from my hand. I kept a firm grip on my knife as I crashed down on the ground.

"Enough!" Ellyda's sharp voice cut through the house.

My head spun and pain pulsed through my body as I pushed myself into a sitting position. Through the mess of furniture and scattered inventions, I could see Vendir and Heldan standing in the doorway between the two rooms. Hadeon and Idra were standing back to back, ready to fight the two wooden attackers that surrounded them. Mordren, Eilan, and Ellyda must have been flung into the room on the other side of the corridor because I couldn't see them from where I was.

The tangle of wooden arms and legs that was standing a few strides away from me stopped jerking. Across the fluffy green carpet, the two monstrosities facing Idra and Hadeon stopped moving as well.

Vendir, who was still standing with his arm raised in my direction as if preparing another blast of air, tore his gaze from me and turned to look towards the room across the hall.

"Enough," Ellyda repeated.

A few seconds later, she came stalking into the living room. Vendir and Heldan stared at her with raised eyebrows, but took a step back to allow her into the room. Mordren and Eilan followed her.

Coming to a halt on the carpet, Ellyda swept flashing eyes over the rest of us. "We agreed. Ask *nicely*. Does this look like asking nicely to you?"

"It's not our fault." Hadeon stabbed a muscular arm towards Vendir and Heldan. "They attacked first."

"Do I look like someone who struts through his own home waving swords around?" Heldan flapped his arms as if to drive the point home. "We didn't attack you."

"Your..." Hadeon waved a hand towards the now motionless mass of wood, "whatever these are, did."

"They wouldn't have done anything if you hadn't broken in. So you started it."

"We didn't start it! They–"

"I don't care who started it," Ellyda cut off. "We came here for a reason. Now act like adults."

Hadeon crossed his arms and scowled at Heldan while muttering something under his breath. On the other side of the room, Heldan did the same. Blowing out a deep breath, I pushed myself to my feet.

Captain Vendir's brown eyes locked on Mordren. "I thought I told you that you weren't welcome here."

Mordren brushed some lingering dust from his shoulder before giving the captain a nonchalant shrug. "Indeed. However, we believe that it is in your best interest to help us with a certain problem."

Lightning suddenly crackled to life along Vendir's arm as he shifted it towards the Prince of Shadows. Mordren looked back at him with an amused smirk on his lips.

"*Nicely*," Ellyda repeated in a threatening voice.

Mordren rolled his eyes, but before he could say anything to make things worse, I spoke up.

"The truth is, we need you." Looking straight at Vendir, I kept my eyes soft as I spread my hands. "We need your help."

Confusion, and a slight hint of surprise, creased his pale brows. But then he wiped the expression off his face and straightened his spine. "Why should I help you? After everything you have done to ruin my life, why would I spend even a second helping you now that I'm finally free?"

"But you're not free, are you? Anron threw you to the wolves and now you're a wanted fugitive suspected of high treason."

"Because of you."

"Yes. But it still doesn't change the fact that you need the emperor and empress to be convinced that Anron is actually trying to overthrow them just as badly as we do."

Holding my gaze with a hard stare, he raised his chin. "And it still doesn't change the fact that this is all your fault."

I blew out a deep breath and then started across the floor. Dull pain pulsed through my body. After sheathing my knife, I rolled my shoulders to ease the ache even though it did little to actually relieve it.

Captain Vendir watched me warily as I closed the distance between us. His hand, still crackling with lightning, swung towards me. Idra took a step in my direction in response to it, but I waved her back. From the corridor beyond, our two thieves watched the proceedings play out from halfway down the stairs.

"Fine. You want revenge." I stopped right in front of his raised arm. White bolts of lightning danced between his fingers. "Go ahead. Take your pound of flesh."

I could feel Mordren's lethal stare burning holes in my

back. And probably Vendir's body too. If the captain actually took the shot I was volunteering for, the Prince of Shadows was going to retaliate regardless of our previous agreements. Hopefully, it wouldn't come to that.

Surprise and hesitation blew across Vendir's face. I spread my arms.

"Go ahead," I repeated.

He frowned down at me for another couple of seconds before clicking his tongue and breaking my stare. The lightning died out as he lowered his arm.

"No?" I looked up at him. "Then what? Do you want us to get down on our knees and beg you for help? Is that it? Because we will. Just say the word."

Vendir adjusted his bronze armor but said nothing.

"But that's not what you want," I said. "Is it?"

His eyes slid back to mine and he raised his eyebrows. "Maybe it is. How would you know?"

"Because I saw you. In that tent back in the Court of Trees. You were writing a letter when two elven ladies came in and then got down on their knees and bowed before you. You looked incredibly uncomfortable." I shrugged and then began lowering myself to my knees. "But if that is what you want, then…"

"Stop." Vendir's hand shot out. With a firm grip on my arm, he stopped my movements and pulled me back up. Embarrassment flickered in his warm brown eyes. "Don't…"

When he trailed off and awkwardly shook his head, I looked up and met his gaze again. "This is what I meant. You're nothing like Anron. You're actually a nice person and you want peace and quiet." I spread my hands in a helpless gesture. "Do you really think there will be peace if Anron overthrows the emperor and empress and takes the throne for himself?"

Indecision swirled in his eyes. Twisting to the side, he exchanged a glance with Heldan. The brown-haired High Elf shrugged in reply. Vendir's gaze slid to Ellyda. She was standing halfway between her brother and one of the wooden monstrosities that had attacked him. There was no judgement, no expectations, and no ill feelings at all on her face. She just looked back at him with an open expression, waiting for him to make whatever decision he thought was best.

A deep sigh echoed through the room. "Fine." Captain Vendir shifted his gaze back to me while dragging a hand through his long blond hair. "What do you need?"

Smug victory sparkled inside me. I had already known that he would agree. After all, I had carefully planned this entire conversation so that it would take us down the road of topics I wanted to broach. Ellyda had told us to ask nicely. I preferred to hedge my bets. So instead of just hoping that this backup plan of a backup plan would work, I had stacked the deck in my favor by manipulating Captain Vendir into seeing things the way I wanted him to. Maybe it wasn't 'asking nicely', but I figured 'manipulating nicely' was close enough.

"We're going to turn Anron and the empress against each other," I explained. "So we need to know everything there is to know about her personality. Her habits. What she likes. Things she can't stand when people do. Stuff like that."

Vendir rubbed his chin. "I see."

"Do you know her well enough to know things like that?"

"Yes, and no. What we–" Turning towards the doorway, he abruptly cut off and instead let out a loud, "Gah!"

Valerie and Theo were standing right in the doorway, watching him with casual expressions on their faces.

"How long have you been standing there?" Vendir blurted out as he recovered.

The two thieves looked at each other before meeting his gaze again.

"A while," Valerie said.

"Yep," Theo filled in.

"We're thieves."

"I think he knows that."

"Clearly not, if he's surprised that we managed to sneak in here without him noticing."

Theo gave her an acknowledging nod. "Good point."

"Thanks."

Captain Vendir expelled a forceful breath and grumbled something about the gods. Massaging his brows, he turned and swept a hand to indicate the room we had broken into and fought a battle in. "Do you people ever do anything other than... *this*?"

Wicked smiles spread across several lips as we all exchanged glances.

"No, not really," Hadeon announced with a satisfied grin on his face.

"Figured as much." After shaking his head at us, Vendir turned to his friend. "Heldan, will you be okay fixing all of this and taking care of your inventions?"

"Oh, of course." Heldan's gray eyes sparkled with pride and mirth as he looked out over the three wooden monstrosities that had attacked us. "This was a great trial run for my burglar alarms. Now I know that both the panels in the corridor and the guards work the way they should."

"Great." Vendir gave him a warm smile and a pat on the shoulder before he jerked his chin at us. "Let's go."

"Where?" Idra asked as we all followed him towards the front door.

"If you want detailed knowledge about the empress, there is a person we need to go see. Someone who knows Empress Elswyth better than me."

"And who is that?"

Dread and apprehension blew across Captain Vendir's face as he opened the door and stepped out into the morning sunlight. Raking a hand through his hair again, he swallowed nervously before finally replying.

"Someone I haven't seen in a very long time."

CHAPTER 23

At the edge of the city, a small meadow spread out before the forest began in earnest. This forest looked more similar to the one we had walked through when we landed than Poisonwood on the other side of the city. Green leaves swayed as a warm breeze stroked the hanging branches of the birch trees, while proud pines stood resolutely between them. Butterflies and bumblebees flew through the sea of colorful summer flowers that rose from the grass.

We walked along a path made of flat stones that had been placed in a winding line from the final street and towards the front door of the house that sat amid the flowers. Pale green tiles shone from the roof of the white stone building, and a bright yellow door added another splash of color to the scene. I drew a hand over a cluster of lavender as we walked. The scent of grass and summer flowers filled the warm air.

"What is this place?" Hadeon asked.

"It's, uhm..." Captain Vendir trailed off as we reached a patch of grass a short distance from the door. He stopped.

Apprehension bloomed in his eyes as he turned back to us. "Could you... Could you just wait here for a moment?"

"Of course," Ellyda said. Her eyes were clear as she scanned the area before us, taking in every detail.

Vendir nodded.

Silence fell. For a few seconds, he just remained rooted in place. Then he forced in a deep breath and turned back towards the house. He started walking.

While he closed the distance to the front door, he adjusted his bronze armor. Several times. And then ran his hands over his hair, smoothening it down.

I arched an eyebrow as I looked over at Mordren. He lifted one shoulder in a shrug. Ellyda, on the other hand, watched Captain Vendir intently.

A few strides from the door, the captain's steps faltered. He briefly paused right there on the grass, but then he gave his body a quick shake and took a step forward again.

Right as his feet touched the grass a few strides from the house, the yellow door was pushed open and a female High Elf strode out.

She was looking over her shoulder, back into the house, while calling, "I'll just be a minute! I think..."

Her words died in her mouth as she turned towards the path ahead and then stopped, staring at Captain Vendir who stood awkwardly on the grass a few steps away. For a moment, nothing moved. Not Vendir. Not the High Elf. Not the wind. I was pretty sure even the butterflies and bumblebees paused to look.

Then the stillness shattered like a smashed mirror.

"Vendir?" the High Elf blurted out. She stared at the captain as if she had seen a spirit. Then she rushed forward. "Vendir!"

Disbelief and utter happiness shone in her eyes as she threw her arms around Captain Vendir and pulled him into a fierce hug. She clung to him like he was a raft in a stormy ocean. Reaching up, Vendir wrapped his arms around her and squeezed her back. Tears ran freely down the High Elf's beautiful face.

"Hi, Mom," Vendir pressed out, his voice breaking on the second word.

Those two words ripped a sob from her throat. Warm brown eyes overflowed with tears as Vendir's mother held her son tightly while crying into his shoulder. I could only see Vendir from behind so I couldn't tell for sure if he was crying too, but his back shook as he hugged his mom.

"Rendir!" she called. "Rendir, you need to come out here! Now!"

Something that sounded like metal cans clattered from inside the house. A moment later, a male High Elf with long blond hair stuck his head out the door.

"Vendina? Did you…" He trailed off. Shock bounced across his handsome features as he stared at the scene before him. "My son."

Paint-splattered sleeves fluttered in the air as he ran towards his wife and son and wrapped his arms around both of them. Vendina cried even harder. As did Vendir, if his shaking body was any indication.

My heart filled with so much joy and sorrow that I thought it was going to burst at the seams. His parents. These people that he hadn't seen in a long time were his parents. And they had missed him so much that they cried when they saw him. This was what family was supposed to be like.

As if he could hear my thoughts and the painful memories that went with them, Mordren slipped his hand into mine.

His warm strong fingers squeezed mine. Letting me know that I wasn't alone and unwanted anymore. I did have a family now.

I swallowed past the emotions blocking my throat, and squeezed his hand back.

Next to us, Theo discreetly wiped a tear from his cheek as he continued watching the display of unconditional love before us. Valerie slung her arm around his shoulders in a casual yet highly comforting gesture.

"Where have you been?" Vendina said when the three of them broke apart. "Why did you just leave? And to run away with the army? I thought you had no interest in the military. Why did you never come back? Why didn't you even tell us that you were leaving? I didn't even know that you were a Wielder. We had to hear from the local gossips that you had become a captain in High Commander Anron's Flying Legion. Why didn't you–"

"Vendina," Rendir interrupted and placed a gentle hand on his wife's shoulder. "Give him a moment to breathe."

Her long brown hair was gathered up in a messy bun, and she ran her hands over it as if to smoothen it down while she nodded and took a step back. The yellow dress she wore was simple yet well-made, and it looked like there were pale clay stains on it. Rendir, in his brown pants and loose white shirt, was covered in splashes of paint. His hands and sleeves bore blue, green, yellow, and red stains that made him look like he had walked through a handful of paintbrushes.

Seeing them standing side by side, I realized that Vendir was a mix of the two of them. He had his mother's warm brown eyes and his father's long blond hair. In his bronze armor, however, he looked completely out of place in front of his parents.

"I was afraid that you..." Vendir began, his voice still a bit shaky. "That you would be... disappointed."

"Disappointed?" Rendir said, complete bafflement evident on his face. "Why would we ever be disappointed in you?"

"I, uhm... There are some things I need to tell you." Captain Vendir cleared his throat and then turned to motion towards us. "These are my fr–" He shook his head. "My associates. They need your help with something, Mom."

Vendina blinked at us as if realizing for the first time that we were there. Her eyes swept over the eight of us, and then snagged on Valerie and Theo. The two thieves gave her a cheerful wave. A surprised laugh bubbled from her throat.

"Of course," she said and motioned for us to approach. "Come inside. I have some lemonade for you so you can cool off from the sun while my son explains where he has been for the past few decades."

Embarrassment flashed over Vendir's face. Clearing his throat once more, he pulled at the collar of his armor and then stepped aside to let us pass. While wiping the lingering tears from his pale lashes, he started towards a set of lounge chairs across the grass.

"The kitchen is just through there," Vendina said as she pointed into the house. "Help yourselves."

"Thank you," Mordren said with a polite nod as he stepped across the threshold.

I nodded in acknowledgement as well before following him inside.

The bright yellow front door led to an equally brightly painted hallway. Colorful leaves and flowers and other nature scenes were painted across the walls of the narrow corridor that led deeper into the house. Something that looked like a cluttered study was visible inside an open door on the right while a wide doorway appeared on our left. The open arch led into a gigantic room that was filled with everything from easels, brushes and cans of paint, to what looked like tools for pottery making. Paintings and different kinds of dishes and sculptures made of clay filled the space in between.

My eyebrows rose as I took in the beautiful artistry on display in there. But we had been told to go into the kitchen, so I tore my gaze from it and continued towards the room at the end of the hall.

A kitchen that continued the same colorful theme as the hallway became visible as I cleared the threshold. Herbs and other plants with dark green leaves dotted the shelves, along with the dried flowers that hung from the ceiling. Beautiful depictions of a serene forest filled the walls, and the wooden furniture added to the feeling that we were really in the woods and not inside a building.

"Wow, this is kind of pretty," Valerie announced as she strolled into the kitchen at the end of our procession.

"Yes," Eilan agreed. His pale green eyes swept across the wall paintings while a smile blew across his lips. "It really is."

Sunlight streamed in through the open windows. We were too far away to hear what they were saying, but we could see Vendir and his parents where they stood among the swaying summer flowers. This must be a very difficult conversation for all of them.

"He hadn't seen his parents in decades," Ellyda said, her gaze fixed on the three High Elves as well. "Decades. He never told them what he tried to do. Why he was forced to join the army. He just left."

"Sometimes leaving is the best thing you can do," Theo said quietly. "For yourself. To protect yourself."

Silence fell over the kitchen as we all just watched the

three of them through the window. A cluster of basil shifted slightly in its pot as a sweet-smelling breeze ruffled its leaves.

"And sometimes the best thing you can do is to come back." Theo smiled at Vendir and his parents. "I'm glad he still had a loving home to return to."

"Yeah." Not taking my eyes off them, I nodded. "Me too."

We stood there in silence, watching Vendir explain the events that had led him to join Anron and all the things that happened afterwards. There was a decanter with lemonade on the table, but no one dared to actually pour any. I glanced over my shoulder.

The room with the art seemed to call to me.

I snuck past Idra and Hadeon, who had stopped glaring at each other and were watching Vendir and his parents instead, and slipped into the corridor we had come from. Entering the great art studio was like walking into another world. Paintings of landscapes, animals, and plants I had never seen before watched me as I turned in a slow circle. My mouth dropped open slightly as I stared up at the works of art.

"It's quite beautiful," a voice said from behind me.

I turned to find Mordren standing behind me, looking up at the paintings as well. His silver eyes glittered in the warm sunlight that streamed in through the large windows.

"Yes, it really is," I answered as I twisted to look at another row of paintings.

Mordren came to stand beside me. The painting before us depicted a glowing forest along with one of those dark blue and silver foxes that we had seen in Mendar's camp. I studied the way the painter had carefully crafted the portrait of the fox to truly make it look like its soft fur was part of the night sky. It was breathtaking.

A pang of sadness hit me. Rubbing a hand over my chest, I tried to ease the ache that suddenly pulsed inside my heart.

"I wish we had more time," I said.

Mordren's eyes stayed on the fox but he blew out a soft breath. "Me too. But this plan will work, even though we're–"

"No," I interrupted. "That's not what I meant. I'm sure the plan will work out, and if not, we'll figure it out anyway." Tearing my gaze from the painting, I turned to face him. "I wish *we* had more time."

A hint of sadness blew across Mordren's beautiful features, but before he could say anything, I pressed on.

"I feel like ever since I met you, we have just had to deal with one crisis after the other. We never have time to just… be. All we can spare are a few stolen moments in between battles and dangerous schemes." Throwing my arms out, I indicated the room around us. "Look at this. Vendir's parents have had decades, if not centuries, together to just live. To wake up next to each other, enjoy each other's company, laugh with friends, and then go to bed without having to sleep with one eye open because someone is hunting them."

"We will have that too one day," he promised. "This plan will succeed. And then we will go home. And we will live."

"I hope so."

Mordren closed the distance between us. Pulling me into his arms, he kissed my forehead. I leaned my head against his shoulder. Behind his back, Ellyda had snuck into the room as well and was walking along the other wall, admiring the paintings. I closed my eyes and let the firmness of Mordren's body keep me steady.

I didn't want to admit just how exhausted I really was. But I could feel, just in the way Mordren held me, that he was exhausted too. We always said that we were skilled at magicking new backup plans from the ashes of disaster, but truth be told, I wasn't sure I could take it if this desperate gamble we had bet on were to fall through.

"When Anron has been dealt with, we will have that time," Mordren promised. "We will create a world where we no longer have to fight every single day."

"So we can focus only on trying to outmaneuver each other," I teased in an effort to lighten the somber mood that had fallen.

Mordren chuckled, making his chest shake against my own. Leaning down, he kissed my forehead again. "Yes. That too. And then you will realize, once and for all, that you really are hopelessly outmatched against me."

I smiled. "We'll see about that, my prince."

"Did your father paint all of these?" Ellyda's voice suddenly echoed through the room.

Mordren and I released each other and turned just in time to see Captain Vendir come to a halt next to Ellyda. Based on the redness around his eyes, he looked to have been crying while he explained to his parents what had happened. But now, as he followed Ellyda's gaze around the room, he raked a hand through his hair and stood up straighter.

"Some of them," he said. Raising an arm, he swept it along the wall they were standing at. "He painted all of these. But those," he motioned towards the paintings along the wall we were waiting by, "are mine."

Ellyda blinked. Her eyes scanned the entire length of the wall as if committing every single piece of art to memory. When she at last reached the far end, she tore her gaze from it and turned back to Captain Vendir.

"You painted them?" she said.

It was halfway between a statement and a question, but

Vendir nodded anyway. "Yes. Before…" He cleared his throat. "Well, everything. I'm surprised my parents kept them all."

"They're breathtaking," Ellyda said, her eyes locked on Vendir's. A sly smile spread across her lips as she cocked her head. "I knew it."

"Knew what?"

"That you were an artist."

Surprise flickered in his brown eyes, but he briefly shifted his attention to us. "We're meeting back in the kitchen."

Mordren and I nodded before starting towards the open doorway.

"Was it after I told you that I wanted to create things?" Vendir asked Ellyda as they disappeared into the corridor ahead of us.

"No."

"You knew before that? When?"

"When you watched me work in the smithy."

"Ah."

Their conversation trailed off as the four of us reached the crowded kitchen. Idra and Hadeon were standing shoulder to shoulder in a corner, looking slightly awkward as they glanced between us and the lemonade glasses that appeared to have been pressed into their hands. I had to suppress a laugh that I knew Idra would've kicked my ass for. The two of them looked like children who had just been scolded by Vendina for not actually helping themselves to the drink they had been offered. The High Elf in question was currently offering a glass to Theo and Valerie, who gratefully accepted.

"So," Rendir began. He had drawn himself up on one of the counters and was sitting with one leg folded underneath him and the other dangling over the edge. "From what I understand, you are responsible for our son's current status as a fugitive wanted for treason."

Tense silence rippled through the room. From his position wedged between Valerie and a green-painted cupboard, Eilan cleared his throat a bit self-consciously. Hadeon and Idra exchanged a glance.

"Yes," Mordren simply answered as he looked back at Rendir with a steady gaze.

Rendir nodded. "Which means that you are also responsible for breaking High Commander Anron's hold on Vendir and finally returning our son to us." A mischievous smile spread across his lips as he drew a paint-stained hand through his long blond hair. "Well done."

Relief blew like a warm wind through the herb-smelling kitchen.

"Don't tease them like that." Vendina slapped Rendir's arm with the back of her hand. "Based on what Vendir told us, our dear son played a rather significant part in wreaking havoc on their lands too."

A sheepish look flashed over Captain Vendir's features.

"Yes, he did," Mordren said. His silver eyes slid to the captain. "However, we then proceeded to kidnap him and blackmail him into betraying his High Commander. So I believe we can consider us even."

Vendir nodded. As did his parents.

"And now," Vendina began as she reached out and ran a hand up and down her son's arm, "Vendir says that you have some kind of plan that would clear his name?"

"Yes. We need to know everything there is to know about Empress Elswyth, and Vendir said that you knew her well."

She nodded. "I do. Before Vendir... left, I worked in the

Palace of the Never Setting Sun. I was on Empress Elswyth's staff."

I raised my eyebrows in surprise. With her clay-stained yellow dress and warm motherly demeanor, I had a hard time picturing her working in the palace. And especially for the stern and authoritative Empress of Valdanar.

"What is she like?" I asked.

Vendina poured herself a glass of lemonade and took a sip before blowing out a long breath. "She's… intelligent. And shrewd. And very good at her job. Because of that, she also hates it when people try to tell her what to do. I once saw her actually shoot lightning at a person who kept offering her unsolicited advice on political matters."

Eilan, Mordren, and I exchanged a knowing look. Oh, we could definitely use that to our advantage.

"If she were to arrange a private meeting with someone like, say, High Commander Anron," I began as I shifted my gaze back to Vendina, "where would she meet them?"

"Her statue garden."

Valerie raised her eyebrows. "A statue garden?"

"Yes. Empress Elswyth has a…" she chuckled and then smacked her lips, "flair for dramatics. You know how she wears that veil to remind people that only widows will be left of those who try to oppose her?"

We all nodded.

"She takes that one step further with her meetings. Unless it's a grand official one that is held in the throne room together with the emperor, she has all of her meetings in her private garden. And this garden is filled with statues… of the people she has killed."

I jerked back slightly. All eight of us stared at Vendina with wide eyes. She huffed out an amused breath and shook her head as if she agreed that it was a very overdramatic custom.

"She makes statues of everyone she kills?" Hadeon blurted out.

"She doesn't actually make the statues herself. She raises a block of stone with her magic, but then an artist hand-carves the actual statue."

Idra narrowed her eyes. "How do you know that?"

Vendina gave her a small smile, as if knowing that the white-haired warrior had already figured it out on her own. "I was one of those artists."

A wave of understanding swept through the room. That was the reason why a creative person such as Vendina had worked for the political leader of their land. And that was why she knew the empress so well.

"But, so she uses the statue garden to... what?" Theo asked, his brows furrowed.

"It's a method of intimidation," Ellyda replied in her stead. "Conducting the meetings surrounded by evidence of what she does to people who cross her serves as a wordless reminder of her power." Her violet eyes shifted to Vendina. "Right?"

"Correct. Not unlike her husband, she enjoys reminding people that she has the power to destroy them at any time. She is not as cruel as he can be at times, but if she feels threatened in any way, politically or intellectually, she will in no uncertain terms remind the person of their place beneath her."

"And High Commander Anron hates it when they lord their power over him," Captain Vendir added. "It's what pushed him over the edge to actually start orchestrating a coup."

"Perfect." A sharp smile slid across Mordren's lips. "Then we have what we need to turn them against each other." He looked between Vendina and Rendir. "Do you by any chance happen to have any messages from the empress saved somewhere?"

"Oh." Vendina blinked and then turned to her husband. "I think so. Rendir, dear, could you...? In the chest, you know, at the..."

"I'm on it," he said as he hopped down from the counter and strolled into the corridor.

Eilan turned to Vendina again. "Is there anything else you can tell us about the empress?"

"Oh." She flashed him a conspiratorial smile. "Lots."

While Vendina began a thorough explanation of the particularities of Empress Elswyth's personality, Ellyda abruptly turned to Vendir. The captain started at the sudden movement and blinked down at the brown-haired elf next to him.

"I need to go into Poisonwood Forest to meet some people that we have promised to help," she announced without preamble. "After that, I am going to need someplace safe to forge a sword. Do you know somewhere I could do that?"

Captain Vendir ran a hand over his jaw while considering in silence for a while. Ellyda simply watched him.

"Yes," he said at last. "I do know a place." Motioning with his hand, he indicated the house around us. "I will be staying here for a while, so just come by when you're ready and I'll show you the place."

She held his gaze without blinking for almost a minute. Then she gave him a firm nod in acknowledgement.

I had to wipe a hand over my mouth to hide my smile.

Sweeping my gaze over the crowded kitchen, I let a sparkle of hope pulse through my chest.

We knew what to do. And we had help from people who actually understood this land and its people.

Our plan was finally coming together.

CHAPTER 24

"Wow, nimble as a steel-infused broom handle."

With a huff, I rolled over the edge of the roof and crawled forward on my stomach until I was lying between Valerie and Theo. Both thieves grinned at me.

"Shut up," I muttered.

Even though the building was relatively short, climbing up the wall to reach the flat roof we had chosen as our vantage point was still a lot more difficult than I wanted to admit. I didn't know how Theo and Valerie managed to do this with two- or even three-story buildings on a regular basis. At least I could comfort myself with the thought that it was only because of my ability to walk *through* walls that we had even made it into this garden in the first place.

Still lying on their stomachs, Valerie lifted an arm and held it out over my back while Theo promptly reached out and fist bumped her. I rolled my eyes.

Morning sunlight fell across the garden below. Neatly trimmed grass and a few grand trees could have given the area a beautiful atmosphere, but it was somewhat ruined by the forest of petrified people. The statues were skillfully carved, but terrifying. With mouths open in silent screams and eyes bulging in terror, the mass of sculpted High and Low Elves made a shiver crawl up my spine. And not just because of the sheer number of statues that filled the garden. If the expressions on their stone faces were any indication, they had all died horribly.

Add to that the building we were currently lying atop, which looked like some kind of mausoleum replica, and it all created a nightmarish landscape.

"Shouldn't he be here by now?" Theo whispered.

"Give it another minute," Valerie answered.

Once we had seen the old messages that Vendina had saved, it had been easy to create a passable note ourselves. Then all Eilan had to do was shapeshift into a High Elf messenger. With both Vendir and Vendina's help, he had been able to learn enough details to create a believable persona. After strolling right in through the gates of the palace, he could drop off the note to High Commander Anron without issue.

Mordren and the others had accompanied Ellyda into Poisonwood Forest to meet with Mendar and figure out a way to get their anklets off, which meant that it was up to me and the two human thieves to supervise how this meeting we had orchestrated played out.

Footsteps sounded from a short distance away.

I pressed myself flat against the roof, only peeking over the edge enough to see what was happening below. Theo and Valerie did the same. But here's the thing about rooftops. When going about their normal business, people very rarely look up. Which was, of course, why we had picked the roof as our vantage point to spy from.

The footfalls drew closer until High Commander Anron became visible in a cluster of screaming statues. Sunlight glinted off his polished bronze armor. Coming to a halt in the middle of the small open patch of grass, he drew himself up to his full height and scanned the garden around him. A scowl lay heavy on his brows.

I suppressed an evil cackle. Apparently, the High Commander did not like being summoned by the empress on short notice. Little did he know that he would be here waiting quite a while.

Shifting my weight on the warm stone roof, I settled in to wait and watch as Anron's mood became more foul when he realized that there was no empress here waiting for him.

At first, he just remained standing immobile on the grass. His chin raised and his spine straight, he waited with dignity for Her Imperial Majesty. A small cloud drifted over the sun. It cast his chiseled features in temporary shadow before the light returned. Anron crossed his arms.

After five minutes, he began tapping his foot against the ground. A rogue breeze whirled through the statue garden and ripped free a few strands of hair, making them flutter in his face. He uncrossed his arms and forced his hair back with clipped movements.

Once ten minutes had passed, High Commander Anron began stalking back and forth across the grass. Dark clouds gathered in his eyes and he muttered something under his breath, but from up here, I couldn't tell exactly what it was. Though, given the situation, it wasn't hard to guess.

Next to me, Valerie was grinning like a fiend.

Flames flickered between Anron's fingers when we were

coming up on twenty minutes. By the rigid set of his shoulders, it seemed to be taking every smidgen of his self-control not to set the garden on fire. Hatred burned in his cold blue eyes.

Resting my chin on the back of my hand, I watched with growing satisfaction as Anron worked his jaw and flexed his fingers. Oh, he truly despised this. He hated being summoned, and being kept waiting was an insult to his pride, but he still couldn't leave because Empress Elswyth was more powerful than he was. The wicked smirk on my face grew.

Movement between the statues drew my attention. I shifted my gaze towards the cluster of statues on Anron's right. The High Commander did the same.

A few moments later, a tall figure became visible.

Theo and I exchanged a glance as Empress Elswyth suddenly appeared. She was wearing a black and silver dress that I hadn't seen before, and her black lace veil barely rippled as she glided across the grass. Lightning crackled up and down her arms, as it always did. Valerie raised her eyebrows as she stared down at her.

The empress stopped abruptly. I couldn't tell because of the veil, but if I had to guess, she probably blinked in surprise. Based on her reaction, I would say that it looked as if she had been on a morning stroll through her beloved nightmare garden and that she was shocked to see someone standing in her usual meeting spot.

"High Commander Anron." She seemingly pulled herself together and started towards him. "Why are you here? You have not been summoned."

Anger flashed in his eyes as he bowed. We could see it from this angle, but I didn't think the empress would be able to. Once he straightened again, the neutral mask was back on his face.

"Yes, I have," Anron explained in a calm and polite tone. "By you, Your Imperial Majesty."

"Nonsense." She flicked her wrist, which made a few bolts of lightning leap from her hand. "I would remember if I had summoned you."

"You did. Perhaps—"

"Are you questioning my intellect, High Commander?" she interrupted, her voice cutting through the air like the snap of a whip.

Anron dipped his chin in deference, but a muscle flickered in his tightly clenched jaw. "No, of course not, Your Imperial Majesty."

"Good."

He bowed again and began to turn away. "I will leave you to your walk."

"Wait." The empress paused until Anron had turned back to face her once more. "Since you are here, there was actually one thing I wished to speak with you about."

"Of course."

"That large island you found, with the humans and the other Low Elves, I am undecided regarding what to do with it. Do they have any strategic resources that would make an annexation worth it?"

I could almost see the wheels turning in Anron's eyes as he tried to figure out which answer would be the most strategic for himself and his own schemes. A planned annexation might provide a fantastic distraction that he could use to blindside them when he finally began his coup. But it might also lead to them discovering what he had done to all of the magic-wielding elves in our lands, which would be proof that we had been telling the truth about his betrayal.

"Well?" Empress Elswyth prompted.

"That is indeed a complex issue," Anron answered diplomatically. "I understand why Your Imperial Majesty is still undecided about it. I would like to think on it before giving my recommendation, if I may?"

"Fine." The lightning along her arms crackled in a slightly wild manner before returning to its usual intensity. "And are there any updates on the matter of locating Captain Vendir and those Low Elves?"

"Not since the update I gave you and Emperor Lanseyo last night." His voice was calm and pleasant, but I could see the irritation bubbling under the surface. "We paid a visit to Vendir's parents two days ago, but they have not seen him since he joined the military. They are hiding somewhere in the city. I am certain of it. And there is only a matter of time before we find them."

I stifled a snort. *Yeah, good luck with that.* The city was huge and there was no way for them to know which empty house we were currently squatting in. And Vendir had gone to his parents' house after Anron's visit, which meant that it was unlikely that he would be found there now.

"Was there anything else?" High Commander Anron asked.

"No." The empress flicked her wrist. "You may leave."

Annoyance rippled in Anron's eyes as he bowed deeply again. After straightening, he turned to leave. I tracked his movements across the grass as he stalked back towards the palace. The farther he got from the empress, the more his walk turned into stomping. I could almost imagine him cursing her under his breath as he left.

Victory sparkled in Valerie's eyes as she twisted her head to grin at me and Theo. I returned the wide smile.

This had definitely been a success. Now, there was just one more thing we had to do before the day was over to really drive that wedge in firmly.

It was time to spread some more lies.

CHAPTER 25

Night had fallen over the city. From deep within the shadows of an alley, I watched the tavern across the street. Fire from the torches outside the door cast pools of orange light on the dark ground and reflected off the bronze armor that every other patron wore. This place was close to the barracks, which meant that this was a bar frequented by soldiers. And that was exactly why we had picked it.

"I don't need the extra backup," Eilan said from where he stood pressed to the wall next to me. "I have been doing jobs like this for a very long time. I know what I'm doing."

"I don't doubt it," I answered.

"But we don't care," Valerie filled in.

"Exactly," Theo said. "If something goes wrong, the three of us can provide a distraction while you get out. Having some backup is never a bad thing."

Holding Eilan's gaze, I jerked my chin towards Theo. "He's right, you know."

Eilan let out a groan. Dragging a hand through his long

black hair, he blew out a resigned sigh. "Fine. But stay out of sight. Off-duty soldiers usually have a lot of pent-up frustration after dealing with their bossy superiors all day, and some of them would like nothing better than to take it all out on people who provoke them. And things will already get heated when they hear what I say."

"Me? Provoke people?" I placed a hand against my chest in mock affront. "I would never."

"Don't worry," Valerie said before he could counter. "We'll be in the ceiling."

"*I* will be in a chair on the floor, thank you very much," I said, and flashed her a wicked smirk.

"Alright." Eilan massaged his brows. "Just be careful."

"Shouldn't we be the ones telling you that?" Theo said.

Eilan forced out a breath and motioned towards the tavern. "Can we just get this over with?"

The three of us chuckled, which only made him scowl even more. After shaking his head at us one last time, Eilan shapeshifted into Gadrien, that blue-eyed High Elf soldier with the arrogant demeanor that he had been when we broke into the White Tower.

"We'll see you inside," I said.

He gave us a curt nod in reply before we disappeared into the darkness. The two thieves made their way towards the roof while I circled the building and approached one of the side walls. After peering through a window to study the layout, I jogged down along the wall to the spot I had marked and then stepped through.

Noise and warmth assaulted me. And the distinct stench of sweat. Moving casually, I slid down on one of the chairs at the back of the room. With my hair covered by the hood of my custom-tailored jacket, I watched the scene before me.

About half of the patrons were ordinary people. The rest were soldiers. They stood out not only by their bronze armor, but by the way they moved. An air of command clung to them, as if they expected everyone in here who was not a soldier to show them respect. I stole a half-empty tankard of ale from the deserted table next to mine and placed it in front of me to help with the ruse.

As soon as I had set it down, the door opened and Gadrien strode inside. That arrogant tilt of his chin was back, as was the coldness in his eyes. With confident moves, he sauntered up to another group of soldiers and started talking as if they had all met at some point. They apparently thought they recognized one of their own when they saw one, so they welcomed him without issue.

Glancing up, I tried to spot Valerie and Theo in the ceiling. I knew they were up there somewhere, but I couldn't see them.

After about half an hour had passed, Gadrien slapped the table in front of him as if he had just remembered something. When he spoke, he did it in a very loud voice, as if he was drunk. Or simply wanted as many people as possible to overhear.

"You know what I heard today?" He paused dramatically as ears from all over the tavern tuned in to his story. "Shit, you ain't gonna believe it."

"Well, spit it out then," someone called from another table.

Laughter echoed through the tavern in response. Gadrien yanked up a hand and flashed the soldier who had spoken a rude gesture, which only made the others howl and cheer.

"I was there, minding my own business, right?" Gadrien began when they had quieted down. "When all of a sudden, High Commander Anron comes stomping out of Empress

Elswyth's statue garden. And I mean proper stomping. Anger just pulsing from him. He doesn't see me, yeah? And you know what he says?"

"What?"

"He says, and these are his words, so none of you lot are gonna go blaming me for it. He calls Empress Elswyth a pompous lunatic who's incapable of admitting when she's wrong."

Shocked gasps rang through the tavern that had otherwise gone dead silent.

"I know, right? And then right before he stalks away towards his house, he mutters that if the empress is so airheaded that she can't even remember when she summons people, then maybe she's not fit to rule."

The dark-haired soldier next to him sucked in a horrified breath and blurted out, "No."

"Yeah." Gadrien nodded, a serious look on his face. "And I'm just pressing myself into the wall, praying to the gods that he doesn't see me. I don't even wanna think about what he would've done if he knew I'd heard him."

"Probably made you disappear. Because if Empress Elswyth got wind of that, she would've killed *him*."

"Exactly!"

"So why did you blab about this to this entire tavern, huh?" a white-haired soldier challenged from the next table. His chair scraped loudly against the floor as he shoved it back and pushed to his feet. "Why go run your mouth about this?"

"Fendon, sit down," one of his friends said while trying to grab the white-haired soldier's elbow and pull him back down.

Fendon yanked his elbow away and took a threatening step towards Eilan. "Why open your big fat mouth, huh?"

"Insurance," Gadrien replied with a nonchalant look on his face. "High Commander Anron can't make me disappear now because other people would know why."

"You betray one of your High Commanders, for what? Your own safety?"

"I will fight and die for my brothers and for our land, but I won't die because High Commander Anron was too stupid to keep his mouth shut inside the palace."

A cry of rage ripped from Fendon's throat. Leaping across the floor, he swung his fist straight at Gadrien. Gadrien, who had seen it coming, nimbly stepped aside and let the strike pass harmlessly through the air. Due to the unexpected lack of resistance, Fendon stumbled into a table as his momentum continued carrying him forwards.

Whipping back around, he snarled at Gadrien, "Don't you dare speak about a war hero like High Commander Anron in that way, you fucking coward."

"Sit down before you embarrass yourself," Gadrien scoffed with an arrogant jerk of his chin towards the seat that the white-haired soldier had previously been occupying.

The comment only served to enrage him further. Snatching up a wooden tankard, Fendon hurled it at Gadrien's head. Ale flew through the air and splashed down on the floorboards as the container spun over and over before slamming into the armored forearm that Gadrien yanked up as a shield. Before he could respond, Fendon sprang forward and swung his fist again.

Gadrien slammed his hand down into the crook of Fendon's elbow, making his arm shoot downwards so that the strike missed. It was followed up with a fist to the jaw that made Fendon's head snap to the side.

Worried murmurs spread through the civilian part of the

room, while the soldiers only cheered the two fighters on as if they were pleased with the entertainment. I flicked my gaze around the tavern, trying to figure out if there was anything I could do to help. Or if I even should. If I interfered, it would raise questions that we couldn't afford.

Gadrien drove his knee into Fendon's groin. A loud *oof* resounded through the tavern as the white-haired soldier doubled over. Not missing a beat, Gadrien used the opportunity to clock his opponent in the side of the head. The hit sent Fendon crashing down right in the small puddle of ale that shone on the floor.

Raising my eyebrows, I sat back down again. Eilan had been right. He was perfectly capable of handling himself even when things went wrong. The effortless way he moved during this fight made me wonder if he had practiced shapeshifting into a High Elf even before we got here. Perhaps even as soon as the High Elves appeared on our coast back home. Learning to master different bodies that all had different heights and muscle mass and everything probably took a lot of time. I would have to ask him about that sometime.

A bang echoed through the tavern as Gadrien yanked up his opponent and slammed him chest first down onto a table. Startled mugs jumped in surprise and a few tipped over to spill even more ale over the already messy tabletop and the floor beneath.

Gadrien clamped a hand around the back of Fendon's neck while using his other to force the soldier's arm up his back. Bent over a table, with his cheek pressing into the damp wood, Fendon struggled uselessly against Gadrien's superior technique.

"You are an embarrassment to your fellow brothers," Gadrien snapped at his captive.

"And you are a traitor!" Pressing his free palm against the table, Fendon tried to push himself up. "You betray a High Commander–"

A yelp ripped from his throat at the same time as a sharp thud rang out that seemed to echo around the room. I shifted my position so that I could see better.

Gadrien had taken his hand from Fendon's neck and instead yanked out a knife. The blade was now firmly lodged in the tabletop only a hair's breadth from the white-haired soldier's hand.

"The next one goes through your palm," Gadrien growled down at him. "Do you understand?"

Fendon struggled to get up from the tabletop, but Gadrien only forced his arm higher up his back, which made the captured soldier cry out in pain. Gadrien yanked out the knife from the wood and instead positioned the sharp tip against the back of Fendon's hand. He stilled.

"You say I'm a traitor," Gadrien began. "But who's the real traitor? Yeah, Anron is a High Commander. But Empress Elswyth is blessed by the gods to rule our land along with Emperor Lanseyo. He is the highest military leader here, and High Commander Anron badmouthed his wife. Our political leader. So don't go screaming at me about treason."

A murmur of agreement rippled through the room.

"I'm not gonna tell the empress about it," Gadrien continued. Glancing up, his cold blue eyes swept over the other soldiers and the civilians. "But maybe someone should."

Several people exchanged looks. Smug satisfaction flashed through me at the calculating glint in a few people's eyes. They were considering what kind of reward they might receive from the empress if they brought this to her attention. Just like we wanted them to.

"Now," Gadrien said as he turned back to Fendon, "I've served this country and its people a hell of a lot longer than you, which makes me your superior. If I let you get up, are you gonna sit down and shut up like the ignorant infant you are?"

Fendon struggled against his grip for only a second before grinding out, "Yes."

Gadrien pressed the tip of the knife harder against Fendon's skin, making a drop of blood well up that trickled down the back of his captive's hand. "Yes, what?"

"Yes, sir."

"That's right."

Giving him a shove down into the table, Gadrien finally released the white-haired soldier. Fendon pushed himself up from the tabletop and whirled around as if to continue the fight. However, one sharp look from Gadrien's cold eyes made him stop in his tracks. An arrogant smirk slid home on Gadrien's lips as he shook his head.

"I've had enough of idiots for one night," he said before whirling around and stalking out the door.

As soon as his bronze armor had disappeared from view, I edged up from my seat and carefully melted through the wall and back into the darkness as well. After rounding the building and darting across the street, I made my way into the alley we had gathered in earlier. A dark shape was standing halfway down the road. I strode towards it.

Right as I closed the final distance, two skinny humans dropped down from above and landed nimbly on the street behind the figure.

"I'd call that a success," Theo announced as I came to a halt next to him.

"Yes." The dark shape turned around to reveal a pair of

pale green eyes set into a gorgeous face. Gadrien was gone and instead Eilan was back, looking like himself. "I marked several people who will no doubt run straight to the palace to tell the empress first thing tomorrow."

"Would you look at that?" I flashed him a wicked grin. "You really do know what you're doing."

He huffed and shot me a half amused, half disgruntled look.

"And you really do know how to twist someone's arm," Valerie added as she winked at him. "Literally."

An embarrassed expression blew across Eilan's features as he dragged a self-conscious hand through his long black hair. "Yeah, I'm... uhm, sorry you had to see that."

"I'm not." While fanning herself with her hand, she wiggled her eyebrows at him. "I actually think it was kind of hot."

Eilan's mouth dropped open slightly.

"I mean," Valerie continued, a wicked grin on her lips, "if you ever want to practice bending someone over a table, I'd be happy to volunteer."

Theo let out a groan that was loud enough that it echoed down the alley, but Eilan only continued staring at Valerie. It was hard to tell in the dark, but I swore his face had taken on an alarming shade of red.

I cleared my throat. "Maybe we should start heading back?"

"Yes," Eilan answered almost before I had finished speaking. Snapping his mouth shut, he turned and began jogging down the alley.

Next to me, Theo slapped Valerie's arm with the back of his hand and then shook his head. She only grinned back at him. Not even bothering to hide the amusement on my face, I turned towards them and motioned that we should get going as well.

As we disappeared into the dark night, I couldn't help wondering just how long Eilan would be able to fend off Valerie's blunt attempts at flirting. Or better yet, why he was even trying to. But I guessed that was something they would have to figure out on their own.

If we survived this.

CHAPTER 26

We had only just closed the front door behind us when it was opened once more. A cloud of shadows faded away to reveal Mordren, Ellyda, Hadeon, and Idra. The lingering sense of worry that had flickered through me ever since they left for Poisonwood Forest dissolved as they strode across the threshold and into the candlelit hallway.

"Any issues?" I asked, my gaze coming to rest on Mordren's beautiful face.

"None." A sly smile spread across his lips as he tilted his head to motion at Idra and Hadeon. "Unless you count these two bickering like children."

Idra's dark eyes shot to the Prince of Shadows. "Careful now, boy. I am older than all the rest of you put together."

"Then start acting like it," Hadeon huffed and crossed his arms. "And not like a toddler who doesn't know how to follow instructions."

"If you weren't so incredibly bad at explaining things, I wouldn't have to constantly figure things out on my own."

"I'm not bad at explaining things!"

Idra jutted out her chin, and arched a pale brow at him. "Really?"

"Yes. You're just incapable of following orders."

Mordren blew out a sigh. Holding my gaze, he flicked a hand towards the two arguing warriors. "I rest my case."

Next to me, Valerie and Theo chuckled as Idra and Hadeon first glared at each other and then turned in unison to narrow their eyes at the Prince of Shadows. Eilan, who was a bit more discreet, wiped a hand over his mouth to hide his smile before the two scowling fighters could see it.

"The visit went well, then?" he asked as he glanced between his brother and Ellyda. "You know how to break the anklets?"

Everyone turned to look at Ellyda. The brown-haired elf in question only continued staring at the wood panels on the wall next to her.

"Ellyda," Mordren said, trying to bring her attention back to the present.

No answer. In fact, I wasn't even sure if she had blinked once since she stepped into the hallway. Mordren was about to open his mouth again when Hadeon's voice instead boomed across the corridor.

"Reality to Ellyda Steelsinger!"

No surprise flashed across her face and she didn't whirl towards him either. Instead, she slowly turned around. After blinking a couple of times, her eyes cleared and she drew her eyebrows down as she fixed her gaze on Hadeon.

"No need to yell, brother," she said.

"Uh-huh," he muttered before flinging his arm out to indicate us. "They were asking how it went, El."

She stared at him in silence for about half a minute before

turning to face us. Her eyes went in and out of focus a few times before finally settling on a spot between me and Eilan. "Good."

"So you know how to break the anklets?" I asked.

"Yes. I'm going to forge a sword." She dragged her gaze to Valerie and Theo. "But I'm going to need you to steal some things for me."

Without waiting for them to reply, she abruptly strode towards the living room. Theo and Valerie exchanged an uncertain glance.

From across the corridor, Hadeon chuckled and waved a hand towards where his sister had disappeared. "I think she wants you to follow."

"Right." Theo cleared his throat before shifting his attention to Valerie. "Well then, after you."

While the two thieves scrambled after the disappearing blacksmith, Hadeon started towards the kitchen.

"I could use something else to eat than stew filled with those blue mushrooms," he announced.

"If you're cooking, I won't say no to some food as well," Eilan said as he followed him.

Still moving towards the kitchen, Hadeon twisted towards Idra and called over his shoulder, "Are you coming or what?"

She glared at him before blowing out a sharp breath. "Fine. I suppose I could eat too."

I let out a silent laugh while she stalked after Hadeon and Eilan. Light from the wall-mounted candles painted gilded highlights in her shining white hair. It brushed her shoulders as she walked. Then she rounded the corner and disappeared from view.

"Mark my words," Mordren said as he started towards me.

"One day, those two are going to kill each other. It is as if they are constantly looking for things to fight about."

"It would be quite entertaining, though," I said. "Watching them battle it out in an actual fight. I wonder who would win."

"Hadeon," he replied without hesitation.

"Oh, my money is on Idra."

Mordren came to a halt in front of me. Tilting his head to the side, he smirked down at me. "When the time comes, and we place those bets, you will lose."

"Cocky, aren't you?"

"It's not arrogance if it's true." He flashed me another smug smile before jerking his chin towards the kitchen. "Do you want to join them for something to eat?"

Lifting one shoulder in a shrug, I gave him a sly look. "I actually had something else in mind."

"Did you now?"

"Yes."

Mordren let out a dark laugh. "Good. So did I."

Draping a possessive arm over my shoulders, he turned me around and steered us towards the staircase. Right before I could put my foot on the first step, Mordren reached down and swept me up into his arms. A surprised laugh escaped my lips.

"What's this?" I asked, raising my eyebrows at him.

He kissed me while carrying me around the staircase and instead down the corridor. "This is me making time for us. Right now. We keep saying that we will have more time when all this is over, but I do not want to wait. I want us to have more time right now."

Looking up into his beautiful face, I smiled. "Me too."

This part of the house lay dark and deserted. I glanced up as if I could see the door to our temporary bedroom through the floor, but Mordren kept heading farther away from the stairs. Surprise flickered through me while he strode down the hall with confident steps.

"Uhm," I began, glancing between Mordren and the stairs we were rapidly leaving behind. "Our room is up there."

A sly smile slid home on his lips. "I know."

Narrowing my eyes, I watched the smug amusement on his face as he waited for me to ask more. I refused to give him the satisfaction, so I kept my mouth firmly shut.

At the end of the hall, he shifted his grip so that he could edge open a door. My eyebrows rose.

With a smirk on his face, Mordren carried me into the luxurious bathroom and set me down on one of the lounge chairs. "I have spent the entire day traveling back and forth from Poisonwood Forest. And you have broken into the palace and a seedy tavern. I think a bath might be in order."

I chuckled. "You know what? I think you might be right."

While Mordren went to lock the door, I lit the candles throughout the large room. Golden light bloomed and cast the whole area in a cozy glow. Not only was the family who lived here rich enough to afford four bedrooms, they were thankfully also able to afford indoor plumbing. And not just any plumbing either. There was a shower in the corner opposite the lounge chairs, and then the whole back part of the room was taken up by a sunken bath that had been dug into the ground below the house and then tiled to match the floor. It wasn't nearly as big as the one back in my bathroom in the Court of Fire, but it was still a lot fancier than most people were able to afford.

Footsteps sounded behind me. A moment later, Mordren's gentle fingers swept my long curls aside and draped them over my shoulder. My skin prickled with pleasure as he leaned down and kissed my neck.

His hands trailed down my shoulders, my arms, and then towards my hips. I arched my back as he gripped the hem of my shirt and began pushing it up my stomach. A shiver coursed through me as he kissed the crook of my neck while he edged my dark shirt over my breasts, caressing them with his hands.

"Arms up," he whispered into my ear.

I raised my arms. Mordren brushed his lips over the side of my neck again before he pulled the shirt over my head. The dark fabric fluttered through the air and then came to rest on one of the lounge chairs. I turned around.

Mordren had only worn his black dress shirt today, probably to avoid attracting too much attention as they crossed the city, so there was no tie or suit jacket to wrestle with. Reaching up, I trailed my fingers over his chest as I started on the first button. He brushed a hand over my cheek before running it through my hair. With a firm grip on my loose red curls, he leaned down and stole a kiss from my lips. I closed my eyes and continued unbuttoning his shirt by touch alone.

When the final button at last yielded its hold, I ran my hands over Mordren's lean muscles. His skin was warm underneath my touch. Drawing my fingers up his abs and chest, I pushed his shirt off his shoulders. He released my hair to allow the fabric to fall to the floor.

Before he could renew his grip, I slid the knife from my thigh holster and placed it against the skin right above his pants. Mordren raised his eyebrows at me. I flashed him a wicked grin.

Brushing the sharp point very lightly against his skin, I

trailed the knife up his abs and chest while backing him towards the wall. His back hit the wall at the same time as I adjusted my grip and positioned the edge of the blade across his throat. Rising onto my toes, I slanted my mouth over his but stopped just short of kissing him.

"Don't move," I breathed against his lips.

I sank down onto my heels again. For a moment, I only continued holding the knife against his throat while locking eyes with him. Then I slowly lowered the blade.

Challenge glittered in Mordren's silver eyes, but he didn't move. A wicked smile spread across my lips.

After placing the knife on the small side table next to us, I grabbed the front of Mordren's belt. While holding his gaze, I slowly unbuckled it and then slid it out of the belt loops. The buckle's metal frame clinked against the tiles as it landed on the floor.

"Shoes," I said.

The look in his eyes informed me that he would take pleasure in exacting revenge on me for ordering him around, but he toed off his shoes and then used his foot to push them to the side.

I flashed him a satisfied smile that only made his eyes glint once more with the promise of retribution.

Holding his gaze, I undid the fastenings on his pants and began sliding both them and his underwear down his legs. He drew in a long breath. Still not breaking eye contact, I knelt down before him as I pushed the garments the final bit down and then made him step out of them. They joined his shoes and belt on the floor next to the table.

I ran my hands up his legs. Still on my knees, I took a firm grip on the back of his thighs and then leaned forward. He sucked in a shuddering breath as I teased his tip with my tongue. My fingers tightened on his thighs. Glancing up, I shot Mordren a sly look before parting my lips and sliding them forward.

He let out a dark moan. A tremor passed through his body as I continued my movements. His hand shot forward and he threaded his fingers through my hair as I worked my lips. With his back still pressed against the wall, he braced one hand against the tiles behind him while the other kept a firm grip on my hair.

Another shuddering breath ripped from his lungs. It was followed by a low growl that seemed to come all the way from his chest. His thigh muscles flexed underneath my hands and his fingers tightened their hold on my hair as I continued pleasuring him with my mouth.

I pushed him to the edge several times as I used my tongue, my lips, and the slight graze of my teeth to make him tremble above me, only to pause right before release found him. Shadows flickered wildly around his forearm as he alternated between squeezing his hand into a fist and splaying it against the wall. When his chest was heaving with desperate breaths and he looked like he would shatter completely, I stopped torturing him and finally followed through.

A loud moan tore from his throat and he gripped my hair hard, holding me in place, as release coursed through him. He collapsed back against the wall.

Satisfied with my ability to make him come undone before me, I slowly rose to my feet again and wiped my lips with my fingers. There was a slightly dazed expression still on Mordren's handsome features. I flashed him a victorious smile and then shoved him towards the shower.

"Don't worry," I said with a sly smile when he raised his eyebrows in surprise. "I'll join you."

Water splashed against the stone tiles as Mordren turned on the faucet while I stripped out of the rest of my clothes. Gathering up both my clothes and his, I dumped them on the lounge chair that already housed my shirt before I sauntered towards the open shower.

The pipes must have been running through the ceiling as well because water rained down from a flat metal square rather than just a small showerhead. I stepped into the shower right as Mordren finished soaping his body.

Warm water washed over my face and body. Closing my eyes, I shifted into position in front of Mordren so that I would stand directly in the pleasant rain as well. And then I blew out a deep sigh.

Gentle hands roamed my body as Mordren began running the lavender soap over me. I leaned back against his chest. His palms scrubbed my arms, my stomach, and my legs. Drawing my fingers through my soaked hair, I pushed a few curls out of my face.

A faint thud sounded as Mordren placed the soap back on the small rack.

For a moment, we just stood there in silence, letting the warm water wash away the soap and our tiredness. Then, soft fingers appeared on my skin again.

Still standing behind me, Mordren slid his hands over my hip bones and then up my stomach. I released a deep sigh as he massaged my breasts before his hands continued in two different directions.

One hand trailed down my stomach while the other continued upwards instead. I tilted my head back as Mordren wrapped a hand around my throat and pushed me harder against his body. His other hand dipped below my waist and down between my legs.

I sucked in a breath as his fingers began stroking my sensitive areas.

Water rushed down our naked bodies as Mordren returned the favor. I gasped and a pleasant shudder went through me as his fingers found just the right spot. He tightened his hand around my throat, tilting my head higher up and forcing my back to remain pressed against his chest. My legs trembled.

He kissed that sensitive spot behind my ear while his fingers continued their torturous movements. A moan slipped my lips. I clenched my hands and tried to rise up on my toes to escape his brilliant fingers when he brought me to the edge over and over again without giving me release. His hand around my throat forced me down on my heels again. I trembled against his heated skin while water continued running down our naked bodies.

"Please," I begged when I couldn't take it anymore.

He smiled against my skin as he kissed the back of my neck, and then his fingers started up their expert movement again. Release built inside me. He kept going. My vision flashed white behind my closed lids and my body shook violently as the long-awaited release crashed over me like an ocean wave. If it hadn't been for his hand around my throat keeping me upright, my legs would've given out. I slumped back against his muscled chest as the final tremors passed through my body.

Mordren's hot breath caressed my ear as he let out a dark laugh. "I do so love it when you do that."

When he finally loosened his grip on me, I turned around and cocked my head as I looked up at him. "Beg or climax?"

A sly smile spread across his lips as he pushed me up against the wall. Water ran down his lethal body and clung to his shining black hair as the current from above shifted to his back. Tilting my chin up, he slanted his lips over mine.

"Both," he breathed against my mouth.

I blew out a dark laugh. After turning off the water, he reached down and positioned his arms around my ass so that he could lift me off the floor. I wrapped my legs around his waist. He stole a kiss from my wet lips before carrying me towards the sunken bath.

Once he had made it to the second step, he sat down on it so that the warm water wrapped around us at waist level. I shifted my legs so that I straddled his lap. Drops of water clung to his dark lashes and hair. The golden light from the candles made them glitter like stardust as he tilted his head to study me.

"You really are stunning. And brilliant." Raising both hands, he drew his fingers through my hair before lowering them so that he cupped my cheeks. His lips met mine in a gentle kiss. When he drew back, there was a wicked glint in his silver eyes. "I am so glad that I decided to blackmail you that day we met."

I laughed against his mouth and then stole another kiss before replying, "I'm so glad I decided to poison you to clear my debt."

His hot breath caressed my lips as he let out a dark laugh as well. I locked my hands around the back of his neck and kissed him deeply while he adjusted his hips between my legs.

We would have more time. For this. For everything. And if we didn't have time, we would make time.

For each other.

Always.

CHAPTER 27

A thin haze of shadows helped the morning sun cast a deep shade over the rooftop. Mordren, Eilan, and I lay on our stomachs atop the mausoleum and watched the empty statue garden below. We had been there since sunrise as we had no way of knowing if or when this meeting would take place, but we had played our cards well last night so we were confident that we had gambled correctly.

Footsteps echoed between the stone statues. We perked up. Peering over the edge, we found High Commander Anron stalking across the fresh green grass. Annoyance flickered like storm clouds across his face. When he reached the empty circle close to the mausoleum, he stopped and crossed his arms.

This time, only a minute or so passed before Empress Elswyth came gliding across the grass. Morning dew sparkled like stars in the light from the rising sun, as well as in the bolts of lightning along Elswyth's arms. The train of her black and silver dress produced a faint rustling sound as it slid across the damp grass.

Anron bowed at the waist. "Your Imperial Majesty."

"High Commander Anron." She came to a halt two strides in front of him and drew herself up to her full height. "I will get straight to the point. Last night, a soldier told an entire tavern full of people that he overheard you say that I was not fit to rule."

"I..." Anron trailed off and genuine confusion blew across his face. Whatever he had been expecting her to say, that had not been it. "What? Why would I ever say that?"

Lightning bolts clung tightly to her arms. "You tell me."

"This is a mistake." A hint of panic flashed in Anron's sharp blue eyes. "I would never speak in such a way about you or Emperor Lanseyo."

Matching smiles that dripped with wickedness spread across Mordren and Eilan's lips. I stifled an evil laugh. Anron might not have said it to a random soldier yesterday, but he had certainly thought it. And perhaps even said it to his accomplices Lester and Danser. I could almost see him racking his brain for a time when the empress, or anyone, could possibly have overheard him.

"Take a good look around you," Empress Elswyth said as she raised her arm to gesture towards the screaming statues all around them. "This is what happens to traitors and malcontents."

Anron's eyes flicked around the garden before returning to the empress. "I know."

"Yes, I suspect you do. But the question remains whether you are about to become one of them."

"In the end, that is of course your decision alone. But it would be a mistake. I would never speak badly of you or Emperor Lanseyo in such a way, and I never have. All I have done is serve you well during my entire career. I have put down uprisings, hunted down traitors, and rounded up malcontents. I have never been one of them."

Empress Elswyth studied him from behind her black veil.

I had to admit, I was impressed by his ability to skirt the truth. No, he would never speak badly of them *in such a way*. Only privately, with no one else around. And he had never been one of them before, but he was about to be one soon. Not to mention that he was able to completely bury his anger and hatred behind a mask of innocence and worry. No wonder we had been outmaneuvered by him so many times.

"You are telling the truth," she finally announced, probably having seen the same sincerity in his eyes that I had. "However, that still begs the question of why a soldier would spread such lies about you."

Anron straightened his armor while a serious look settled on his face. "When I selected the soldiers who would join my Flying Legion, I had to pass some of them over because there simply wasn't room. Some of those didn't take it well. My guess is that, now that I have returned, one of them decided to get back at me for not selecting him."

"I see. Yes, I suppose that does sound reasonable."

"Petty jealousy can be a dangerous thing if it is allowed to fester. With your permission, I would like to hunt down this pathetic excuse for a soldier and have him face the consequences of his misguided actions."

"Granted."

"Thank you, Your Imperial Majesty." Anron inclined his head before looking up again. "I have also considered the fate of the magicless island, and I have some advice for you."

The controlled bolts of lightning spread from Empress Elswyth's arms to her chest as she cocked her head. "Advice? You do not give me advice, High Commander."

"No, of course not," he amended quickly. "I only meant that I have given some thought to what we should do about the island we found."

"*We?*"

"You, Your Imperial Majesty. What *you* and Emperor Lanseyo might want to do about the island." It seemed to be getting increasingly difficult for Anron to keep the irritation out of his voice and eyes. Blinking, he cleared his throat before continuing. "The island does not have any native magic. Nor any magical creatures. As far as strategic resources go, they have nothing that can't be found in our lands or our other colonies. Therefore, I would recommend you not to try to annex it."

Apparently, High Commander Anron had decided that it was too risky to use an invasion of our island as a distraction while he overthrew the empress and emperor. To be fair, I reckoned he was right. If Empress Elswyth had actually decided to travel there herself and seen all the elves with black bracelets, she would have easily figured out what Anron was up to.

"There it is again," the empress said, her voice cutting through the silent morning like a knife. "That tone and those words. It is almost as if you believe that you are the one making the decisions here."

"Of course not. I was just–"

"Perhaps there is some truth to that soldier's words after all."

"What? No. Please, Empress Elswyth, I was merely offering my humble opinion on something that I do have a lot of knowledge about."

Lightning split the air. I shrank down and pressed my body into the warm stone roof as a white bolt hit the side of the mausoleum, missing Anron by a hand's breadth. Chips of marble flew and rained down onto the damp grass below us.

When I peeked over the edge again, I found High Commander Anron standing straight-backed on the ground, staring at the empress who had shot a calculated and well-aimed lightning strike at him. War raged behind his eyes. Two steps away, the empress stood facing him and her back was also like a rod. Controlled lightning crackled over her body, as if she was still deciding whether that one warning shot had been enough or if she should make the next one actually hit. I couldn't see her face, but there was no mistaking the anger that rippled off her.

"Choose your next words carefully, High Commander." Her voice was low and deadly. "Because every word out of your mouth right now only serves to dig your grave deeper."

Furiously banking his rage, Anron unclenched his hands and instead bowed deeply. "My sincerest apologies, Your Imperial Majesty. I meant no offense."

"For your sake, I hope not." Bolts of white lightning spread down her black skirt. "Do not presume to have more knowledge than me. I have ruled this great land for far longer than you have even drawn breath."

Anron bowed again.

Raising her arm, she stabbed a hand towards the path behind Anron. "Get out. Before I decide that your words were insincere after all."

After bowing a third time, High Commander Anron turned and made his way towards the entrance he had used. I only managed to get a brief look at his face once he had turned around, but it was enough to confirm that he was completely livid. My gaze drifted back to the empress. And so was she.

Whirling around, she stalked back through the statues in the same direction that she had arrived. Lightning clung to her entire body. A wide grin spread across my lips.

"Go," Mordren whispered. "Split up."

Eilan nodded. "We'll meet back up outside the living quarters."

After a quick nod to confirm that I had heard them, I rolled over the edge and lowered myself to the ground. Dew from the damp grass clung to my boots as I hurried towards a cluster of statues.

Soft thuds sounded behind me as Mordren and Eilan did the same.

I cast a quick look behind me to make sure we were covering all directions. When I saw them moving towards the predetermined places, I turned my attention back to the path ahead. Morning sunlight warmed my face as I followed the empress while Eilan disappeared in the same direction as Anron, and Mordren snuck towards the other exit.

High Commander Anron might have been able to convince the empress that he hadn't been badmouthing her to a soldier yesterday, but his own words during this meeting had fortunately been enough to still make her angry.

Now, all we had to do was keep applying pressure until this small crack in their relationship turned into an unbridgeable chasm.

CHAPTER 28

None of the others were here yet. Walking right through the wall, I ended up in the deserted living room of a house that belonged to one of the other High Commanders. Thanks to Eilan's careful investigations, we had learned that this particular military leader was currently on a mission abroad, which meant that he would not object to me using his home as a vantage point for spying. Well, he would never know, anyway.

I pressed myself up against the wall and scanned the area outside before edging the window open so that I could hear the conversation about to happen. Warm air blew through the gap and caressed my cheeks. Leaning one shoulder against the pale wooden wall, I settled in to wait for the second meeting that Mordren, Eilan, and I had orchestrated this morning.

Footsteps echoed against the white stone ground outside.

A villainous smile spread across my mouth.

They had managed to time it perfectly. Lester and Danser came striding towards the place we had picked, with no

Anron to accompany them, right as an angry empress rounded the corner on the other side.

Both the empress and the two High Commanders jerked to a halt as they almost collided with each other. I shifted my position in the window so that I could see all three of them properly.

"Empress Elswyth," Lester and Danser said in unison while bowing at the waist.

"Lester. Danser." Lightning bolts danced over her arms. "Are you in such a hurry that you cannot even be bothered to look where you are going?"

"Our apologies, Your Imperial Majesty," Danser said smoothly as he bowed again. "We should have been paying more attention."

"Yes, you should have. However, since you decided to make my already infuriating morning even worse, I do have a question for you."

"Of course."

"Word has reached me that High Commander Anron was overheard questioning my ability to rule. What are your thoughts on those accusations?"

A hint of alarm flickered in Lester's eyes. His long blond hair rippled across his bronze breastplate as he shifted his stance to hide it. But from my position, I had seen it clear as day.

"I would say that it has to be some kind of mistake," Danser continued in his steady voice.

"Are you saying that I have made a mistake?"

"Of course not, Your Imperial Majesty. However, I do believe that your source is mistaken. Anron would never speak ill of you or Emperor Lanseyo. He has always served you faithfully. As have we."

"Or perhaps you are in on it."

Danser's face drained of color. Next to him, Lester flicked his gaze between the empress and his co-conspirator while opening his mouth to protest. I wasn't sure if the horrified expressions were a calculated way to lend credibility to their supposed innocence, or if they had truly let their masks slip for a few seconds as panic overtook them.

"We would never conspire against you, Empress Elswyth," Danser said while raising his hands in an entreating gesture. "Your cunning is legendary and you have made this land into the prosperous nation that it is."

Rogue bolts of lightning leaped from her arms and zapped the stones in front of the two High Commanders. They flinched back the tiniest bit.

"Do not think to flatter me," she said, her voice cold and deadly. "I have had enough of smooth talkers for one morning who think themselves in a position to give me advice or assess my competency."

"We meant no disrespect," Lester said, having recovered from the flash of panic. "And I swear, we would never question your ability to rule. And neither would Anron."

"I hope not. Because do you know what I would do if I found out that you have tried to undermine me in any way?" Her black veil rippled as she turned her head towards Danser. "You have a wife." She shifted her attention back to Lester. "And your parents still live in town."

They nodded slowly, uncertain whether that had been a question or simply a statement.

"If you ever do anything to compromise my rule," she continued in that cold voice, "I will ensure that your families die horribly before they become part of my statue garden. Then, once I have made you watch as I kill them slowly, I will hand both of you over to my dear husband. I assume you are aware of his natural cruel streak? Imagine what he would do to the people who tried to undermine his wife."

The tiny bit of color that had returned to Danser's face drained from his skin with every word she spoke. Bronze armor glinted in the morning sunlight as Lester uncomfortably shifted his position again. Wicked satisfaction swirled inside me. I already knew that he was terrified of Emperor Lanseyo. This not-so-subtle threat was sure to add more fuel to that fear.

"So if you ever do hear High Commander Anron question my ability to rule, I would suggest that you inform me swiftly." Another few lightning bolts flickered out of control and zapped the stones around the empress as she cocked her head. "That way, we can avoid any misconceptions regarding your own involvement in such sordid affairs."

"Of course." Danser cleared his throat and dipped his chin. "We are ever your loyal servants, Your Imperial Majesty."

"Good." Empress Elswyth flicked her wrist. "You may leave."

Both High Commanders bowed deeply before hurrying away at the quickest pace they could without being disrespectful. I watched the anger and fear that blew across their faces as they exchanged a pointed glance once they thought no one could see their expressions.

After straightening her spine, Empress Elswyth stalked away in the direction she had been heading before Lester and Danser had almost collided with her. The white lightning bolts along her arms were crackling out of control now and leaped down to strike the ground around her. Then she rounded the corner and disappeared from view.

A victorious smile slid home on my lips.

This morning had been a complete success. Not only had we managed to drive a wedge between Empress Elswyth and Anron, but thanks to this carefully arranged meeting, we had also forced Lester and Danser to consider the grave consequences that would befall them if their scheme with Anron was discovered. Cracks were forming in all of Anron's important relationships now. If we kept this up, it wouldn't be long before they snapped completely.

With glittering hope sparkling in my chest, I phased back through the wall and then slunk away to rejoin Mordren and Eilan.

Things were finally looking up.

CHAPTER 29

"How did it go?"

Mordren and I looked up to find Hadeon and Idra striding in through the door. Evening had fallen outside the windows. After our excursion to the Palace of the Never Setting Sun, Mordren, Eilan, and I had returned to an empty safe house. Theo and Valerie had been out stealing supplies for Ellyda, while the blacksmith in question had been escorted to Vendir's parents' house by Idra and Hadeon. The two thieves had since returned, but the two warriors hadn't gotten back until just now.

"It went well," Mordren replied. "All relationships are now properly strained."

The door to the living room clicked shut behind Idra. I shifted in my armchair to look behind her.

"Where is Ellyda?" I asked.

Hadeon threw himself down on the couch next to Mordren and propped his boots up on the low table. "Still at Vendir's place. She's in the middle of forging her sword and said she didn't want to be disturbed."

Idra snickered. "I believe her exact words were 'stop hovering, Hadeon' and 'you're ruining my concentration.'"

"That's not what she said."

"No? Perhaps it was 'get out before I hit you with my hammer'?"

Grimacing at her, Hadeon raised his hand and flashed her a rude gesture. A sharp smile spread across Idra's mouth, but she only lowered herself into the armchair next to mine.

"How long before the sword is done?" I asked before they could start fighting about something else.

"El says tomorrow afternoon, if nothing goes wrong," Hadeon answered.

"And if no one interrupts her," Idra added with a smirk.

"I already told you, I–"

Glass shattered and rained down around us as the windows exploded. Panic pulsed through my whole body. I leaped up from the armchair and yanked out my knife right as soldiers welled in through the broken windows. Candlelight reflected against bronze armor.

"The gear! Get out!" I screamed at the top of my lungs.

While hoping that Eilan, Valerie, and Theo, who were all upstairs, understood that they needed to grab our packs and escape through the upstairs windows, I vaulted across the nearest couch and sprinted for the hallway along with the others.

Mordren threw a thick blanket of darkness around us to hide us from view, but magic hummed in the air and attacks were imminent. Clanking noises echoed through the house as a pile of metal slid down the stairs. Gratitude bloomed inside me. Someone upstairs had made the fantastic decision to slide our weapons down before they escaped with the rest of our gear. I snatched up my sword and then whirled around right as stomping boots closed in on us from the windows in the living room and the front door.

"Split up," Idra snapped as she and the others grabbed their weapons as well. "Before they box us in."

"Meet at the White Fire tavern," Mordren added.

The world exploded.

"Go!" Hadeon bellowed.

White light pulsed through the shadows around us as someone sent a storm of lightning into the darkness. I dove forward. Sliding along the floor on my stomach, I narrowly avoided getting struck by a crackling bolt.

Bronze-plated legs appeared before me. I rolled to the side and phased through the hallway wall right before a wave of water hit the shining wooden floor I had been occupying. Drops clung to the bottom half of my hair as I leaped to my feet in the next room.

A blast of wind slammed straight into my chest.

I flew backwards. Hoping that I was at least going in the right direction, I phased through the wall I would otherwise have crashed into.

Cool night air wrapped around my body as I cleared the outer wall and flew through the street outside. I sucked in a gasp as I slammed into something hard. The surprise roadblock let out a startled yelp as well and we both went down in a heap.

Torchlight flickered around me and made the bronze-clad limbs I was entangled in gleam. Rolling over, I tried to get away from the High Elf soldier I had crashed into.

"They're splitting up!" High Commander Lester screamed from somewhere on the other side of the building. "I have eyes on the shadow prince. In pursuit."

Yanking out my left hand from underneath an armored

elbow, I stabbed my knife towards the soldier trying to pin me underneath him.

"With me!" Danser yelled from somewhere terribly close by. "The two warriors are escaping this way."

"She's–" began the soldier underneath me.

My knife sank into the unprotected skin of his neck before he could finish. Shock bounced in his eyes and blood spurted across the stones as I yanked out my blade after severing his carotid artery. I struggled to my feet and got ready to run right as a tall figure darted out from the house and into the street a short distance from me.

High Commander Anron.

Even though I had managed to kill the soldier before he finished his sentence, his shout had been enough to draw the attention of the one person I didn't want to face. Despite all of my power and cunning, I was still hopelessly outclassed against Anron in a one-on-one fight.

"She's here!" Anron bellowed as he shot a blast of water straight towards me. "Half of you, follow Lester. The rest of you, with me."

With a flick of my sword, I threw up a wall of fire to block his attack. Dark red flames shot up from the ground and licked the sky far higher than I had anticipated. Panic pounded through my veins. The blast of water hit my fire shield and exploded into a cloud of hissing steam. Not wasting a second, I whirled around and sprinted towards the nearest building.

I couldn't fight Anron head on. My only chance was to make him lose track of me.

A pair of soldiers darted into the alley mouth in front of me. Magic hummed in the air. Pushing off from the ground, I leaped through the outer wall of the building I had been aiming for. Flashes of lightning lit up the world outside the windows while I dove into a deserted kitchen and rolled across the floor. A chair scraped against the floorboards as I shoved it aside and took off towards the opposite wall. From outside, High Commander Anron was bellowing orders.

Zigzagging through purple armchairs and dark wooden tables, I made it through the living room behind the kitchen before I phased through the outer wall. Warm evening air washed over me. It tasted like ozone.

"She's here!" a soldier yelled.

Lightning crackled down the street.

Without even turning to look, I sprinted across the narrow gap and disappeared through the next wall. A loud *crack* echoed through the street and the building around me trembled as a bolt of lightning smacked into the wall where I had been only seconds before. Screams cut the air from somewhere upstairs. I ignored them and instead darted towards the wall leading to the next house.

A brightly lit kitchen appeared before me as I leaped through yet another wall. Wood clattered against stone as a family of four shot up from their seats, knocking the chairs over in their surprise. I opened my mouth to apologize, or perhaps to tell them to move, but I never found out which one because the dark-haired female by the window snatched up an iron skillet and threw it at me.

Terrified vegetables flew through the air and rained down around me as the pan spun over and over before crashing into the doorframe right next to me. I brushed a piece of fried broccoli from my shoulder while sprinting into their living room.

Bronze armor flashed past the windows on both sides of the building.

With my heart slamming against my ribs, I raced towards the wall that would take me to the next interconnected building. As long as I stayed indoors, I was safe. They could sprint along the street outside, but it would take too much time for them to actually open a door and try to catch me in here. Now, all I could do was hope that I would be able to carve out a sufficient head start so that I could make it across the empty street once this row of interconnected buildings eventually ended. The only problem was of course that since I was running indoors, I had no idea when that would be.

Fresh air slammed into me like a block of stone as I cleared a wall and abruptly found myself outdoors. I continued sprinting forwards while looking for the next place to hide.

"She's out!" someone bellowed on my left.

I had ended up in an open courtyard. Panic shot up my spine. There was a round tower of some kind a short distance ahead, but other than that, the area was flat and empty before more rows of houses boxed it in farther away.

Boots thudded on both my left and right.

Sucking in desperate breaths, I hurtled towards the tower. If I could just get there, I could use it as a halfway point that would temporarily shield me from view before I made a break for the other row of buildings. My lungs were on fire, but I forced myself to keep sprinting.

A wave of water sped towards me from the left. I flicked my sword, shooting a blast of fire at it while throwing myself through the tower wall. Steam exploded over the courtyard right as I phased through the wall and stumbled into a darkened room filled with sewing machines.

Leaping over a pile of fabric, I weaved through the next room and then the next while hurrying towards the other wall. As I reached it, I cast a quick glance through the window.

Three High Elf soldiers in bronze armor were taking up position at the back of the tower. Dread sluiced through my veins. Shoving it aside, I sprinted to one of the side walls.

More soldiers blocked that part too.

The dread inside me was transforming into full-blown panic as I darted to the final wall only to realize that the same thing was happening there as well. Somehow, Anron had anticipated my movements and sent soldiers here to trap me.

"Shit, shit, shit," I hissed.

At the front of the building, a door creaked open.

"Ah, Kenna." High Commander Anron's voice was laced with smug victory. "You forget that this is my city and that I know all your tricks."

While silently sliding my sword and knife back in their sheaths, I edged away from the window and moved to one of the inner walls. The sound of Anron's boots slowly moving towards me echoed through the quiet building.

"As soon as I knew which direction you were heading in, I knew exactly where to trap you," he continued in that same mocking tone.

If I could just stay one step ahead of him, I might be able to find a way out later.

"Being able to walk through walls won't save you when the whole building is surrounded," he taunted.

I snuck around a large loom and then weaved between a few baskets of yarn so that I could get to the wall on my left. Anron's voice was coming from the right, so if I moved in the other direction, I should be able to avoid him. I phased through it.

Another room filled with sewing machines and looms

appeared before me. This had to be some kind of factory. I scanned the darkened room for anything I might use to my advantage. Soft piles of fabric and machines too heavy for me to lift stared back at me uselessly. While continuing to move to the left, I cast a quick glance out the window.

Soldiers were standing a short distance away.

Suppressing a curse, I phased through yet another wall.

"I don't know how you did it," Anron said from a few rooms away on my right, "but you somehow managed to convince Empress Elswyth that I questioned her ability to rule. I know that it was you. No random soldier would ever just decide to do that on their own. Luckily, I was able to reassure her that I would never do such a thing."

I would have scoffed at the blatant lie if it wouldn't have given away my position.

"But I am getting tired of these ridiculous games, Kenna. If I had known that you would be this much trouble, I would have persuaded Volkan Flameshield to kill you long before you could even begin plotting your rise to power."

The next room held a spiraling staircase that led up to the second floor, and presumably the other floors above as well. I scanned the room around me while sneaking towards the wall on my left once more. Anron's footsteps had fallen silent, as if he was trying to figure out where I had gone. Pressing myself up against the outer wall, I glanced out the window.

Bronze armor gleamed in the torchlight outside.

I bit back another curse. There had to be a way to get the soldiers to shift their positions so that it would open up an escape route for me. Moving back from the window, I edged around the wooden staircase.

My heart stopped.

Anron strode in through the door just a short distance in

front of me. A look of surprise blew across his face as his eyes landed on me. He shouldn't have been on this side of the building. Based on my calculations of where his voice and his footsteps were, he should have been moving on my right. When the surprise in his eyes gave way to a cunning glint, I realized that he had done it on purpose. He had talked so that I would think that I knew where he was, and then he had moved in the opposite direction.

Terror pulsed through my body. Acting on instinct, I grabbed the railing and swung myself onto the first step.

Magic hummed in the air and the primal fear that it caused inside me screamed at me to surrender. I smothered it and instead sprinted up the stairs. Lightning shot through the room. It hit the railing right next to me. White light exploded from it and a stray bolt zapped my arm. I sucked in a gasp at the pain that flashed through me and I almost stumbled as I reached the landing.

Boots pounded against the floor below. A moment later, they reached the stairs.

Whipping my head from side to side, I tried to find a way to safety but there were only more rooms with desks and supplies. Not to mention that I had lost my way out of the building. I couldn't jump from the second floor since the nearest buildings around the tower were too far away. Slipping through several walls, I tried to put some distance between me and Anron. If I could just lead him away from the staircase, I could make my way back down again.

"That was just a taste of what I will do when I catch you," Anron said. His voice was coming from only two rooms away. "Or perhaps I will use water. Do you know what it feels like to almost drown?"

My skin tingled from the elbow and down to my left hand

after the stray lightning strike. I tried to flex my fingers, but the muscles wouldn't cooperate. Fear spread like cold poison through my body. One shot. All it would take was one clear shot with his lightning, and I was done for. My heart pounded in my chest.

Shaking my hand, I tried to get the tingling sensation to disappear and to get full control of my arm back.

"Yes, I think I will go with drowning. You're too familiar with lightning. Especially since Lester is probably torturing your precious little Mordren with lightning right now. I remember the look on Lester's face as he watched Emperor Lanseyo do just that in the throne room. Oh, you should have seen his smile when you crawled up and licked the emperor's boot to get him to stop. I'm sure Lester is recreating that scene with Mordren right now."

I knew what he was trying to do, that he was trying to rattle me, but unfortunately it was working. Images of Mordren twitching uncontrollably on the ground flashed before my eyes. Drawing in a deep breath, I tried to force them away.

"How about this?" His voice followed me as I slipped into a room filled with bookshelves and ledgers. "Come out and throw yourself on my mercy, and I might spare a few of your friends. The humans, perhaps?"

I phased through another wall. Bolts of fabric had been piled into neat stacks along the walls. Staying silent, I crept towards the next room. I had almost made it back to the room with the staircase. Only two more, and then I could sprint back down.

Water slammed into me.

Slapping a hand in front of my mouth, I narrowly prevented myself from gasping. The water hit me with enough force to throw me off my feet and completely encase me. A twisting ball of clear water, with me inside it, filled most of the room.

Pure terror pulsed through me and washed away all clever thoughts. All I could feel was the panic as I tried to move while being trapped in an ever-shifting bubble of water that kept pushing me back to its center.

A tall figure in bronze armor strode in through the door.

"I gave you a chance to surrender," Anron said, his voice muffled through the water.

Kicking my legs, I tried to swim towards the edge of the ball but I kept getting swept back to the middle of it. Water rushed in my ears when I tried to move, only to go completely silent once I was back where Anron wanted me.

"Now, you will feel what it is like to almost drown," he said through the thick shield of water. "Remember that feeling, because when I allow you to breathe again, you will tell me exactly where the other princes on your island are hiding. If you refuse, we will start from the beginning again. And then I might add some lightning to the water too. It will be a never-ending cycle of painful brushes with death until you finally give me what I want and tell me everything I want to know. And then, and only then, will I show you mercy before I take you and your friends to the palace to receive proper punishment from the emperor and empress."

My lungs burned for air. While trying to stifle the runaway panic that was making me dumb, I desperately cast my mind around for something that would save me. I had fire magic. Fire would turn water into steam. How could I create fire while I was surrounded by water? It felt like jogging in mud to try to get any thoughts through my brain.

Anron was in the room and he had me trapped in water.

Even if I could get out of this watery prison, he would still be standing only a few strides away.

Cold waves washed me back to the center of the ball again and again.

I had to fight my instincts to keep from drawing breath as my lungs screamed for oxygen. Blood pounded in my ears.

The world was beginning to darken at the corner of my eyes.

I needed air.

I needed fire.

I needed…

CHAPTER 30

Dark red flames exploded around me. The world turned into a thick cloud of white steam as my survival instincts sent an uncoordinated ring of fire magic blasting out around me. Even though I was underwater, the sheer strength of the attack was enough to neutralize the watery prison I'd been trapped in.

I fell towards the floor.

Making a split-second decision, I phased through the wooden floorboards and hoped that I would land on something soft in the room below. Anron's angry shout was abruptly cut off as I disappeared downstairs.

Pain shot up my side. I hit the edge of a large loom and flipped over before landing in a pile of fabric. From upstairs, Anron was already sprinting towards the stairs. While sucking in desperate breaths, I struggled to my feet.

Black spots flickered in my vision and I stumbled as I tried to round the loom.

"She's making a break for it!" someone bellowed from outside the tower. "East side!"

The soldiers who had been guarding the area on this side sprinted past the window. Surprise flashed through me, but I wasn't about to let this miraculous opportunity pass me by, so I ran right through the wall and out into the now unguarded west side. The door to the tower crashed open, but when I heard Anron's voice, it came from the other side of the building. Whoever had falsely called out my escape on that side had just saved my life.

With pain pulsing through my body and my left hand still tingling, I closed the final distance to the next row of buildings.

A hand shot out and grabbed my numb arm. I gasped as I was yanked into the shadows of a side alley and slammed up against the wall. Warm fingers pressed over my mouth.

"You really don't make it easy to rescue you, do you?" Valerie whispered.

My eyes finally focused on her face. She looked winded, and worried, but otherwise unharmed. When she saw that I recognized her, she took her hand from my mouth. I sagged back against the cold stone wall.

"We didn't even know where you were until I saw through the window how you fell down from the ceiling," she whispered while motioning for us to start moving. "The bloody ceiling, woman. Are you crazy?"

It took all my strength to push myself off the wall and follow her as she jogged down the street.

"How?" I asked. My lungs were burning and I was still trying to battle the shock and fear of almost drowning, so I only managed that one word.

"Eilan," she replied. "He shapeshifted into a High Elf soldier. Once we knew which side you were on, he could call out to make them move away from where you were."

I gulped in more air before pressing out, "Thank you."

She flashed me a grin. "Anytime."

For a few minutes, we said nothing. Mostly because I couldn't jog and breathe and speak at the same time. When we had put enough streets behind us, Valerie mercifully slowed to a walk.

"Does all that water covering you have anything to do with why you're so out of shape?" she teased, and waved a hand towards my soaked body.

"Shut up," I muttered between heavy breaths. Once my heart had stopped pounding in my chest, I carefully sent a wave of fire up and down my body to dry it while asking, "The others?"

Worry crept back into her warm brown eyes. "Not sure yet."

Oppressive silence fell across the street. That image of Mordren's body twitching from continuous lightning strikes reappeared in my mind. Focusing on my breathing, I tried to ignore it once more.

Running footsteps sounded behind us.

I yanked out my sword and whirled around. Since I still didn't have full control over my left hand, it hung uselessly at my side as I raised the blade with my other.

A moment later, Eilan became visible through the darkness.

My breath whooshed out in a deep sigh of relief. He came to a halt before us. After sliding the sword back in its sheath, I reached out and squeezed Eilan's arm.

"Thank you," I said.

He nodded. "They're searching the streets in the other direction now, so we should be okay."

Not wanting to waste breath on talking, we simply started

towards the White Fire tavern once more. It was a tense and quiet jog. Every step brought us closer to finding out if everyone had made it to safety, but I didn't dare hope.

When the tavern finally came into view, my heart was pattering in my chest like an erratic butterfly.

"Val," a soft voice drifted through the air.

The three of us whipped towards our right. Only the shadows of a deep doorway stared back at us. Then they began to dissipate. Relief flooded my chest as Mordren and Theo became visible behind the shadow shield.

Valerie leaped over and drew Theo into a bear hug. A smile spread across my lips as Eilan stalked over and embraced Mordren as well. I rubbed my left arm while closing the distance to them. The shadow shield sprang back up as soon as I reached the doorway.

"Hadeon and Idra?" Eilan asked as he stepped back from his brother.

"Not here yet," Theo answered from next to them.

Mordren raked perceptive eyes over my body before his gaze locked on mine. "Are you hurt?"

"No," I lied. "You?"

He narrowed his eyes at me as if he could see straight through the lie, but in the end only shook his head. "No."

Folding me into his arms, he held me tightly for a few moments. I rested my cheek against his shoulder and allowed myself to take a deep breath.

"They're not here," a worried voice came from down the street.

"Of course not," another voice snapped back. "If they're here, they're hiding. Not standing right out in the open."

The final bit of worry seeped from my bones as Idra and

Hadeon came striding towards us. I sagged back against Mordren while he dropped his shadow shield.

Idra and Hadeon whipped their heads towards us.

When they came closer, I realized that both of them were covered in blood.

"Is any of it yours?" I demanded.

They looked down at themselves in unison, as if they hadn't realized that they were splattered with blood, and then exchanged a glance.

"No," Idra said in a confident voice.

Hadeon shrugged. "Maybe some."

"We need to get off the street," Idra continued before I could respond. Her dark eyes slid to Eilan. "I saw a deserted-looking guesthouse back there. Can't you shapeshift into a High Elf soldier and commandeer a few rooms for us?"

"That's actually not a bad idea," Hadeon said as he raised his eyebrows.

"All my ideas are good," she sniped back before jerking her chin at Eilan. "Enough chitchat. Get to it already."

I blew out a tired chuckle and shook my head at Idra while Eilan shapeshifted into a High Elf soldier once more. We followed him towards the guesthouse Idra had spotted. A few orders and thinly veiled threats later, and the proprietor did as commanded and let us all in. When we poured across the threshold, he opened his mouth as if to ask how such a random group of people came to be present at his inn at this hour. But then he took one look at Idra and Hadeon's bloody clothes and wisely enough decided not to ask any questions.

"The baths are that way," he said as he pointed down a narrow wooden hallway. "But there are only two. I can bring you some food while you wait your turn."

The implied request that we take a bath before dirtying his beds was clear enough. Eilan in his shapeshifter form nodded in acknowledgement before jerking his chin at Hadeon and Idra.

Idra narrowed her eyes at him, but then she just stalked away towards the baths with Hadeon next to her.

"That move you made with the wall was pretty damn impressive," Hadeon said as they disappeared down the corridor.

"Yeah." She was silent for a few moments before continuing. "I wouldn't have been able to do it if you hadn't been covering my back, though." By the tone of her voice, she sounded reluctantly impressed. "You really do know how to read a battle."

I let out a soft laugh as I sank down on a frayed brown couch. The worn piece of furniture creaked as Mordren sat down next to me. Valerie and Theo did the same on the opposite sofa. Staring at the door, the High Elf that was Eilan remained standing until our host had brought a tray full of bowls filled with steaming meat stew and some mugs of water. Only once he had left and closed the door to the common room behind him did Eilan shapeshift back into himself.

Raking a hand through his long black hair, he let out a deep sigh and sank down on the couch next to Valerie. I grabbed a couple of bowls from the tray and handed one to Mordren before drawing up my legs underneath me. For a few minutes, we all just ate in silence.

For the keeper of a more or less deserted guesthouse, the tall elf was a very accomplished cook. Or maybe I was just that hungry. The warm lamb stew tasted of thyme and rosemary, and the meat was perfectly cooked. I scraped the spoon against the bottom of the bowl to gather up the final mouthfuls and closed my eyes as I savored it.

Wood clanked faintly around the room as the others finished their food as well and returned the spoons to the empty bowls. Mordren placed mine and his back on the tray before shifting in his seat so that he sat facing me. On the couch across the low table, Theo and Valerie spoke in quiet voices while Eilan closed his eyes and rested his head against the backrest.

"Are you hurt?" Mordren asked, proving that he knew I had lied the first time.

I flexed the fingers on my left hand. The tingling had stopped and I had regained control of the muscles. My side, on the other hand, still pulsed with pain from where I had hit the loom when I fell through the ceiling.

"A little," I admitted.

Mordren must have seen me wince when I moved because he knew exactly where to look. Reaching out, he pushed up the hem of my shirt and inspected the skin above my hip. An angry red mark bloomed there. Gently, he pressed soft fingers against it. I suppressed another wince.

"Nothing appears to be broken at least," he said.

"I could have told you that." I gave his hand a weak swat and pulled my shirt back down before flashing him a sly smile. "Bossy."

His eyes glittered as he stroked my cheek. "You know you like it."

"Well, I–"

"No," Valerie interrupted in a loud voice. Pushing to her feet, she began pacing back and forth in front of the two couches. "You know what? I don't have time for this anymore. We almost died today. Again. And with the lives we're living, we don't have time to wait for appropriate times and places to say stuff, and I don't care that we have an audience so here we are."

"We can leave if–" Theo began but Valerie just kept talking.

"I am not a subtle person," she declared.

A soft chuckle escaped Eilan's lips as he opened his eyes to look at her. "Really? I hadn't noticed."

"Shut up." Slamming to a halt, she stabbed a finger in his direction and locked eyes with him. "I'm being serious."

Uncertainty blew across Eilan's face. Blinking at her, he sat up straighter. Mordren and I exchanged a glance but said nothing as Valerie continued staring Eilan down.

"I am not a subtle person," she repeated while holding his gaze. "And I thought I was very obvious with my flirting, but apparently not. So I will just tell you plain and simple. I like you. A lot."

Eilan stared at her in stunned silence, his mouth hanging open slightly.

"And I sometimes get the feeling that you like me too," she continued. "But you never do anything about it so I'm just gonna ask you straight out. Are these feelings I have one-sided?"

"No," Eilan answered immediately.

"Then what's the problem?" Valerie threw her arms out in a gesture of bewilderment and exasperation. "If the feelings are mutual, why do you never do anything about it?"

"Because you're human."

Valerie rocked back as if he had slapped her. I frowned at Eilan in confusion, but his eyes were locked on Valerie's. The couch groaned as he pushed himself to his feet and stalked forward until he was standing right in front of her.

"I haven't done anything about it because you're human and I'm an elf," he repeated.

Anger pushed out the hurt on Valerie's face and she gave his chest a shove. "What the hell does that have to do with anything? I'm not good enough, is that it? I'm just a poor little human, huh?"

She kept trying to shove him backwards, but with the difference in height and strength, it did nothing to actually make him back away. Theo shot to his feet, which made Mordren do the same. I stood up as well while Mordren held out an arm to block Theo's path. When I furrowed my brows in silent question, Mordren only shook his head as if telling me to wait.

"You're going to die in about sixty years," Eilan snapped back, his voice rising.

"So?" She raised her hands to shove him again.

"You only have that short time, while I'm going to live for a very long time. Why would you want to waste those short precious years you have on me?" Eilan caught her by the wrists, trapping her in place, as he locked serious eyes on her. A disbelieving laugh ripped from his lips as he shook his head. "How could you ever believe that *I* would think *you* are not good enough? *I* am the one who is not good enough for *you* to waste your life on."

Stunned silence fell across the cozy common room. For a moment, the only things that moved were the flames from the fluttering candles on the tables. Mordren lowered his arm, but Theo didn't try to approach Valerie and Eilan anymore. I stared at the two of them. When it became apparent that

Valerie was no longer planning on shoving Eilan back, he released her wrists and let his arms drop back by his sides.

"What?" Valerie finally pressed out. Confusion danced across her face as she studied him. "What are you saying? Are you saying that you actually do want to be with me?"

"Of course I do." Raw emotions bled into Eilan's voice as he looked at her. "I have never met anyone like you. Someone who laughs easily, loves freely, and just shrugs off problems with a mischievous wink. Every time you walk into a room, my heart does this ridiculous little backflip. I can't stop listening to you. Staring at you. It's as if the sun itself just walked through the door and commanded all the presence in the room."

Valerie's mouth had dropped open and she just looked up at him, speechless for what had to be one of the first times in her entire life.

"I kept my walls up, as I always do, but you didn't sneak into my life to stealthily chip away at them." He laughed and shook his head. "You swaggered in and began blowing them up with bombs. And all I've wanted to do since I realized that you were actually serious with your ridiculously blunt flirting is to push you up against a wall and shut you up by kissing you senseless."

"So why don't you?" she finally blurted out.

"Because I would only complicate your life. I will stay the same while you grow older and–"

"Will you stop liking me when I'm old and gray?" Valerie interrupted.

"No. Never."

"Then I don't understand the problem. Yes, we might only have sixty years together. But so what? Yes, it might only be a short time for you, and you will have to move on once I'm dead, but I don't care because we will still have had sixty fucking awesome years together. I will have had a damn good life because you were in it. I don't understand at all how you could think that being with you could somehow make my life worse."

"Because you don't even know me." Desperation crept into Eilan's voice. "I'm so many people and you haven't even met a fraction of them all yet."

"I like this version. The kind gentleman." Valerie drew her finger up Eilan's chest. A sly smile spread across her lips as she cocked her head. "And I like the ruthless authoritative High Elf version too, and that arrogant the Void that Kenna told me about."

Eilan stuttered out something incoherent.

She laughed and let her hand drop. Holding his gaze, she flashed him a wide grin and shook her head. "Don't you get it? I like all versions of you. And the ones I don't know yet, I look forward to meeting eventually." She spread her arms. "Do I really look like someone who wants a dull life with a boring and predictable man? I like you *because* you are mysterious and complicated and kind and ruthless and gentle and possessive and everything all at once. And I can't imagine anything better than to spend an entire lifetime exploring all versions of you."

His pale green eyes sparkled with emotion. Then he closed the distance between them and pulled her towards him. Their lips met in a kiss so passionate that it had both me and Theo letting out a little cheer. With a firm hand on the back of Valerie's neck, Eilan backed her up against the wall while continuing to kiss her senseless. Her hands raked over his lean muscled back before she grabbed the front of his shirt and pulled him harder against her.

Pressing a hand over my mouth, I tried to hide the wide smile that had slid across my lips.

Hope for a future. A bright future. It really was a wonderful thing to behold.

And given what we were about to do, we would need all the hope we could get.

CHAPTER 31

"Remember to put it where it can be seen, but not directly in the center."

Turning, I arched an eyebrow at Valerie. "I know how to plant fake documents. I'm a spy, remember?"

"Right." A wicked grin spread across her face. "I must have just forgotten since you needed so much help getting up on this roof."

I swatted at her arm with the back of my hand, but she dodged it easily and instead flashed me another satisfied grin.

Morning winds blew across the roof of High Commander Anron's home inside the Palace of the Never Setting Sun. We needed to set up another couple of traps before we could move into the final phase of our scheme, and one of them involved a fake report in Anron's office. I studied the area around us while we waited for Theo to climb back up.

All ten High Commanders had a house inside the palace grounds. They were identical and arranged in a circle, but the name of the person living there was engraved on a golden plaque next to the wall, which was how we had been able to find the right building. The bright morning sun glinted off the mirror-like surfaces that made up the walls and houses all around us. It was like standing in the middle of a sunrise.

"We're good to go," came a whisper from down the side of the building. A moment later, Theo nimbly climbed up over the edge and straightened on the roof next to me and Valerie. "Anron, Lester, and Danser are all downstairs."

"Alright." I nodded. "Keep an eye on the street."

Both thieves nodded as well.

Moving over to the edge of the roof, I sat down and then carefully twisted around. With a firm grip on the edge, I lowered myself to the windowsill below while keeping my eyes on the window right in front of me. I still wasn't a fan of climbing around the side of buildings, but dropping down from the ceiling would have made too much noise and I couldn't take the stairs since there were three High Commanders sitting downstairs.

My heart lurched with a flash of panic as I let go of the roof and only balanced on the windowsill. Resisting the morbid urge to look down, I instead stepped right through the window and into High Commander Anron's study.

It looked just like I had imagined it would. Bookshelves lined the room. A grand desk and chair were positioned at the back wall, facing the door, so that the person sitting there could see everyone walking in. Almost as if it were a throne. Most of the floor space between the desk and the door was taken up by a large round table that held small figures to represent armies and soldiers. And the entire room was of course neat and organized.

Muffled voices came from below where Anron, Lester, and Danser were most likely discussing the events of last night. I snuck forward silently as I approached Anron's desk. There was a stack of reports on the left side. It was impossible to tell if he had read them already or not, but I hoped that if he had, he would at least sort through them one last time before putting them away. Planting documents was a lot easier if the room was less neat, but I had done this enough to know how to make it work anyway.

After placing our fake document in the pile in a way that would make it look like it had just stuck to the paper above it, just in case he had already gone through the stack, I made sure that the desk looked exactly as it had when I arrived. Right when I was finished, the front door banged open downstairs.

Chairs scraped against the floor as Anron, Lester, and Danser no doubt shot up from their seats. A flash of alarm went through me at the sound, but I shoved it down and instead snuck towards the door that would take me into the corridor. Walking straight through it, I found myself in a glittering hallway that led to the open staircase.

"Anron," said a voice that I now knew very well.

While I edged forward so that I could peer down at the entrance hall just inside the door, three other High Elves arrived from the other side.

"Empress Elswyth," High Commander Anron said in a, given the situation, surprisingly calm and steady voice. "We did not expect to see you this early."

Anron, along with Lester and Danser, stood facing a straight-backed Empress Elswyth. Since no one could see her face, her body language was the only indicator of her mood. And based on the straightness of her spine and the rigid set of her shoulders, she looked furious. Not to mention that the lightning along her arms was more out of control than it had been during my own encounters with the empress.

"Lester and Danser," Empress Elswyth said while the three High Commanders bowed. "You are here as well. Excellent. That saves me the trouble of hunting you down."

"Your Imperial Majesty," the two of them mumbled as they all straightened.

"I have been informed that you attacked the traitors' safe house last night but that you were unsuccessful in capturing them." The black veil rippled as she cocked her head. "But that can simply not be true."

Danser and Lester glanced towards Anron, who kept his eyes on the empress. A malicious smile spread across my lips. Staying pressed to the wall upstairs, I studied the almost imperceptible hints of panic displayed by Lester and Danser. Only Anron remained cool and unaffected.

"I'm afraid it is true," he said, sounding entirely unapologetic.

Lightning leaped from the empress and zapped the gold-shimmering floor. "How is it that three High Commanders can be outsmarted by a bunch of foreign Low Elves?" Her voice was low and vicious like a snake. "You have access to the Great Current, and yet you cannot apprehend some lowlifes with a few stolen powers. You are a *disgrace* to your race and your ranks."

"Because their magic is so specialized," High Commander Lester blurted out while spreading his arms. "They don't have the range of elemental magic that we do, but they have these strange specialized powers that we have never encountered before. That shadow prince, he can inflict pain without touching people. And when he's hiding in a cloud of shadows, I can't even counter the pain magic thing because I can't see him!"

"I am not interested in your excuses. I want results."

Anron shot Lester a warning look before returning his attention to the empress. "Please do not worry, Your Imperial Majesty. I dealt with Mordren Darkbringer and Kenna Firesoul back in their courts, and they are slippery like White Water eels, but I will find them and deliver them to you."

Suppressing a chuckle, I decided to take that insult as a compliment instead.

"You'd better." She turned her head as if looking from face to face. "Because the way things stand now, I am beginning to wonder if your failure to capture them is deliberate."

"I can assure you that it is not."

"I hope so. For your sakes."

A rogue lightning bolt leaped from her arm and struck Lester's shin. His knee buckled and he had to grab Anron's forearm to steady himself. Fear and anger blew across his face while he looked down, but when he straightened again, it was gone. Danser watched him intently, but none of the High Commanders dared to say anything.

"This is your last chance," Empress Elswyth said in a voice dripping with threats. "One more mistake, one more hint that you are failing in your duties, and I will personally hand you over to my husband." Her face was turned to Lester, as if to show that she knew that he feared Emperor Lanseyo the most. "Then I will watch while he shows you exactly what he does to incompetent commanders and traitors to our realm. And only once you are begging him for death will I step in and make you a part of my statue garden. Am I making myself clear?"

Anron clenched his jaw in rage. On his left and right, Lester and Danser looked more worried than angry. However, all three of them only bowed deeply while answering, "Yes, Empress Elswyth."

"We will speak more about this later." She whirled around, her black and silver dress rustling against the shining floor, before she strode back towards the front door. "Do not fail me again."

The front door shut with an ominous bang as the Empress of Valdanar disappeared back outside. I stayed up on the landing, grinning from ear to ear.

"Anron," High Commander Danser said in a voice full of quiet warning. "She knows."

"She doesn't know," he snapped back.

"Didn't you hear her? She said 'traitors to our realm'. What else would that mean?"

"If she knew, we would not be standing here."

"He has a point," Lester added while looking at Anron. "But so does Danser. This plan of yours is getting dangerous, Anron."

"It has always been dangerous," he countered.

"Yes, but ever since you allowed your captain and those Low Elves to get here, to our lands, things have started spinning out of control." A shiver passed through Lester's body as he drew a hand through his long blond hair. "And I will not be dragged in front of Emperor Lanseyo as a traitor."

"Nor will I," Danser agreed.

"Pull yourselves together," Anron snapped. His sharp blue eyes seared into his two co-conspirators as he stared them down. "We will not lose. The Low Elves got lucky last night because we had to divide our forces and chase them through the city. All we need to do is corner them with overwhelming numbers, and even their pain magic and walking through walls trick won't be able to save them from the sheer power we can channel through our soldiers."

"We still need to be careful," Danser cautioned, his dark

eyes holding Anron's gaze. "The empress suspects something now. Once we have the shadow prince and the fire lady, and we've made them tell us where the other princes are hiding on their island, we need to re-evaluate our plan."

"I agree," Lester said.

A calculating smile spread across Anron's mouth. "I already have. Once we finish things here, we will go back to their island not only to find the other princes, but also to find something else that I'm almost certain they have been lying about. Their magic."

My stomach dropped. *Shit*. Did he know that we had lied about there only being one source of magic for each court?

"What does that mean?" Danser asked.

"I will tell you when the time is right. For now, let's find a way to end this." He motioned towards the stairs. "I have received some reports from our night scouts. Let's see if we can't find these Low Elves before the day is over."

As soon as he lifted his arm, I ducked back and silently sprinted towards the door to his study. Footsteps sounded on the stairs behind me, but I was already climbing up onto the windowsill. After phasing through the window, I straightened and held up my arms.

Theo and Valerie grabbed my wrists and swiftly pulled me back up onto the roof.

I drew in a deep breath of clear morning air.

We had not only planted the fake document, but also further strained Anron's relationships. However, he had somehow figured out that we were lying about our magic.

We had to finish this.

Today.

CHAPTER 32

Nervous anticipation hung over the camp. Even the multitude of strange animals that lived alongside the exiled elves seemed to have gone silent and still as Ellyda unsheathed the sword. A small smile graced her lips as she waved Mendar forward.

After sneaking into High Commander Anron's house earlier that morning, we had returned to Vendir's place to find that Ellyda had finished forging her magical sword. It was time to fulfill our promise to the elves of Poisonwood Forest. With the sword secured along with our gear, we had crossed the busy city and then disappeared into the woods where we were met by Mendar, Endira, and some of their people. Finally back in their camp, everyone had gathered around to see if the sword actually worked.

Mordren draped a possessive arm over my shoulders while Idra and Hadeon crossed their arms next to us. A proud smile was present on Hadeon's lips as he watched his sister. Theo, who along with Valerie had insisted on coming too, appeared to be watching the firebirds and blood panthers more than the people around him. Eilan chuckled at the stunned look on Theo's face as a firebird soared past above us. The light from the flames in its plumage made the already golden afternoon sunlight even more vibrant. Standing a little to the side, looking slightly awkward, was Captain Vendir.

"He is a Wielder," Endira said, her eyes fixed on the captain. "Are you sure he can be trusted?"

"Yes," Ellyda answered without hesitation. "He helped me make the sword. Now, Mendar, if you please?"

The leader of the Poisonwood elves hesitantly closed the final distance between them. There was a guarded and skeptical look on his face. My heart cracked a little when I saw it. I knew what it was like to be trapped and to hope for freedom, only to have that hope crushed over and over again. Wrapping an arm around Mordren's back, I leaned closer to his solid warmth. He tightened his hold on my shoulders in response.

"Put your foot on the log, please," Ellyda directed. Her hair was tied up in its usual messy bun and her clothes were dusty and rumpled after all the hours of forging and the trip across the forest, but her violet eyes were clear and sharp. "And turn it a little to the side."

Mendar was furiously trying to bank the hope shining in his observant brown eyes as he placed his foot on the log before Ellyda. The rest of his people pressed in closer around us. The ring of elves was so thick that it was barely possible to see any of the wooden buildings around us. A fox with midnight blue fur dusted with silver snuck between a redheaded elf's legs and sat down at the front of the circle. Cocking its head, it watched the scene curiously.

Ellyda lifted the sword. It was a fairly ordinary-looking weapon, apart from the faint red glow that swirled over the steel blade. With practiced hands, she positioned the sword between Mendar's leg and the red anklet around it.

The elves around us drew in a breath.

And then they held it.

Not seeming to notice any of it, Ellyda only studied the sword in her hands for another few seconds. Then she pushed it outwards using both hands.

A sound like shattering glass filled the silent woods.

The red band around Mendar's ankle hit the log and then fell to the grass below in pieces.

No one moved.

Everyone only stared at the black-haired leader and the broken anklet that lay in the grass beneath his raised leg.

Then a raw cry of heartbreaking relief ripped through the warm afternoon air. Pressing a hand over my mouth, I tried to stop myself from gasping. The elves around us let out even more cries of relief and pure joy as they each turned to hug the person next to them.

When Mendar finally looked up from the broken pieces on the grass, he had tears in his eyes. Stepping over the log, he drew Ellyda into a fierce hug. She stiffened and blinked in surprise, but then raised her free hand to awkwardly pat Mendar on the back.

Hadeon chuckled and elbowed Idra in the side. "Told you."

"I never doubted her," she replied.

The usual neutral mask was present on Idra's face, but she couldn't quite hide the raw emotions swirling in her dark eyes. She, more than anyone, knew what it was like when a physical bond of imprisonment was finally severed.

Mendar released Ellyda and stepped back to wave Endira and the rest of his people forward. Shifting on her feet, Ellyda cleared her throat as if to recover from the sudden display of gratitude that she didn't really know how to handle.

As soon as Endira had placed her foot on the log, Ellyda positioned the blade and broke the anklet around it. Another rush of giddy relief blew through the camp. Endira squeezed Ellyda's arm before moving aside to let another elf take her place. The blue and silver fox twitched its ears and trotted after the redheaded elf as she moved to join the line of people queueing up across the grass.

I watched with a smile on my face while Ellyda continued shattering anklet after anklet.

Once every elf in Poisonwood was finally free of their shackling jewelry, they all remained gathered around the cold firepit where we stood, as if they didn't quite know what to do now. Someone had brought out food and drinks, and a few of the elves cheered and laughed with their friends while others just stared up at the golden sky or out towards the ring of tall trees that surrounded the camp. Endira had taken a seat on one of the logs and kept drawing her hands through her long white hair while shaking her head. Next to her, Mendar watched his people with the same look of disbelief on his face.

"What will you do now?" Mordren asked.

The black-haired leader tore his gaze from his people and shifted it to Mordren. "Honestly? I don't know."

"Will you find somewhere else to live or will you stay in the forest?"

"I don't know." Mendar raised a hand to massage his forehead while a look of exhaustion passed over his face. "Even though we're free of the anklets, we still won't be able to settle in town. The empress and emperor would just try to imprison us again. And even if we could, I'm not sure if we'd like to live in a city. Living outdoors, surrounded by nature and animals, has been our life for quite a while now. But at the same time, I don't want to stay here in this forest because this will always be our prison."

The elves around us still cheered and laughed, but silence fell over our small group as Mendar blew out a deep sigh.

"You could come with us when we leave," I said.

Endira's head jerked up. Standing up, she met Mendar's gaze, and for a while they seemed to be engaged in some kind of silent conversation. Mordren and the rest of our group only nodded in support since we had discussed this offer before even going into the forest.

"Where would we live?" Mendar asked carefully as he shifted his attention from Endira to me.

"There is a forest." It was Idra who answered. That carefully constructed mask that revealed nothing was back on her face as she spoke. "No one lives there. And no one has for a very long time. But perhaps it's time for new life to grow there now."

"I… we…" Mendar trailed off. After another glance at Endira, he tried again. "We will need to discuss it with our council."

"Of course," Mordren said. He looked up at the sky above to estimate the time. "It is a big decision and we understand if you need time to discuss it in private. We need to leave as well."

Mendar nodded. "Yes. Right. I will show you the way."

From a couple of steps away, Hadeon blew a low whistle and made a circling motion with his hand. Theo, Valerie, and Eilan, who had drifted away from our small group while Ellyda worked, turned to look at him. Tipping her head back, Valerie let out a groan.

Theo stroked a gentle hand over the firebird's red and

orange flames one last time before nodding goodbye to the elf next to him. While he started towards us, Eilan picked up the pink cloud-like animal that had been sitting on Valerie's shoulder and handed it back to a pair of giggling elves with long golden hair. I wiped a hand over my mouth to hide my smile as Valerie patted it on the head and then reluctantly followed Eilan towards us as well.

Once we had geared up, Mendar led the way back into the forest.

A blood panther fell in beside him as soon as we left the ring of trees behind and started into the woods. Mendar absentmindedly ran a hand over the panther's back while we turned right and followed a path only he could see.

As we walked, the sky turned into a canvas filled with orange and pink streaks. But thankfully, sunset was still some time off. Fresh green leaves rustled in the branches above us, but soon the dark purple moss and brightly colored flowers began dotting the area. Mendar stuck a hand into one of his belt pouches and withdrew a stack of pale blue mushrooms.

"Here," he said as he handed them out to us. "A little extra insurance."

I took one gratefully and popped it in my mouth. The taste of mint spread across my tongue as I chewed.

"You didn't have to keep your promise," Mendar finally said after a long stretch of silence. "Why did you?"

"Because we know what it is like to be trapped," Idra answered, her voice devoid of emotion and her eyes locked on the trees straight ahead.

Hadeon studied her profile for a second before shifting his gaze to Mendar. "And we've dealt with people who take advantage of others' hospitality only to betray them."

"Exactly." Ellyda glanced at her brother before nodding.

"Which is why we would never do that to someone who helped us."

For a few moments, Mendar only swept his gaze over our strange group of nine. At the edge of our procession, Captain Vendir seemed to be doing the same, as if both of them were trying to figure out exactly what we had been through that had made us all like this. A bit damaged. But also honorable in our own way.

In the end, Mendar just nodded in acknowledgement. "Thank you. Truly."

He trailed to a halt. Thick yellow mist spread out before us and hung like a cloud between the tree trunks. I studied the way it swirled even though the wind didn't blow in this part of Poisonwood.

"This is the area I talked about," Mendar said as he motioned towards it. "The flowers in this part of the forest are in full bloom right now so this whole area is thick with pollen. You should be okay for a while since you have eaten the mushrooms, but I don't recommend breathing it in for extended periods of time. It makes you hallucinate wildly and once you come down from the high, your memory will be incredibly patchy." He pointed towards our left. "If you stay to the left of this cloud, you will find your way back out of the forest without having to enter into the pollen."

The blood panther next to him let out a low growl and backed up a few steps as if it didn't want to get too close to the yellow pollen cloud either. I ran a hand over the hilt of my sword and knife.

"I will return to our camp," he continued while turning to face us. "And discuss your offer with my council. Afterwards, we will find you and tell you what we decide to do."

I gave him a small smile. "If we're still alive at that point."

"You will be." His intelligent brown eyes met each of our gazes in turn. "I know you will be."

Even though I wasn't so sure about that myself, I gave him a grateful nod. He returned it before starting back the way we had come. The blood panther stayed. As did the handful of firebirds who had been following us from above.

"Good luck with your scheme," he tossed over his shoulder before disappearing behind a thick sheet of purple hanging moss.

"Thanks!" Valerie called after him.

"We'll need it," Theo added in a quiet voice.

Hadeon looked up at the flaming birds who were almost camouflaged against the fiery sky, before clearing his throat and waving a hand towards the left side of the pollen cloud. "Alrighty then."

We started forward once more. Taking care to stay a safe distance from the hallucinogenic yellow mist, we marched the final stretch towards the edge of the forest. We had put a strain on all of Anron's important relationships. We had planted fake reports. We had freed the elves of Poisonwood Forest. And now, there was just one final push left.

My heart thumped in my chest as the orange and pink sky became visible between the thinning trees ahead. What we were about to do would not only require an enormous amount of skill, but also impeccable timing and no small amount of luck. And I couldn't help the flash of fear that shot up my spine. What if we had gambled wrong?

I flicked a gaze up and down the line of people spreading out on both sides of me. Captain Vendir and Ellyda were walking together on one end while Theo and Valerie made up the other flank. Idra and Hadeon, their gazes constantly moving across the forest, stalked forward on my left. On my right, Mordren and Eilan prowled. I swallowed the dread rising in my throat. I suddenly had a bad feeling about all of this.

What if it didn't work?

It had to work.

It had to.

The tall trees around us thinned out. Golden light from the afternoon sun painted the grass with gilded hues. I drew in a calming breath as we at last cleared the forest and stepped out into the grasslands that separated the city from Poisonwood.

My heart lurched.

Screeching to a halt just outside the tree line, all nine of us stared out at the fields before us.

An army of bronze clad soldiers stared back. At the very front were five people. High Commanders Anron, Lester, and Danser flanked two figures covered in magic. Empress Elswyth, in a black dress to match her veil and lightning crackling down her arms, stood next to Emperor Lanseyo. The sun emblazoned on his breastplate gleamed in the firelight from the flames that rippled down his rich blue cloak and flickered along the length of his hair.

Blood pounded in my ears.

Working my tongue around my parched mouth, I swallowed. Magic hummed in the air. A ripple went through our group as everyone subtly shifted position. The High Elf soldiers drew their gigantic bows in response. The sight of those weapons, along with the primal fear that the High Elves' magic still caused, made my heart race even faster in my chest.

There were so many of them.

Too many.

CHAPTER 33

Only the swaying grass moved in the breeze while the High Elf army stared us down. I edged a step forward. Bows creaked in response as the soldiers drew their arrows farther back. The three High Commanders raised their right hands and pointed them straight at us. Water swirled around Danser's forearm while air spun around Lester's. White bolts of lightning crackled up and down Anron's arm.

"You're getting careless," Anron said. "After days of successfully sneaking through the city, you got too bold and our scouts saw you head into Poisonwood Forest."

"Or maybe we just wanted you here," I called back in challenge to buy some time. Lowering my voice, I spoke to Captain Vendir while keeping my eyes on the mass of soldiers ahead. "How many of them can you channel magic through?"

"Only the ones from my own Flying Legion," Vendir replied, "and only from the ones who haven't forsaken their oath of loyalty to me."

"More false bravado," High Commander Anron answered

to my challenge. "Just what I expected from you, Kenna. But there are no walls or floors to escape through this time."

"Aren't there?" I called to Anron before lowering my voice and asking Vendir, "And how many is that?"

"Not enough," Vendir said softly.

Emperor Lanseyo slashed a hand through the air. "Enough. You are outnumbered, outmatched, and cut off from the city. A true leader knows when it is time to surrender, and that time is now."

"Do what you can," I said to Vendir. "The rest of you…"

"Wild goose chase," Theo said as he moved closer to Valerie.

"Get down on your knees," Emperor Lanseyo continued in a booming voice that pulsed with authority. "And surrender."

"El," Hadeon said, and cast a quick glance at his sister. "Vendir will keep you safe. I'll see you afterwards."

"Now!" the Emperor of Valdanar bellowed.

"Kenna." Idra's voice was tense. "Now would be the time."

Worry shot through my body. I had no idea if this would work, if it would be enough, but all our lives depended on it. With my heart slamming against my ribs, I took another step forward and spread my arms wide.

A smug smirk slid across Anron's mouth.

I drew in a deep breath. "Run."

Fire exploded from me.

Dark red flames rose in a tidal wave as tall as the trees behind us and swept across the field towards the High Elves on the other side. Shouts rang out and magic flashed through the air to counter it, but I didn't stay to watch. As soon as the wall of fire shot towards Anron and his army, I turned and ran after my friends.

Through the fear in my chest, a sense of awe and wicked

satisfaction bloomed. The attack had been a lot more powerful than I had expected. I grinned as I darted back into the trees while floods of water slammed into my fire wall and sent it exploding into steam. I had definitely made the right choice.

During our failed attempt to steal magic from the White Tower, I had passed by the wide bowl of fire, and the magic there had reached towards me as if it recognized the magic in my blood and wanted it back. I had no intention of giving it back. Quite the opposite. Since I already possessed fire magic that had come directly from that source, I figured that I might as well take some more. Just in case. So I had drunk from that bowl. The extra magic had made my control slip, which was why I had barely used my fire magic when we were inside the city. But out here? The raw power had come in handy indeed.

Angry hissing ripped through the air as the High Elves neutralized my flaming attack with water, and a thick cloud of white mist momentarily covered our escape before it dissipated. Theo and Valerie split away from the group and sprinted to the right. Up ahead, Vendir and Ellyda were already disappearing through the trees. I was just about to open my mouth to call out instructions to the rest of my friends when roaring winds cut through the forest.

I sucked in a gasp as the gust of wind barreled straight into me and flung me off my feet. Mordren, Eilan, Hadeon, and Idra flew through the air in different directions while I spun over and over before slamming into a tree trunk farther in. Pain pulsed through my shoulder blades. Pushing myself off the ground, I whipped my head from side to side to see where the others had landed, but all I could see was a mass of bronze-clad soldiers swarming towards me. At the front was the Emperor and Empress of Valdanar.

Yanking out my knife, I slashed it through the air and sent a scythe of fire straight towards Empress Elswyth. She shoved it aside with a flick of her wrist and a concentrated burst of water. I sent another one. While she deflected that one as well, I whirled around and sprinted away.

"You insolent little girl," she snapped behind me, her voice cutting through the clamor in the forest.

"Elswyth," Emperor Lanseyo said.

"I have her," she replied. "Get the shadow prince."

"You and you, with me," the emperor called. "The rest of you, find the others!"

My head spun and dull pain pulsed through my shoulder blades with every step but I darted deeper into the forest. Magic hummed behind me. On instinct, I threw myself behind a thick tree trunk. A moment later, lightning cracked into the tree. Purple moss rained down around me and the whole tree shook with the force. I pushed off from it and ran.

Screams split the air somewhere to my left. Terror welled up inside me as I tried to identify if they belonged to any of us. Hopefully, it was only soldiers who had met the full force of Mordren's pain magic.

I veered left.

Bronze armor flashed between the trees. *Shit.* Screeching to a halt, I swung myself around and continued sprinting forwards instead. The soldiers were spreading out. If this kept up, they would have me surrounded. While running, I slashed my knife through the air.

A scythe of flames much wider than my usual ones shot forward and sped towards the High Elves. Shouts of alarm rang out as some of them ducked while someone else threw up a shield of water. Lightning crackled through the air. I dove forward right as another bolt cleaved the air where I had been only moments before.

Rolling across the roots and stones, I barely managed to get behind a moss-covered boulder before the entire forest was lit up by a storm of white lightning bolts. Squeezing my eyes shut, I tried to stop it from blinding me. The crack as it hit trees and boulders around me drowned out the blood pounding in my ears. The empress was mad now.

When the light died down, I leaped up and slashed my knife through the air to regain some of the distance I had lost. Water washed through the forest and turned it into steam. I dared a quick glance over my shoulder as I sprinted towards my left.

Soldiers were closing in on all sides and the empress had almost reached me. She wasn't running. As if such an activity was beneath her. Instead, she strode through the forest in her black dress and veil like death incarnate. Lightning clung to her arms. And then it shot towards me again.

I zigzagged between the gnarled tree trunks to avoid being struck by her attacks. Panic screamed inside me as the bronze-clad soldiers drew in closer and closer. I sent another few fire attacks, but the empress neutralized them all regardless of which direction I sent them in. And all the while she continued shooting lightning at me.

My throat burned with every breath as I hurtled through the trees, trying to get out of the ever-closing ring of soldiers before it was too late. Chips of wood rained down around me as lightning bolts cracked into the trees. I grabbed a trunk and swung myself around it to change direction.

A gust of wind smacked right into me. Green and brown and purple and yellow bled into a messy canvas in my vision as I spun through the air at breakneck speed. Dread spread through my chest. This landing was going to break some of my bones.

Something colorful flashed amid the other already spinning hues and yanked at my clothes. Instead of breaking my bones while colliding with a boulder, my momentum was halted somewhat and I crashed down onto the grass. My breath exploded from my lungs and pain shot through my hip, but it wasn't nearly as bad as it should have been and I even managed to keep the grip on my knife.

Struggling to my knees, I took in the area around me.

I was in a depression. Almost like a large bowl with sides made of dirt and grass. The ground sloped upwards all around me until it leveled out and the trees began again. Where I was, there were no trees or boulders. No cover. And High Elf soldiers stood in a ring around the edges with their bows drawn. Lightning crackled above the ridge, informing me that the empress was quickly closing in as well.

Hopelessness washed over me. There was no way to get out without being shot full of arrows.

"She's here," one of the soldiers called over his shoulder to what I presumed was the empress.

My chest heaved. Desperation flashed through my body. *Damn it all*. I would just have to make a break for it and hope for the best. Shifting my weight, I got ready to jump to my feet and send a fire magic attack towards one side while I ran up the slope.

"Don't," one of the soldiers warned as if he had read my move.

Shit. This was going to hurt.

I leaped to my feet.

Screams ripped through the afternoon air and echoed between the trees as a mass of something red and black shot through the woods. I stared in stunned disbelief as a pack of blood panthers pounced on the unsuspecting High Elves from behind. Sharp claws and lethal teeth cut deep ruts into their bronze armor. Panicked chaos spread out around me as the soldiers tried to reorganize themselves and face the new threat while another swarm of animals sped out of the woods.

Flat except for the green spikes on their backs, the four-legged animals thundered out of the trees and snapped giant maws at the High Elves while four blue eyes tracked them. A screech cut the air as three firebirds swooped down from the canopy and distracted the soldiers from the threats on the ground. Fear and panic rippled through the clearing.

Not hesitating a second, I sprinted up the grassy slope and leaped over one of the four-eyed animals, dodged a couple of blood panthers, and hurtled away while sending a silent but heartfelt thank you to the animals of Poisonwood for helping me out. Or maybe they just hated the High Elf soldiers so much because of what they had done to the elves who were forced to live in the woods. Either way, I was grateful. And I sent an extra thank you to the firebird who had broken my bone-shattering flight by grabbing me in the air and redirecting my path.

"Left!" someone screamed behind me. "She's running left!"

Another lightning storm lit up the forest. The animals behind me disappeared into their hiding places while I took cover behind a tree that was thick with purple hanging moss. When the light died down, the sound of thumping boots started up behind me. Pushing away from the tree, I took off again.

At least I had broken their ring and they were all behind me now.

However, their longer legs and insane physique had them

closing the distance at an alarming rate. With my heart pounding in my chest, I leaped over roots and dodged the lightning strikes that cracked into the trees behind me.

Suddenly, a thick yellow mist became visible before me. There was so much of it that it stretched out all the way on both my left and right. And it came closer with every step.

I knew exactly what it was.

The cloud of hallucinogenic pollen.

CHAPTER 34

The thick cloud of pollen drew closer with each step. Behind me, the soldiers were closing in. Lightning crackled through the air.

"She's heading into the cloud!" someone screamed from somewhere to my left. "Those two warriors and that other black-haired elf also ran into that yellow cloud earlier."

So Idra, Hadeon, and Eilan were already in there as well. Sucking in one final deep breath, I leaped into the mist.

The colorful forest around me was immediately replaced by a thick yellow haze. I continued running straight ahead until I was sure that I was a safe distance inside. Then I stopped. Turning around, I only stared back the way I had come. I had no idea how far the cloud stretched on the other sides, so I had to leave the same way I had come.

"Box them in," the same voice screamed. "Empress Elswyth, she ran right in there. Do you want us to follow you or spread out through the cloud?"

"Spread out," the empress said. "If more of them are here, I want them surrounded from all sides."

My heart slammed against my ribs but I forced myself to remain standing completely still, staring into the thick yellow mist before me. From somewhere to my right, there was a clashing of swords. If Hadeon was in here, it was probably him. I drew my sword as well.

I had to make them come into the cloud before I could slip past them and get out unseen. But I might have to fight my way through.

Winds whooshed through the forest.

"Stop," Empress Elswyth snapped. "Whoever is using air magic, stop immediately. You are only making the cloud bigger."

Cocking my head, I listened to the sound of boots against the ground. They were spreading out as if in a long line. Smart. They had probably guessed what my plan had been. I continued drawing shallow breaths.

Mendar had said not to breathe it in for extended periods of time. Now I desperately wished that I had asked him to clarify what exactly constituted an extended period of time.

The soft thumping of feet drew closer.

A soldier in bronze armor appeared a few strides before me.

I drew in a sharp breath between my teeth. He seemed as surprised to see me as I was to see him, because he blinked for a second as if to make sure I was really there. Using that second, I sprang forward and swung my sword at him.

He yanked up his own blade to block it. Metallic clanging filled the air as our swords collided. I knew I would lose against his superior strength so I immediately disconnected our blades and jumped back out of reach from his counterattack.

"She's here!" he yelled.

"Fuck," I swore.

Thudding feet sounded on both sides as the soldiers hurried towards us.

The soldier lunged at me. Making a split-second decision, I sidestepped while sliding my sword back in its sheath and instead grabbed his outstretched wrist. Fire bloomed in my palm.

A scream ripped from my attacker's throat as the searing flames burned through his armor and melted it all the way to the bone. Surprise flitted through me. My magic really was incredibly powerful now.

The High Elf's sword fell from his hand as he tried to yank his arm back. I released it and used my other hand to slash his carotid artery while he stared in shock at his ruined wrist. He toppled backwards.

I ran.

Boots thudded all around me as the other soldiers closed in. Hoping that the distraction would be enough, I darted back towards the edge of the cloud. It was much farther than I remembered. Or maybe the wind had blown the border that wide.

"Where is she?" someone snapped from where I had fought the soldier only seconds ago.

The thick yellow mist hid the forest around me except for a few strides in every direction. I kept running.

"What's that?"

"What's what?"

"That." Terrified screams accompanied it. "There's something else in here."

"Empress Elswyth, why are you taking your clothes off?"

"How dare you?" the empress snapped back. "I would never undress among you. Soldier, why do you have a knife?"

"I don't have a knife!"

"Of course you do. I can see it clearly in your right hand. It is glowing bright blue."

"My hand is blue?"

"Empress! Why are there two of you?"

"My hair is on fire!"

"No, it's my eyes."

"Something's wrong."

"Where's the girl?"

"Where's the forest?"

"Where are my feet?"

Something hard crashed into me from the side. I was thrown off my feet and crashed down on the ground in a tangle of limbs as a High Elf soldier collided with me. His brown eyes were wide and panicked. The hallucinogenic pollen must be kicking in hard.

He whipped his head around as if looking for something before his gaze zeroed in on me below him. Recognition flashed across his face. Struggling for control, he rolled to the side and yanked his arm out from underneath me while pinning my own arm with his knee. I drove my leg upwards to force him off.

His eyes flashed and he winced as my knee connected with his groin, but he managed to stay in place above me. Then he blinked as if having trouble keeping focus.

My knife was useless in my pinned hand and my sword was sheathed across my back so I closed my fist and swung my free hand at his temple instead. He grabbed my wrist right before the blow landed.

While straddling my hips and keeping me trapped below him, he forced my arm towards the ground. My muscles shook as I tried to stop him but he was far stronger than me.

A spike of fear flashed through me. My hand slammed into the ground at the same time as he used his free one to pull out a knife of his own. Desperately struggling underneath his weight, I tried to get away. His grip on my wrist tightened until I had to bite back a scream.

Blinking, he tried to get his eyes to focus again while bringing the knife down towards my throat.

I thrashed in his grip.

This could not be happening. I was so close. So close.

His head snapped to the side.

With quick jerky movements, he scrambled off me and shot to his feet while holding out the knife in front of him. "No. How did you get here?"

Surprise crackled through me as I stared at the empty yellow mist next to us, but I wasn't about to let this opportunity go to waste. While the soldier continued bargaining with someone who wasn't really there, I struggled to my feet. And then I ran.

Dull pain pulsed from where he had grabbed my wrist, but I ignored it as I rammed the knife back in its sheath and sprinted the final distance to the edge of the pollen cloud.

Clear air rushed into my lungs as I broke through. Since I wasn't sure what was on the other side, I immediately dove for cover behind a gnarled tree trunk. Rolling to my feet, I got ready to run.

A hand around my throat slammed me back into the tree while another hand was pressed over my mouth to stop my scream. I struggled against it for a second before the shadows behind the tree lightened. Glittering silver eyes stared down at me.

The panic drained from my body and I slumped back against the tree trunk. Mordren slowly released me.

"Are you okay?" he breathed into my ear.

I nodded. "You?"

He replicated the gesture.

Before I could say anything else, a figure stumbled out of the thick yellow mist. Empress Elswyth, with one hand over her veil to further cover her mouth and nose, staggered out into the forest and collapsed against the closest tree. The lightning along her arms flickered erratically. Bending over, she coughed and wheezed several times before recovering enough to move a few more strides away from the cloud of pollen.

"To me!" she screamed, and then coughed again.

A few moments later, a small group of soldiers came running through the trees.

"Empress Els–"

"Do not go in there," she cut off before he could finish. "There is something in the air that makes people lose their minds. Get my husband and the High Commanders."

"But they're chasing–"

"Now!" Lightning shot from her arms and zapped the ground between her and the soldiers.

They hurried away to obey her orders.

Mordren shifted his gaze from the empress to me. I nodded. While continuing to scan the area for soldiers, we snuck from tree to tree until we had an empty clearing behind us and the yellow cloud a short distance on our right. Screams and clanking metal and muffled orders still came from inside. I swore two of the voices snapping orders belonged to Hadeon and Idra.

The soft cracking of twigs and thumping of boots came from our left. Mordren's arm shot out to block my way. Placing a palm against my chest, he pushed me back against the tree we had been about to leave. I twisted around so that I could see the people who were about to arrive while Mordren layered a thin haze of shadows around us.

A moment later, Emperor Lanseyo, High Commanders Anron, Lester, and Danser came striding through the trees.

CHAPTER 35

Fire licked the air as Emperor Lanseyo stalked towards his wife with his flaming cloak billowing behind him. Rage flashed in his eyes. The three High Commanders walking behind him couldn't quite hide the uneasiness on their faces.

"Are you unharmed?" the emperor said as he came to a halt before Empress Elswyth.

"Yes," she replied. "The veil protected me from the worst of it, but that yellow cloud is filled with something dangerous."

He nodded in acknowledgement. "Where are the rest of our soldiers?"

"They are stumbling around inside that hallucinogenic mist."

"All of them?"

She flicked a hand towards the five who had gone to retrieve the emperor for her. "All except those. And the ones with you, of course."

"There are no soldiers with us."

"Excuse me?"

Emperor Lanseyo shot a scathing look at Anron. "He said that you were in danger and that you needed more soldiers."

"Yes," Anron immediately said, a defiant tilt to his chin. "A soldier came running to say that Empress Elswyth had disappeared and that he heard screaming but couldn't find you so he needed everyone else to come and help look for you and protect you. So naturally, I sent them to do just that."

"What about everyone else?" the empress demanded.

Lester and Danser exchanged an uncertain look.

"Those two warriors lured most of my soldiers into the mist as well," Danser replied carefully. "When I heard the screaming, I realized that something was wrong so I didn't pursue them. Then I thought I caught a glimpse of Vendir, so I followed him until I ran into Lester."

Lester grimaced and crossed his arms. "Yeah. The two humans did much the same as those two warrior types. Or I think so. They're so tiny that they're hard to see."

"I am not interested in your excuses." Empress Elswyth's voice was dripping with cold threats. "Do you honestly mean to tell me that practically every soldier we brought is trapped inside that yellow cloud?"

Danser and Lester exchanged another uncertain glance. The scowl on Emperor Lanseyo's brow deepened as he stared them down until they finally nodded. Anron kept his chin up and his shoulders squared.

"And you?" Empress Elswyth continued in that same cold voice as her gaze locked on Anron. "You are supposed to be a High Commander. How could you let this happen?"

"I was pursuing Mordren Darkbringer with Emperor Lanseyo," Anron said through clenched teeth. "He was heading in this direction and we almost had him, but we had to stop our hunt when we were told to come here instead."

A sly smile spread across Mordren's lips. I glanced up at him before returning my attention to the scene ahead. Purple moss hung like thick sheets from the branches. The sky had turned from orange and pink to red and purple. Sunset was close now.

"Enough," the empress snapped. Turning, she stood so that she faced Anron head on. "I have had enough of your insubordination. You have been second-guessing my every decision for days now."

Anron drew himself up to his full height. "I have not been second-guessing anything. I have been offering my opinion on important matters."

"Why would you presume to do such a thing?"

"Because you asked for my advice!"

"I do not need advice from the likes of you." The lightning along her arms crackled even more out of control. "I am the Empress of Valdanar. *I* make the decisions. *I* give the orders. *You* obey."

Something snapped in Anron's usually so cool blue eyes. "Yes, you are the Empress of Valdanar. But I am a High Commander. If you ask for my advice, I am going to give it. So with all due respect, Your Imperial Majesty, stop summoning me to ask for my opinion on something only to later act as if I am offending you by responding to your own inquiries."

Tension crackled through the air.

"You made me grovel for forgiveness after I offered you advice on what to do with the magicless island," Anron continued. "Even though *you* had asked for my opinion on the matter."

"Tread very carefully, High Commander." Threats dripped from her words with enough malice to make Lester and

Danser edge a step back. "I do not need your help." She cocked her head. "Perhaps that rumor was true that you had questioned my ability to rule."

Flames spread from Emperor Lanseyo's cloak to cover his whole suit of armor. Turning with deliberate slowness, he fixed Anron with a lethal stare. "You did what now?"

Lester and Danser shrank back another step, but Anron stood his ground.

"I did no such thing," he replied, his chin raised.

The Emperor of Valdanar grabbed the edge of Anron's breastplate and yanked him forward. Leaning down, he growled in the High Commander's face, "Watch that tone."

Anron held his gaze for another few seconds before dropping his eyes and lowering his chin in submission.

"My apologies, Emperor Lanseyo. Empress Elswyth." He kept his eyes downcast and his voice soft. "I meant no disrespect. I'm afraid that I am simply... frustrated with this situation with these foreign Low Elves."

The emperor stared him down for another moment before releasing his armor. Anron took a step back. Even though he kept his chin lowered, I could see how tightly he was clenching his jaw. Submitting like this infuriated him.

A wicked grin spread across my lips.

Next to me, Mordren nudged my side and then motioned behind us. I nodded. After casting one last glance at the empress, who was still facing Anron, I edged a step backwards.

Then another.

And another.

Side by side, Mordren and I snuck backwards towards the empty glen behind us. With every step, the sound of the High Commanders voices grew fainter. They appeared to be discussing how to best get us out of that pollen cloud without suffering the effects themselves. Little did they know that we were already out.

Once we reached the clearing, we turned and quickly scanned the area. It was empty. Moving with confident steps, we strode across the grass and took up position at the back of it. Twisted trees full of purple hanging moss formed a barrier on our left, as well as behind and in front of us. To our right, the thick yellow cloud of pollen created another boundary. I tipped my head back.

Dark red streaks stretched from the west to cover the sky. We were running out of time. If we were going to do this, it would have to be now.

A gust slammed into the left side of my face. I turned to look towards the tree line but I couldn't see anything between the hulking trunks. After running a hand over the hilt of my weapons, I rolled my shoulders and then raked my fingers through my hair. Next to me, Mordren did the same.

"Tell me this will work," I said.

Mordren glanced down at me. "It will work."

"I almost believed that."

"Me too."

"And if it doesn't?"

"We will be dead, so who cares?"

I huffed out an amused breath. "You're a good liar."

He gave me a small smile. "So are you."

Leaves rustled faintly in the canopy above and a few twigs creaked as a strong afternoon wind swept past above Poisonwood Forest, but the breeze never reached us on the ground. The screaming inside the cloud of pollen had gone silent. Given the amount of time that had passed since our sneaky group of nine had lured the High Elves inside, they had all probably passed out by now. I blew out a calming breath.

This was it.

This was our last chance.

If this didn't work, we would be captured, Anron would take over our island and leave it in Princess Syrene's power-hungry hands, and then he would overthrow the Emperor and Empress of Valdanar. And it all came down to the next few minutes.

Mordren brushed a hand down my arm. "Ready?"

"No." I laughed softly and shook my head. "But let's do this anyway."

As one, we raised our right hands straight up towards the sky. And then we let our magic loose.

Two columns shot towards the clear sky above.

One made of shadows.

And one of flame.

CHAPTER 36

Shouts rang out. Mordren and I spread our arms and kept our hands clearly visible, palms out, to show that we were not planning on attacking. A few moments later, three High Commanders came running into the clearing. They were followed by Emperor Lanseyo and Empress Elswyth. Confusion blew across all of their faces as they saw us standing there.

Magic swirled around the arms of the High Commanders as they pointed them towards us, but they glanced back at their rulers for instructions. Emperor Lanseyo and Empress Elswyth strode forward until they were standing in the middle of the empty glen. Anron, Lester, and Danser moved into position on either side of them. Their boots left faint imprints in the grass as they walked.

"What is the meaning of this?" Emperor Lanseyo demanded.

His flames had retreated from his entire armor and now only covered his rich blue cloak. In the dying light of day, his fire magic helped brighten the otherwise dusky area.

"We only wish to talk," Mordren answered.

"Surrender, and then we can talk."

"No."

Rage darkened Emperor Lanseyo's face. "Choose your next words carefully."

"If you take us back to your palace," I began, still keeping my hands raised, "Anron will make sure that you never hear what we have to say."

"Is this about those absurd allegations against me again?" Anron cut in.

"They're not absurd," I said, my eyes locked on the emperor's. "Please. We only want to talk."

Silence filled the forest for a few seconds. Emperor Lanseyo continued staring me down, as if trying to read the truths and lies on my face. I kept my gaze soft as I looked back at him. They controlled the situation. I knew it. And he knew it.

At last, the empress cocked her head, making her black lace veil ripple. "You are aware that we could kill you at any time?"

"Very."

"And yet, you only stand there."

"Yes."

"Why?"

"Because we are telling the truth." I looked between her and the emperor. "We have been telling the truth all along."

"Enough of this—" Anron began.

Empress Elswyth slashed a hand through the air. "Silence."

Irritation flickered in his blue eyes, but he closed his mouth. Turning back towards me and Mordren, he glared at us as if daring us to say any more. I suppressed the urge to smirk at him. The empress lowered her hand and turned her head in our direction once more.

"Speak," she commanded.

"Anron is trying to steal your throne," I said. "He invaded our lands and put those black bracelets on everyone so that he could siphon enough magic to overthrow you."

"You have already said that," Emperor Lanseyo said. "But what proof do you really have of that?"

"We kidnapped Captain Vendir, locked one of those magic-suppressing bracelets around his wrist, and then tortured him until he agreed to fly us all the way across the world to get here. Why would we go through all that trouble if it wasn't true?"

"You have already used that argument."

"It's the truth."

"Or it is a lie to make us forsake one of our best military leaders because he successfully ended a war you started against our Flying Legions."

"Do you really believe that?"

"You are not presenting us with any other plausible explanations," Empress Elswyth said before the emperor could reply. She flicked a wrist towards Anron, Lester, and Danser. "Are we truly supposed to believe that three of our highly-decorated, and longest serving, High Commanders are secretly plotting to overthrow us?"

A hint of a smirk tugged at Anron's lips as he looked back at us expectantly. Lester and Danser kept their faces carefully blank. I watched the way Emperor Lanseyo's flames cast dancing reflections in their bronze armor for a few seconds.

"No," I finally answered.

"Then why are we wasting time on this?" the emperor snapped.

My heart pounded in my chest but I kept my gaze steady as I looked him straight in the eye. "No, three of your highly-decorated and longest serving High Commanders are not trying to overthrow you." I nodded towards Anron. "But he is."

Anron drew back a fraction and blinked in surprise.

Tearing my gaze from him and the emperor, I instead met the eyes of the other two High Commanders. They looked even more shocked than Anron. A pair of pale eyes and a pair of dark eyes stared back at me in confusion.

"High Commanders Danser and Lester know nothing about this." I nodded towards them. "You can see on their faces even now that they have no idea what I'm talking about. That's because Anron has duped them too."

Wheels began turning behind Lester and Danser's eyes.

"They still believe that you, Emperor Lanseyo and Empress Elswyth, were the ones who approved the use of those black bracelets on us back on the island because we supposedly rebelled," I charged on. "So that all of our power would go to *you*. They have no idea that the bracelets are linked only to Anron."

Thoughts and plans spun frantically behind Lester and Danser's eyes. My heart pounded so hard in my chest that I thought they might hear it. This was a critical point that might sink or sell our whole scheme. We had created situations where the two High Commanders were faced with the empress and emperor's wrath and where they began to believe that their plan was about to be discovered. We had sown fear. Worry. Dissent between them and Anron.

And now we had given them an out.

If they backed up my claims, they would get out of this precarious situation entirely unscathed. But they would have to betray Anron and give up their chance to gain more power from Anron's plot to overthrow Lanseyo and Elswyth. They would have to decide if their fear of the emperor and empress was worth a shot at more power now that their scheme was no longer a complete secret. And they would have to decide right now.

I barely dared breathe.

Looking back at Danser and Lester across the dead silent clearing, I desperately hoped that they would do the right thing. Only two seconds had passed since I had stopped speaking, but it felt like an eternity.

High Commander Anron opened his mouth.

My heart thumped in my chest.

"What is she saying?" High Commander Danser furrowed his dark brows and turned towards the emperor before Anron could get a single word out. "Did you not order the use of the bracelets on all the Low Elves of the island?"

It took all my self-control to stop myself from heaving a deep sigh of relief. Keeping the blank mask on my face, I settled for a soft breath that they couldn't detect from across the grass.

"Of course not," Emperor Lanseyo answered. "Those bracelets were decommissioned ages ago." Suspicion crept into his blue eyes as the rest of Danser's words sank in. The tiny flames in his long blond hair flickered when he turned towards Anron. "All the Low Elves? You are using them on *all* the Low Elves? And you told them that we ordered the use of them?"

"No," Anron protested.

"Yes, you did," Lester said, making his decision as well. "You said that it was to increase their power. Are the bracelets connected to *you*?"

Pure rage flooded Anron's sharp eyes as he stared down his former co-conspirators. "Liars."

"No, it's true."

Everyone whirled around to face the source of the new voice. A High Elf in bronze armor came striding out of the trees on my left. Captain Vendir.

"It's true," he repeated as he came to a halt halfway between the line of twisted trees and the surprised High Elves in the middle. "What Kenna and Mordren are saying is true. As is what High Commanders Danser and Lester are saying."

"If it is true," Emperor Lanseyo began, "then why did you not report it yourself? According to these Low Elves, and your own words in our throne room, they had to force you to take them here."

Captain Vendir kept his chin up but met the emperor's scrutinizing stare with soft eyes. "Because I owed High Commander Anron a life debt. As you know, he saved me from drowning in White Water Bay, and after that I was bound to him. I did not agree with High Commander Anron's plans, but I could not defy him either. Until these Low Elves forced my hand." He raised his chin a little further. "I am a trained captain. I can withstand torture quite well. But in the end, I decided to help them of my own free will. Because once I was free of High Commander Anron's control, I had a chance to expose his treachery and prove my loyalty to you. That is why he turned on me and made up those lies about me."

A frown creased the emperor's pale brows.

"You would believe the words of a turncoat over me?" High Commander Anron said. "A weak boy who tried to drown himself before I found him and turned him into a real High Elf Wielder?"

"I believe him," Empress Elswyth suddenly said, speaking for the first time in a while. "I believe Captain Vendir."

Lanseyo blinked in surprise and turned towards her. "You do?"

"Yes. It always struck me as odd that Vendir would be a traitor to his own people. He has always been loyal to his superiors." The lightning along her arms decreased a little. "His mother used to work for me, if you remember? They are a good family. Loyal."

The emperor drew a hand over his jaw. "That is true, I suppose."

For the first time, a hint of fear flashed across Anron's features. He edged a step towards the tree line.

"You asked what proof we had," I called across the grass. "We have now produced three powerful and loyal witnesses who corroborate what we have been trying to tell you. Anron is plotting to overthrow you using the magic of our people to boost his own."

Fabric rustled and armor creaked as everyone turned to face the accused High Commander. He had managed to take a couple of steps away before their gaze froze him in place.

"High Commander Anron," Emperor Lanseyo said in a voice pulsing with authority. "I hereby command you to stand down and surrender."

A haughty look of indignant rage slid home on Anron's face as he stared back at his emperor, but he raised his arms as if to surrender.

Surprise and worry flashed through me.

Then his mouth stretched into a cold smile.

Air exploded around him.

CHAPTER 37

Due to the very short distance between them, Emperor Lanseyo and the others didn't have time to block the whole attack. Lester and Danser were blasted backwards and tumbled across the grass. The emperor managed to shield best of all and was only pushed back a short distance before he raised a block of stone from the ground to stop the hurricane winds from snatching him up. Empress Elswyth, on the other hand, didn't shield at all and caught the full force of it.

Black fabric fluttered through the air as she flew across the clearing and disappeared right into the thick cloud of pollen.

Mordren and I were hit with the edge of the attack and crashed down on the ground a few strides from where we had been standing. A sharp whistle echoed through the forest. Pushing myself up on my elbows, I whipped my head from side to side and only caught a glimpse of High Commander Anron before a great white air serpent shot down from the sky.

"Elswyth!" the emperor screamed while racing towards the barrier of yellow mist.

The raw emotion in his voice tore at my chest and made me sincerely doubt the rumors that she wore a veil because he had burned her face. Panic had pushed out the rage on his face once he realized that she had been flung into the dangerous cloud, and he barreled towards it with incredible speed.

A wall of shadows shot out.

Wings boomed from my left. As I jumped to my feet next to Mordren, I saw Anron leaping up onto his white air serpent at the same time as Emperor Lanseyo slammed to a halt in front of Mordren's shadow wall. Terrible rage flared in the emperor's eyes as he whirled to attack the Prince of Shadows.

"If you go in without protection, you will lose yourself before you find her," Mordren pressed out right before a lightning bolt took him in the chest.

"I was going to leave your island alone afterwards," Anron bellowed from high above the trees. "But now I will take that as a consolation prize instead. Well done, Kenna. You might have saved our lands but you just doomed your own."

The emperor sent a blast of fire magic that roared over the heavens, but Anron was already speeding across the forest. Mordren was lying on the grass next to me, his body shaking uncontrollably. Dropping to my knees, I placed a hand on his chest. My heart bled.

"What did he mean 'without protection'?" Emperor Lanseyo demanded as he stalked towards us. Flames flickered in his hair and his cloak was more fire than cloth at this point. "Answer."

"He wasn't trying to stop you," I answered, unable to keep

the sharp note from my voice as I looked up at the emperor. "He was trying to help you. That cloud is so thick that you can't see more than a couple of steps in front of you, and it's filled with pollen that causes hallucinations and memory loss. So if you go charging in there right now, you will just be trapped too."

Emperor Lanseyo clenched his jaws. If he hadn't attacked Mordren, he would have received these answers much faster.

"The protection?" he ground out.

"These," said another voice from across the clearing.

We all turned to find Ellyda standing next to Captain Vendir. The captain was still staring in the direction that Anron had escaped, but Ellyda's sharp eyes were locked on the Emperor of Valdanar. Sliding a hand into one of her belt pouches, she withdrew a pile of pale blue mushrooms.

"If you eat one of these, it will make you immune to the effects of the pollen for a while." She held out her hand. "Long enough to find your wife."

Lanseyo narrowed his eyes at her.

Tearing his gaze from the darkening sky, Captain Vendir blew out a sigh and picked up one of the mushrooms. With his eyes now locked on the emperor instead, he popped the blue mushroom in his mouth and chewed. Emperor Lanseyo snapped his fingers at Lester and Danser, who hovered awkwardly at the edge of the clearing. They cleared their throats and approached.

Once they had also eaten the mushrooms and not died of poisoning, Emperor Lanseyo stalked up to Ellyda and grabbed one as well.

Mordren's body had stopped twitching, but he was still lying on his back in the grass, staring up at the sky while his chest rose and fell with short breaths.

"Are you okay?" I whispered.

His gaze slid to my face. "Soon."

I squeezed his hand.

Flames licked the air as the emperor stalked towards the yellow cloud as soon as he had eaten his mushroom. For a few seconds, I considered not saying anything. But in the end, reason won out because we needed him clear-headed.

"You have to wait about five minutes for the mushrooms to take effect," I called before he could storm into the pollen.

"Five minutes?" He whirled to face me while stabbing an arm towards the yellow mist. "My wife is in there."

"I know." I pushed to my feet. All the fear and worry and exhaustion from the past weeks bled into my voice and gave it a razor-sharp edge. "I know that you are worried about the love of your life. And I am worried about mine after you hit him with lightning when he was trying to *help* you."

A dangerous expression flashed across the emperor's face. In a few powerful strides, he closed the distance between us and grabbed the front of my shirt. With his fist buried in my collar, he forced me up until I was standing on my toes.

Leaning down the final bit, he growled in my face, "Watch that tone."

"All we have done since the day we got here is try to warn you about a coup." I held his gaze. "And all you have done is hurt us and try to kill us. I think we're allowed to be a bit angry."

"Kenna," Captain Vendir said from a few strides away, his voice full of worry and warning.

"No, you are not." Emperor Lanseyo tightened his hold on my collar. "No one speaks to me or my wife with such a tone."

I only continued glaring at him. His eyes flashed. Lightning flickered through my body. I sucked in a breath between my teeth, but said nothing else. Another current went through me, making my limbs shake. From the corner of my eye, I could see Ellyda trying to take a step forward, but Vendir held out an arm to block her way. An even stronger bolt of lightning crackled through my body.

Swallowing my pride and anger, I at last dropped my gaze.

Emperor Lanseyo released my collar and gave me a shove backwards.

I stumbled a step back before straightening again and brushing a hand down my clothes. "Anron did."

"Anron." He practically spat out the name. "Even though my wife said that she believed Captain Vendir, I have to admit that I did not believe it entirely myself until I heard it from Anron's own mouth right before he fled on his air serpent."

"But you believe us now?"

"Yes," he reluctantly admitted. "And now, I am going to find my wife because five minutes have passed. Lester. Danser. With me."

Before any of us could protest, he stalked towards the yellow barrier. The two High Commanders scrambled to follow. When they passed us, they looked from face to face as if trying to decide where we all stood now. In the end, Danser just gave us a slow nod in acknowledgement of the secrets we now shared, and then they disappeared into the cloud of pollen after the emperor they had plotted to overthrow.

Silence fell over the glen. I raised a ball of fire in the middle of it to light up the quickly approaching evening. The red and purple streaks were starting to give way to a dark blue as the sun sank lower. Branches snapped from somewhere deeper into the trees.

While Ellyda and Vendir drifted closer to us, Mordren let

out a low groan and sat up. I knelt down and helped pull him to his feet.

"I won't even ask how you're feeling," I said as I draped his arm over my shoulders to lend him support.

He drew his other hand through his now messy hair. "I'm fine."

"Liar."

A huff of laughter escaped his lips. It immediately made him wince. Wrapping an arm around his waist to keep him steady, I turned to Ellyda and Vendir.

"The others?"

"They're all safe," Ellyda said. "They should be on their way here as we speak."

Relief washed over me. Blowing out a deep breath, I gave her a nod.

For a while, we just remained standing there in silence. Watching the darkening forest and the swirling cloud of pollen. Waiting for the emperor and empress to reappear. At last, voices came from inside the yellow mist.

"She must have wandered around, trying to find her way back out," High Commander Danser said carefully.

"Yes," Lester agreed. "But she appears unharmed."

"Unharmed?" Emperor Lanseyo snapped. "She is unconscious."

A few seconds later, the three of them strode out into the firelit clearing. The emperor was carrying a limp Empress Elswyth in his arms. For the very first time, there was no lightning along her arms. However, the black lace veil lay neatly draped over her face.

"She is unconscious," the emperor repeated, this time as an accusation directed at us.

"She has probably been hallucinating wildly," I replied.

"And she will have memory gaps. But other than that, she will recover quickly and without issue."

"I have to get her back. You," he turned to Lester and Danser, "get the soldiers out of the mist."

"What about Anron?" I called before he could leave. "Will you send a force after him to kill him?"

"No."

My blood froze. *No?* What did he mean 'no'? After everything we had done to make this plan work, how could he refuse now?

"What?" I shook my head. "Why not?"

"Anron is a war hero. He is well liked and celebrated by the people." Lanseyo shifted his arms so that his wife lay in a better position. "And betrayal breeds betrayal. If others were to find out that someone like Anron had planned to overthrow us, they might start getting ideas." He leveled a hard stare on Lester and Danser until they dipped their chins in acknowledgement of the unspoken order. "And we cannot have that."

"So you'll just let him get away with it?"

"Not necessarily." A shrewd glint appeared in his blue eyes. "If Anron were to die in an ill-advised war in another land, then we would consider the matter closed."

Mordren narrowed his eyes at the emperor. "You are going to make us deal with him on our own so that you will not be implicated in his death."

"Yes." He flashed us a calculating smile. "But at least we will not retaliate when you kill him."

Before we could reply, he jerked his chin at Lester and Danser. While the two High Commanders disappeared back into the cloud to help the lost soldiers out, the Emperor of Valdanar strode back towards the

Palace of the Never Setting Sun with his unconscious wife.

"Fantastic," I muttered.

"At least Anron's betrayal has been exposed now, and he has been cut off from the empire." A sharp smile spread across Mordren's lips. "Killing him ourselves will be a pleasure."

"Shouldn't we–" Vendir began before being cut off by a cheerful voice.

"We brought some help!" Valerie called as she came strolling out of the forest with Theo beside her.

Frowning, I was just about to open my mouth to ask what kind of help she was referring to when a gigantic pink cloud poured into the clearing. Surprise shot up my spine. Then the large cloud split into a multitude of small pink clouds. They sped into the yellow mist, and a moment later, it started shrinking. Those pink cloud-like animals from the elves' camp were eating the pollen.

An exhausted laugh bubbled from my throat. Shaking my head at the grinning thieves, I eased Mordren over to a fallen log at the edge of the clearing and sat us down on it. The others followed. For a while, we just sat there watching as the hallucinogenic cloud disappeared. Along with the soldiers.

Idra and Hadeon came striding out of the now clear patch that had previously been covered with yellow mist. They smirked at each other when they thought we couldn't see, but as soon as they noticed us, they wiped it off their faces and stalked over to join us.

Once the area around us was clear of soldiers and the High Commanders had followed their emperor back out of Poisonwood Forest, I dared a deep sigh of relief. I couldn't believe we had actually pulled this off.

Branches snapped from the woods across the clearing. I

turned towards it, hoping to see Eilan's beautiful face appear between the tree trunks.

An involuntary spike of fear flashed through me as another figure became visible.

Empress Elswyth, her black dress flowing around her and lightning crackling over her arms, stalked out of the forest and advanced on us. When she spoke, her voice was dripping with poison and threats.

"Did you really think I would let you off the hook that easily?"

CHAPTER 38

Lightning bolts leaped from her arms and zapped the grass between her and us. We all pushed to our feet as she came to a halt a few strides away. Empress Elswyth cocked her head, making the black veil over her face ripple.

"I am not done with you yet," she said. "Before I consider this business done, I want you all to bow before my feet."

Hadeon and Ellyda exchanged a look while Vendir raised his eyebrows in surprise. The forest seemed to be holding its breath.

Mordren snorted. "Nice try."

With deliberately slow movements, the empress raised one hand and grabbed the edge of her veil. Another bolt of lightning hit the grass before her. Then she lifted her veil and draped it over her long brown hair instead.

A perfectly ordinary-looking face stared back at us. No scars. No burns. Nothing special about it at all. In fact, it barely even had the usual traits of a High Elf's face.

"Well, it was worth a shot," she said.

The edges of her body blurred.

And then Eilan appeared on the grass in her place.

Lightning still clung to Eilan's arms and leaped out around him for another few seconds before he managed to snuff it out.

"That was a top-class performance," Valerie announced with a beaming smile. "We were watching from the trees back there and, man, you played the part to perfection."

A slight blush crept into his cheeks. "Well, I've had a lot of practice at this point."

I didn't even try to hide the wicked grin that spread across my mouth. Yes, what a performance it had been. What a *scheme* it had been.

This absolutely insanely brilliant plot had all started with a thief. A thief with a complete disregard for rules and a penchant for finding loopholes.

After Eilan had announced that he could not shapeshift into someone who already existed, everyone else had dropped the issue and tried to think of another plan. But not Valerie. When we visited the elves' camp here in Poisonwood for the first time, on our way to steal the magic from the White Tower, she had shared a backup plan that she had secretly been cooking up in case it wasn't possible to actually steal the magic.

Her chaotic examples of forged bills that were only properly done on the front and pigeons that looked like doves from far away had led to an explanation of the loophole she had found. Eilan could not shapeshift into someone who already existed, but how did the magic define someone who already existed? Someone who looked and sounded exactly like someone else. But what if you changed something? Then it would no longer be the same person. Only someone *similar*.

Eilan could shapeshift into someone who sounded like Empress Elswyth and who had the same body shape as her, but then pick a completely different face. That would mean that he had not shapeshifted into someone who already existed, because Elswyth's face was completely different from the vaguely human-looking face that Eilan had picked.

Loopholes.

Bloody brilliant loopholes.

So then when Eilan and I broke into the White Tower and realized that we couldn't take the magic with us when we left, we adopted Valerie's crazy backup plan. But to sell Eilan's performance as Elswyth, he needed to have lightning constantly flickering up and down his arms. And there was no way to fake that. So we had to go for the real deal.

Since I already possessed fire magic, I drank some more from the bowl to test if we could do that. When the magic accepted me without issue, we considered that proof enough that it worked the same way that our stolen bowls of magic did when we crowned a new prince. So we sent a prayer to whatever gods and spirits were listening, and then Eilan drank from the bowl of lightning.

Thankfully, the magic accepted him without issue too.

However, he didn't get a lot of time to practice his control over it before we had to start the ruse. That was why the lightning along Elswyth's arms was always less controlled, and leaped away to zap the ground, when it was Eilan and not the real empress. And that was quite often.

We needed to create bad blood between Anron and the empress, as well as between Anron and Lester and Danser. But to do that, it wasn't enough to orchestrate meetings. We had to control what was being said in those meetings. Which was why we had Eilan as Empress Elswyth ask Anron for advice so that he would then offend the real empress by giving the advice that she had in fact never asked for. We also needed to make Danser and Lester afraid of discovery, so we had Eilan go in as the empress and threaten to turn them over to Lanseyo and make them part of her statue garden.

In fact, the only meeting that I had spied on where it had been the real empress, was the one in the statue garden when she had summoned Anron to confront him about the rumors that he had questioned her ability to rule. During all other meetings between Elswyth, Anron, Lester, and Danser, the empress had actually been Eilan. All we had to do was make sure that they all got to the meeting when we wanted them to, and then Eilan did the rest.

But we also knew that those meetings would never be enough. We needed a final push. So that was why I had planted a fake report in Anron's study this morning that said that we had been spotted heading into Poisonwood Forest. We wanted to have them waiting for us in that exact spot when we came out of the woods. After consulting with Mendar, we had picked that massive cloud of pollen as the stage for our final act, which was why we were so close to it when we exited the forest to find the army there. I hadn't expected there to be quite so many of them, but we had figured it out anyway.

After my high-powered fire magic attack, we had split up, as previously agreed. Everyone had tried to lead all the soldiers into the cloud, while making sure that the emperor and the High Commanders stayed out of it. My job had been to make sure that the empress went inside.

After a few close calls, I finally got her to follow me into the cloud of hallucinogenic pollen where Eilan was already waiting. That soldier who saw two empresses had actually not been hallucinating.

Once inside, Idra and Hadeon made sure that she stayed long enough for the pollen to take effect. And while the real Empress Elswyth was passing out inside the cloud, Eilan stumbled out of it in his shapeshifter form and coughed and called for soldiers to get the emperor and the High Commanders. We needed all four of them for our final act.

Mordren and I had positioned ourselves in the preselected glen that was oh-so-conveniently placed next to the cloud. Lester and Danser's testimony was a part of the scheme, but we couldn't be sure that they would turn on Anron, and even if they did, we didn't think that it would be enough. We would never have been able to convince the real empress and her husband, but with Eilan controlling what the empress said, we were able to persuade Emperor Lanseyo. The fact that he heard it from Anron's own mouth in the end only sealed the deal.

And the real empress would of course not remember this meeting since she was never at it. Which was why we couldn't make Eilan say all of this just anywhere at just any time. We had to make sure that there was a plausible explanation for why she would not remember such an important meeting afterwards. And given that she just happened to fly right into a cloud of pollen that just so happened to cause memory loss, it wouldn't matter that she had no recollection of this momentous occasion.

The damage was already done.

Emperor Lanseyo knew the truth.

Anron was cut off from the empire and we were finally free to kill him.

I could barely believe that this desperate gamble had actually worked.

"How was the landing?" Captain Vendir asked as his eyes found Eilan.

The shapeshifter chuckled and rubbed his shoulder. "Rough."

"Sorry. I had to make sure that you flew in the direction we wanted, and that it was far enough to land you inside the mist."

"Oh it was far enough, alright. I caught part of Anron's attack before your blast of wind smacked into me and sent me in another direction." He rolled his shoulders and then raked his fingers through his long black hair. "If it's all the same to you, I'll leave that as the one and only time we do that."

Captain Vendir hid a small smile behind a sincere nod. Letting his arms fall back down by his sides, Eilan opened his mouth to say something to Valerie when his gaze snagged on Mordren.

"What happened to you?" he asked.

Mordren leveled a flat stare at him. "I was on the receiving end of Emperor Lanseyo's revenge-filled lightning strike."

"Ouch. How did–"

"I thought I would find you here," a voice said from behind.

We all whirled around to see a mass of elves, blood panthers, firebirds, midnight foxes, and more of those pink cloud things. I blinked at them in surprise. How such a large group had managed to sneak up on us without making a sound was incredibly impressive. And a bit terrifying.

"I take it everything went well?" Mendar continued as he closed the distance between us and came to a halt in front of us.

The crown of spiky red branches that sat atop his black hair looked formidable in the flickering firelight. Around us, the forest had turned dark. A blood panther followed after the tall leader of the Poisonwood elves.

"Yes," I answered. "More or less, anyway. Anron is fleeing back to our lands, but the emperor has given us permission to kill him without any threat of retribution. So now we're going back to do just that."

"I see." Mendar stroked the panther's black and red fur. "And we have made a decision."

My heart rate sped up. The others drew a little closer as well.

"We are coming with you," Mendar declared.

A smile spread across my mouth. "You are more than welcome."

The elves of Poisonwood Forest let out a cheer. Valerie joined in and then snuck over to pet one of the pink cloud animals.

"I only have Orma." Captain Vendir cleared his throat when Mendar turned to frown at him in confusion, and then clarified, "My air serpent. I only have one so I'm not sure how to…" Trailing off, he motioned at the mass of elves around us.

"We have firebirds. And…" A mischievous spark twinkled in Mendar's brown eyes. "Well, you will meet them later. But let's just say that we won't have any problems crossing the ocean."

"Oh, that's good. I…" Vendir trailed off again when he noticed Ellyda's stare.

"You're coming with us," she said, her eyes locked on Vendir. Her words were halfway between a statement and a question.

"I, uhm... Yes." He adjusted his armor a bit self-consciously. "If you'll have me."

For a few very long seconds, Ellyda only continued staring at Vendir with those intense violet eyes of hers. Then she gave him a firm nod.

Hadeon chuckled and elbowed Idra in the ribs, which only made her turn and glare at him. I suppressed another smile.

"So... we're going home now?" Theo asked.

"Yes." I swept my gaze over the group of elves and humans and strange magical animals gathered around us. "We are going home."

We were going home to take back our courts.

To fight High Commander Anron and his Flying Legion one last time.

With no help from the Empress and Emperor of Valdanar, we would have to rely solely on our own strength and cunning. To create a new scheme. A new plan. To somehow win a fight against an opponent who was far stronger than us and who still kept most of our people trapped with bracelets that blocked their magic. Magic that Anron could instead use against us.

In terms of people who were free to fight, we were outnumbered.

In terms of raw magical power, we were outmatched.

But we would still fight.

For our home. Our freedom. Our power. Our courts. And the people we love.

One last time.

One last stand.

BONUS SCENE

Do you want to know what happens when Kenna and the thieves take on a fun challenge to once and for all decide who is the best at breaking into houses? Scan the QR code to download the **exclusive bonus scene** and find out who's the sneakiest of them all.

ACKNOWLEDGMENTS

People like Valerie truly are amazing. People who laugh easily, love freely, and just shrug off problems with a mischievous wink. If you are a person like that, thank you for being that big ball of sunshine mixed with a box of fireworks that so many of us need. And if you have a person like that in your life, please treasure them. Lastly, if you don't know someone like that yet, I truly hope that one waltzes into your life soon and starts throwing their spectacular energy around.

As always, I would like to start by saying a huge thank you to my family and loved ones. Mom, Dad, Mark, thank you for the enthusiasm, love, and encouragement. I truly don't know what I would do without you. Lasse, Ann, Karolina, Axel, Martina, thank you for continuing to take such an interest in my books. It really means a lot.

To Oskar Fransson. Thank you for being that big ball of sunshine mixed with a box of fireworks that I talked about above. Spending time with you always makes me happy and gives me a boost of energy. I truly am lucky to have a friend like you in my life.

Another group of people I would like to once again express my gratitude to is my wonderful team of beta readers: Alethea Graham, Deshaun Hershel, Luna Lucia Lawson, and Orsika Péter. Thank you for the time and effort you put into reading the book and providing helpful feedback. Your suggestions and encouragement truly make the book better.

To my amazing copy editor and proofreader Julia Gibbs, thank you for all the hard work you always put into making my books shine. Your language expertise and attention to detail is fantastic and makes me feel confident that I'm publishing the very best version of my books.

I am also very fortunate to have friends both close by and from all around the world. My friends, thank you for everything you've shared with me. Thank you for the laughs, the tears, the deep discussions, and the unforgettable memories. My life is a lot richer with you in it.

Before I go back to writing the next book, I would like to say thank you to you, the reader. Thank you for joining me and Kenna on this mission. If you have any questions or comments about the book, I would love to hear from you. You can find all the different ways of contacting me on my website, www.marionblackwood.com. There you can also sign up for my newsletter to receive updates about coming books. Lastly, if you liked this book and want to help me out so that I can continue writing, please consider leaving a review. It really does help tremendously. I hope you enjoyed the adventure!

Printed in Dunstable, United Kingdom